mpressive
as Laura McHugh's *The Weight of Blood*. It is a
chilling portrait of a small town in the Ozarks
where violent men are protected and
young women vanish.'
Joan Smith, *Sunday Times*

'One of the best books of the year . . . Beautifully
written and cleverly plotted with memorable,
deftly drawn characters, *The Weight of Blood* is
an unmissable debut.'
Sunday Express

'Very accomplished technically, and a scary psychological
study of an introverted rural community.'
Independent

'*The Weight of Blood* is an outstanding debut.'
Sunday Times

'There's a haunting, hypnotic quality to this book that
gives a splendid tautness as the secrets of a suspicious and
inward-looking community isolated in a magnificent
but dangerous – even deadly – landscape
are uncovered. An accomplished debut.'
Guardian

The Weight of Blood

Laura McHugh

arrow books

1 3 5 7 9 10 8 6 4 2

Arrow Books
20 Vauxhall Bridge Road
London SW1V 2SA

Arrow Books is part of the Penguin Random House group of companies whose
addresses can be found at global.penguinrandomhouse.com.

Penguin
Random House
UK

First published in Great Britain by Hutchinson in 2014
(First published in the United States by Spiegel & Grau in 2014)
First published in paperback by Arrow Books in 2015

www.randomhouse.co.uk

A CIP catalogue record for this book is available from the British Library.

ISBN 9780099588368

Printed and bound by CPI Group (UK) Ltd, Croydon, CR0 4YY

For Brent, Harper, and Piper

The Weight of Blood

I

Lucy

That Cheri Stoddard was found at all was the thing that set people on edge, even more so than the condition of her body. One Saturday in March, fog crept through the river valley and froze overnight. The morning sun crackled over a ghostly landscape across the road from my uncle's general store, the burr oaks that leaned out over the banks of the North Fork River crystallized with a thick crust of hoarfrost. The tree nearest the road was dead, half-hollow, and it leaned farther than the rest, balanced at a precarious angle above the water. A trio of vultures roosted in the branches, according to Buddy Snell, a photographer for the *Ozark County Record*. Buddy snapped pictures of the tree, the stark contrast of black birds on white branches, for lack of anything better to print on the front page of the paper. It was eerie, he said. Haunting, almost. He moved closer, kneeling at the water's edge to get a more interesting angle, and that was when he spied the long brown braid drifting in the shallows, barely visible among the stones. Then he saw Cheri's head, snagged on a piece of driftwood: her freckled face, abbreviated nose, eyes spaced too wide to be pretty. Stuffed into the hollow of the tree were the rest of Cheri's pieces, her skin etched with burns and amateur tattoos. Her flesh was unmarked when she disappeared, and I wondered if those new scars could explain what had happened to her, if they formed a cryptic map of the time she'd spent missing.

Cheri was eighteen when she died, one year older than me. We'd lived down the road from each other since grade school, and she'd wander over to my house to play whenever she felt like it and stay until my dad made her leave. She especially liked my Barbies because she didn't have any dolls of her own, and we'd spend all day building little houses for them out in the woodpile, making swimming pools with the hose. Her mom never once called or came looking for her, not even the time I hid her in my closet so she could stay overnight. My dad found out the next morning and started hollering at us, but then he looked at Cheri, tears dripping off her face as she wolfed down the frozen waffles I'd made her, and he shut up and fried us some bacon. He waited until she finished eating and crying before giving her a ride back home.

Kids at school—including my best friend, Bess—thought Cheri was weird and didn't want to play with her. I knew Cheri was slow, but I didn't realize there was actually something different about her until fourth or fifth grade, when she disappeared into the special ed class for most of the day. Newspaper articles after the murder described her as "deficient" or "developmentally disabled," with the mental capacity of a ten-year-old. We weren't as close in high school—I'd outgrown her in certain ways and spent most of my time with Bess—but we still shared a bus stop at the fork of Toad Holler Road, and she was always there first, sitting on a log under the persimmon trees, smoking cigarettes she'd steal from her mother and picking at her various scabs. She always offered me a cigarette if she had one to spare. I didn't know how to inhale, and she probably didn't, either, but we sat there every morning, elbow to elbow, talking and laughing in a cloud of smoke.

One morning I beat Cheri to the bus stop. I got worried when the bus rumbled up the dirt road and she still wasn't there, because her mom always sent her to school, sick or not, if only to get her out of the way. Days passed with no sign of her, so I walked through the woods to her mom's trailer and knocked and knocked, but nobody answered. There were rumors she'd dropped out of school, and when somebody from the county finally went to check it out, Doris Stoddard said her daughter had run away. She hadn't reported her missing because she figured she would come back.

Flyers were posted in shopwindows around town, and I taped several up at my uncle's store, Dane's, which had been in our family for generations. Above Cheri's picture, in thick black print, was the word RUNAWAY. I wasn't convinced that she'd left on her own, but no one shared my concern. In time, the flyers faded and curled, and when they came down, no new ones went up in their place.

A year passed between Cheri's disappearance and her murder, and during that time hardly anybody spoke of her. It felt like nobody missed her besides me. But as soon as her body turned up, it was all anybody could talk about. It was the biggest news to hit our tiny town of Henbane in years. Camera crews arrived in hordes, parking their vans by the river to get a shot of the tree, which had sprouted a modest memorial of stuffed animals and flowers. They barged into Dane's demanding coffee and Red Bull and complaining about the roads and poor cellphone service. People who had ignored Cheri while she was alive were suddenly eager to share their connections to the now-famous dead girl. *I used to sit behind her in health class.... She rode on my tractor one year in the Christmas parade.... I was there that time she threw up on the bus.*

The whole town jittered with nervous speculation, wondering where she'd been for that missing year and why she'd turned up now. It was common knowledge that in the hills, with infinite hiding places, bodies disappeared. They were fed to hogs or buried in the woods or dropped into abandoned wells. They were not dismembered and set out on display. It just wasn't how things were done. It was that lack of adherence to custom that seemed to frighten people the most. Why would someone risk getting caught to show us what he'd done to Cheri when it would've been so easy to keep her body hidden? The only reasonable explanation was that an outsider was responsible, and outsiders bred fear in a way no homegrown criminal could.

In the wake of Cheri's murder, Meyer's Hardware ran out of locks and ammunition. Few people went out after dark, and those who did were armed with shotguns. My dad took precautions, too. He worked construction jobs where he could get them, usually a couple hours away in Springfield or Branson, and he had been letting me stay home alone a couple days at a time while he was gone. After Cheri's body was found, he went back to driving the round-trip every day, spending hours on the road so he could be home with me at night.

I replayed our mornings together, Cheri's and mine, sifted through our last conversations. She'd talked mostly about her "boyfriends," pervs who hung around her mom's trailer and told her she was pretty and tried to feel her up. Boys our age, the ones at school, were cruel. They called her a retard and made her cry. I told her to ignore them, but I never told them to stop, and that's what I remembered when Cheri's body turned up in the tree: the ways I had failed her. Like how I'd been her best friend but she wasn't mine. How I'd worried something bad might have happened when she went missing, but I didn't do anything about it. All the way back to when we were little, me being less of a friend than she thought I was. I gave her my Happy Holidays Barbie, not because it was her favorite but because I had ruined its hair.

Spring was short-lived. The hills were ecstatic with blooms, an embarrassing wealth of trees and wildflowers: dogwoods in cream and pink, clouds of bright lavender redbuds, carpets of phlox and toothwort and buttercups. Then the leaves filled out the canopy, draping the woods in shadow. The vines and underbrush greened and resumed their constant creeping, and the heat blossomed into a living thing, its unwanted hands upon us at all times. Cheri had been buried at Baptist Grove in a child's casket—which was cheaper and plenty big to hold what was left of her—but I couldn't stop thinking about her, how she'd shared so much with me but hadn't said a word about running away.

By the end of May, there were no real leads in Cheri's case. Everybody in town still talked about the murder, arguing about whether the tree where she was found should be cut down or turned into some type of memorial, though most folks had gone back to their normal routines. Dad got tired of his daily commute and went back to leaving me alone for a day or two while he worked. As time passed, it seemed less and less likely that what happened to Cheri would happen to anyone else.

The shock and fear over Cheri's death had faded to the point that kids joked about it at school. Most of my classmates thought Mr. Girardi, our former art teacher, had killed her, despite his alibi. He had returned to Chicago around the time Cheri disappeared, having lasted less than a semester in Henbane. Back then, kids gossiped that Cheri had run away with him, that he was hot for retarded girls. Why else, they asked, would he have encouraged her pathetic attempts in class or let her eat lunch in the art room?

Mr. Girardi had been doomed from the start for the simple fact that he wasn't a native, but he made it worse every time he opened his mouth. He didn't know that a *haint* was a ghost or that *puny* meant sick or that *holler* was the way we said hollow. *Ah!* he said when he figured it out. *So a holler is like a valley!* When a kid in class welcomed him to God's country, Mr. Girardi wondered aloud why the churches in God's country were outnumbered by monuments to the devil. It was true: the spiny ridge of Devil's Backbone, the bottomless gorge of Devil's Throat, the spring bubbling forth from the Devil's Eye—his very anatomy worked into the grit of the landscape. Mr. Girardi spent an entire class period comparing Henbane to paintings of hell. The land was rocky and gummed with red clay, the thorny underbrush populated by all manner of biting, stinging beasts. The roads twisted in on themselves like intestines. The heat sucked the breath from your chest. *Even the name*, he'd said before being fired for showing us a Bosch, which was full of boobs, *Henbane. Another name for nightshade—the devil's weed. He's everywhere. He's all around you.*

I'd felt sorry for Mr. Girardi because he didn't understand why everyone treated him like a trespasser. Tourists came through on the river, but strangers rarely moved to town, and they naturally aroused suspicion. Even though I'd lived in Henbane all my life—had been born in the clapboard house my grandpa Dane built not a mile from the North Fork River—no one could forget that my mother was a foreigner, that she had come from someplace else, even if that place was only Iowa. Some folks didn't think it possible that the cornfields and snowdrifts of the North had produced a creature as mysterious as my mother, so they had crafted origin myths involving Gypsies and wolves. As a kid, I didn't know if such things could be true, so I'd studied photographs of her, seeking proof of their claims. Was her long black hair evidence of Gypsy blood? Did her ice-green eyes spring from a wolf? I had to admit there was a hint of something exotic in her olive skin, the fullness of her mouth, the wideness of her eyes. I'd read somewhere that beauty could be measured by scientific means, calculated in symmetry and distance, scale of features and angles of bone. Certainly my mother was beautiful, but beauty alone couldn't account for the effect she'd had on our small town. There was something deep-rooted, intangible, that the pictures couldn't quite grasp.

Part of it was that they didn't know her, Dad said. She came to work for my uncle, and folks didn't get why he'd hired an outsider. She had no family and wouldn't talk about her past. A woman without kin, in the town's eyes, had been cast out, and surely not without reason. Rumor spread that she was a witch. People still told the story of my mother turning Joe Bill Sump into a snake. They said she emitted a scent that would seduce you if you got too close. That her eyes had the same rectangular pupils as a goat's. Some even said that her grave was dug up, revealing nothing inside but a bird. None of these things was true. She had no grave because we had no body. Most of Dad's kin, the aunts and uncles and cousins on his mother's side, broke away, treated us like strangers—like we were tainted because of her. But I didn't mind the talk of witchcraft, however ridiculous it was. All the better if people were wary and left me alone. It was preferable to hearing them whisper about the one undisputed truth: that when I was a baby, my mother had walked into the inky limestone labyrinth of Old Scratch Cavern with my father's derringer pistol and never returned. Before Cheri's death, my mother's disappearance had been the biggest mystery in town.

On the last day of school, I walked home from the bus stop alone. Over a year had passed since Cheri made the walk with me, and I remembered how she used to linger in my driveway before continuing down the road to her trailer. As my house came into view, I noticed that without Dad's truck parked out front, the place looked almost abandoned. The yard was a mix of rock and scrub, with Queen Anne's lace bordering the fence. The house once was white, but the paint had worn down to a dull, splintery gray. It was a simple two-story rectangle with porches on the front and back, one of the nicer homes around when Grandpa built it, before it started to succumb to dry rot and age. It sat in a grove of walnut trees, and Grandpa Dane crowded the foundation with viburnum bushes. Grandma Dane once fell from a second-floor window while cleaning the glass, and Grandpa claimed the viburnum broke her fall and saved her life. Inside, the wood floors had long since lost their varnish, but the walls in each room were the bright cheery colors of Easter eggs, pink and aqua and orange, painted by my mother in a fit of nesting before my birth.

We kept a vegetable garden in a clearing beside the house where I'd spent countless hours picking rocks and pulling weeds. No matter how we tended the soil, the stones never stopped surfacing, denting the tiller blades every spring as they pushed their way out of the earth. Behind the house was a trickle creek that raged in the spring, and beyond that, on three sides of our property, the trees closed ranks and marched up the hillside into the Ozark Mountains.

I was in the kitchen tacking up flypaper when I heard Birdie, our nearest neighbor, warbling *hullo!* from the road. Birdie had been widowed for twenty years and had a habit of wearing her husband's old overalls, the legs cuffed to fit her barely five-feet frame. She came by to check on me when Dad was gone, and even though she'd been in this house for my birth, she always hollered from the property line before coming into the yard. It was old-fashioned etiquette, she insisted, that you didn't step on somebody's porch without permission unless you wanted to get shot. I'd told her that kind of thing didn't happen anymore, but she wasn't one to break old habits.

I walked out to meet her and patted her coon dog, Merle. Birdie squinted into the late-afternoon sun, her face a web of wrinkles. When the breeze ruffled her thin white hair, pink scalp showed through. "You behaving yourself while the gravedigger's gone?"

I held back a smile. Dad worked construction, but Birdie, like a few older folks in town, remembered the Danes as gravediggers and saw

Dad as a continuation of the line. While he knew how to bury a body, he was rarely asked to do it. Still, Birdie called him "gravedigger" the same as she'd call someone "doctor," implying pedigree and respect.

"I'm doing fine, Birdie, how about you?"

She held up the burlap sack she was carrying. "I shot a possum getting into the dog food this morning, and when I went to pick it up, wouldn't you know, it had these darned little babies stuck all over it." She opened the sack and Merle whined softly, glued to Birdie's side.

I peered in. A litter of possums, each about the size of my thumb, crawled over one another. Grown possums are ugly as sin, but the babies in the bag were unbearably cute, with their tiny pink noses and feet and delicate hairless tails.

"What're you gonna do with them?" I asked, assuming she'd probably already diced their mother up in a stew. She ate most anything she shot, with the exception of feral cats, which she threw in the burn barrel without any hint of regret.

"They're too little to cook," she said matter-of-factly. "Hardly any meat on 'em. Figured Gabby might want 'em, seeing how she's got all them animals." She handed me the sack. "Think you could run 'em over there before dark?"

Gabby, Bess's mom, took in every type of stray, man or beast, and couldn't turn away abandoned babies—me being an example. She and Birdie, along with my uncle Crete, had taken turns keeping me until Dad emerged from his whiskey-soaked grief with the realization that Mom wasn't coming home.

"Sure," I said.

"When you get back, you're welcome to come for supper. Spare room's always ready if you care to stay."

"Thanks," I said. "Just depends when I get back, I guess." I had no intention of sleeping at Birdie's if I didn't have to. I used to stay with her all the time when my dad was away on construction jobs, and when he finally agreed to let me stay home alone, it was only so long as Birdie checked in on me. He knew she kept a close watch, shuffling the half-mile to our house periodically to make sure I wasn't burning the place down or starving to death or whatever else he thought would happen without her supervision.

"Don't dawdle, now," she said.

We nodded goodbye and I carried the bag through the backyard, pausing to pluck some pennyroyal and rub it on my arms and legs to ward off ticks. A deer path led from the creek up toward the river, where Bess and Gabby lived in a double-wide behind Bell Tavern. The woods I walked through belonged to my dad and uncle. Each had his own chunk, though it was hard to tell where the property split. Grandpa Dane had left the general store to Crete, who was the first-born and arguably the better businessman. Dad wasn't bitter about it; he preferred construction work anyhow. And he hadn't come away empty-handed. He got the house and took over the family vocation of gravedigging, though it was no longer the profitable business it had been in Grandpa's day. It had diminished to a nearly forgotten craft, like making bentwood chairs or apple dolls, and didn't take much time away from Dad's real job.

Private burial was legal as long as it was done on private property, outside the city limits. Most of Dad's business came from old folks who lacked the funds for a "city" burial, which was what they called any-thing involving a funeral parlor. There were others, too: hippies from the commune on Black Fork who'd rather rot in the woods than be embalmed; a preacher from the snake-handling church who hadn't been worthy enough for God to save from the venom. There were shady circumstances, too, but Dad was known, as Danes have been known for generations, for looking the other way. Sometimes when he was drinking, he'd tell me stories I was not to repeat, of people burned up in meth lab explosions, shot in drug deals, beaten to death by jealous lovers. When he sobered up, he would apologize for scaring me and make me swear he hadn't told me any names.

The trees thinned and I could hear the river where it raked over the shallows. "Lucy-lou," Gabby hollered as I came into view. She was sitting in a lawn chair on the wobbly front deck, with her bare feet propped up on a cooler, her frizzy blond hair bushing around her head like a lion's mane. She wore a terry-cloth swimsuit cover-up minus the swimsuit. "When you gonna listen and call me for a ride? You know I don't like you walking those woods alone."

"Sorry," I said. Bess and I had roamed freely before Cheri's murder, and Gabby had always encouraged it. *Please*, she'd say. *Go disappear for a while*. I kept hoping her newfound concern would wear off.

A joint smoldered between Gabby's thumb and forefinger. "Goddamn," she said as I walked up the steps. "You look more like your mama every time I see you. Got your hair halfway to your ass just like her. And you're finally getting yourself some titties, praise Jesus. I was starting to worry."

I'd always been told I looked like my mother, but over the past year, as my hair grew out and I got taller and slightly less awkward, Gabby had compared me to her constantly. It made me happy at first, to know how much I resembled my mom, but lately Gabby seemed troubled by it. I didn't like the way she looked at me, her face all sorry and sad.

"I brought you something," I said. She took a long drag on the joint, burning it up to her fingertips, and stubbed the roach out on her armrest. I opened the sack for her to see.

"Oh, Lordy!" she said, scooping up one of the possums and cupping it in her palm. "Where'd you get these adorable critters?"

"Birdie," I said.

"I'm surprised she didn't eat 'em." Gabby stroked the possum's silky little tail, and it curled around her finger.

The screen door squeaked open and Bess joined us on the deck, pulling her home-bleached hair away from her neck and fanning herself. "More strays?" The trailer was already home to an unknown number of cats and a rabbit with a mangled leg.

"Just look, Bessie," Gabby said, holding up her finger. The possum hung upside down by its tail.

"Birdie shot their mom," I said.

"Perfect." Bess rolled her eyes at Gabby. "We know how you love the motherless."

Gabby ignored her. "Lucy, I've got a nursing mama cat out in the woodpile. I'll see if she'll take 'em on. We'll start with one, 'case she eats it. That happens, we bottle-feed."

"You think a cat'll nurse a possum?" Bess said, examining the roach to see if there was anything worth salvaging. "You're nuts. That's a crime against nature."

"I've seen stranger things," Gabby said.

"C'mon, Luce." Bess slid her feet into a pair of flip-flops. "Let's go to Bell's. I'm out of cigarettes."

"Forget it," Gabby said. "Gonna get dark here right quick. I don't wanna be picking pieces of you out of the river."

"We could just as easily get chopped up in daylight." Bess ran a finger under the edge of her shorts and tugged them down.

"I said no." Gabby took the baby possums out of the bag one by one and draped them on her chest, where they clung to the terry cloth with tiny paws.

"You weren't so worried about our safety when you used to lock us in the station wagon and whore yourself out at the Red Fox," Bess said.

"If I wasn't worried, I wouldn't have locked the doors." They glared at each other until Gabby stalked off, cradling the possums.

"Why do you have to bring up stuff like that?" I asked.

"It just pisses me off," Bess said. "You know how she had that come-to-Jesus moment after the whole Cheri thing, went back to A.A., started asking where I'm going all the time." She twisted her hair into a bun and then shook it loose. "It's annoying. She thinks she's mother of the year now. I just like to remind her."

"She's still smoking," I said. "How's that work with A.A.?"

Bess laughed. "Pot's not a *drug*, it's her *medicine*—she says it's for her anxiety. Like Xanax or something. It's the only thing that keeps her sane. I'm actually looking forward to working at Wash-n-Tan so I don't have to spend all summer stuck in the trailer with her."

"I wish you were working with me at Dane's."

"Your dad hasn't even said he'll let you."

"I know, but he will. He doesn't have any good reason to say no." For the past two years, he'd told me I was too young for the job, but he could hardly argue now that I was seventeen.

Bess smirked. "Maybe he's worried that if you hang around your uncle too much, you'll wind up like Becky Castle."

"Holly's mom? I don't even know if Crete's still seeing her. And she was a wreck before they started dating." Holly was a few years younger than us, a tiny girl so pale and white-blond that Bess used to call her an albino. The three of us had been in 4-H club back in grade school and had done a team project together, raising rabbits to show at the fair. Holly's mom, Becky, was always forgetting to come pick her up after club meetings.

Bess nodded. "Yeah, but have you seen her lately? She looks like a wrung-out dishrag. She was over at Bell's one night, dancing by herself in front of the jukebox. Had jizz crusted all down the back of her hair."

"How do you know it was *jizz*?" I asked, laughing.

Bess shrugged. "Just saying, if your dad thinks *I'm* a bad influence, I can see where he wouldn't want you around somebody like her."

Crete never bothered to introduce any of his girlfriends to me or Dad, probably because Dad was always telling him that he had terrible taste in women. None of the relationships lasted long enough to get serious anyway.

"All right, I need to get home," I said, wadding up the burlap sack that had held the possums. "Maybe I'll see you tomorrow."

"You know she'll wanna drive you back."

"Tell her you tried to stop me." I smiled and blew Bess a kiss.

She pretended to catch the kiss in her palm, then pressed it to her lips, something dumb we'd done since we were babies. "Try not to get dismembered," she said. *Dismembered*. The word came easily, like she'd said it a hundred times. It was a newspaper word, one that grew too comfortable with repetition, from countless articles in dozens of papers and broadcasts on the Springfield nightly news. It was easy to think of Cheri as *dismembered*. It was harder to think of someone leaning on a blade to saw through her joints, to cut muscle, windpipe, bone. It didn't seem fair to condense what had happened to her into one clean word.

I took the long way home, crossing onto conservation land to stare into the mouth of Old Scratch Cavern, where dogs had tracked my mother's scent when she went missing. Old Scratch, of course, was a nickname for the devil. I didn't go in; narrow tunnels and false floors gave way to an underground river that never saw light. Things lost to the cave stayed lost, and if my mother's bones rode blind currents in the earth, I'd never find them.

When I was old enough to hear the story, I thought the worst part of my mother's disappearance was the uncertainty, not knowing what really became of her. The sheriff was convinced she'd killed herself, but no one could prove she was dead. The search parties Dad pulled together yielded nothing definitive. Bloodhounds followed her scent toward the cave but didn't find her. The most worrisome part was that my dad's pistol had disappeared with her, and she'd left with nothing else, but even that didn't prove anything. I wasn't the only one who didn't take the official explanation as gospel; as with anything concerning my mother, there were rumors and stories and whispers of magic.

That she haunted Old Scratch and roamed the hills at night. That she'd traded spirits with a crow and flown away, or slipped off with traveling Gypsies. Without evidence of her death, I could continue to believe she was alive somewhere, that for some reason she'd had to leave but would someday come back for me. I begged Gabby and Birdie (and my dad, before he stopped talking about her) for stories, details, any scrap of who she was and what she did. I pieced her together over time, a mosaic of others' words: witch and ghost, woman and girl, magic and real. I wanted more, but that was all I had.

When Cheri turned up in the tree, I knew uncertainty wasn't the worst part. It was a luxury, a gift. The worst part was knowing for sure that your loved one was dead, and I was grateful then that my mother's body had never been found. The mystery eats away at you, but it leaves a thin rind of hope.

It was dark already among the trees, fireflies flaring and burning out like flashbulbs, but the path was familiar, and I was more cautious than scared. I'd avoided the woods after Cheri's murder, just like everyone else, but after a while the fear dulled. I knew the land better than any stranger who might wander through. If I paid attention to my surroundings and kept up my guard, I'd be fine. I wasn't like Cheri, who'd been vulnerable as a wounded fawn, the easiest kind of prey. No one looking out for her. Not even me.

When I got home, I fixed myself a peanut butter sandwich and a glass of tea to take up to my room. I snapped on the bedside lamp, sending shadows scurrying up the lavender walls, and turned on the fan in the window next to my bed. Fresh air flowed into the room and slowly flipped the pages of the notebook I'd left on my pillow. It was a journal of sorts, mostly lists. "Things I Know About My Mother" (almost a full page, including a strand of hair I'd found on an old nightgown of hers and taped in the margin). "Boys I've Kissed" (five: four from a spin-the-bottle game at a river party where I got drunk on apple wine, and one a visiting pastor's son Dad caught leading me—willingly—toward sin on the front porch). "What Happened to Cheri?" Her death hadn't answered that question, hadn't narrowed the list of possibilities. She'd run away or she'd been taken, and the last year of her life was a question mark.

When I wasn't scrutinizing Cheri's list, I jotted down notes about places where I wanted to travel. Iowa, of course, to see where my mother had lived, but I wouldn't stay there long. It wasn't far enough away. Sometimes I wanted to put so much space between myself and Henbane that it would take days to cover the distance. Dad had never taken me farther than Branson, and he had no interest in going anywhere else, even if we could afford it. He had my life plotted out in three bullet points: get good grades, stay out of trouble, go to college. He hadn't accomplished any of them himself, but he insisted it was what my mother wanted for me. He'd added a fourth bullet after the incident with the pastor's son: Don't let a boy get in the way of numbers one through three.

Dad couldn't complain about my grades, which came easily. He said I must have gotten that from Mom's side of the family. And I hadn't been in much trouble except the occasional scuffle with Craven Sump, nephew of Joe Bill, who—if you believed the story—had slithered off into the brush, never to be seen again after my mother turned him into a snake. Dad said Joe Bill ran off to avoid paying child support, but Craven and his kin believed in black magic. He called me "witch" or "devil's spawn" every chance he could, and sometimes I got tired of it and called him a dumbass or gave him a little shove and he'd report me to the office. The principal would sigh and tell me I had more potential than anyone else in my class, but I needed to work on my charms and graces if I wanted to get somewhere in life. Sometimes I'd glare at Craven, focusing all my energy on a mental picture of snakes clotted in a den, but he remained in his annoying human form.

If my mother truly had transformative powers, she hadn't passed them on to me.

I sprawled across the bed to eat my sandwich and pulled my paperback copy of *Beloved* out of the crack between the mattress and footboard, thumbing it open to a photocopied bookmark from Nancy's Trade-A-Book. Henbane's tiny library ("library" being an exaggeration — it was just a room in the basement of the courthouse) never had anything good, so I'd made a list for Dad, and whenever he passed through Mountain Home, he'd stop at Nancy's and see what he could find.

When I couldn't keep my eyes open to read any more, I got ready for bed in the pink bathroom across the hall and turned off all the lights. I padded over to the double window opposite my bed, the one that looked out across the backyard and into the hills. We'd learned in science class that stars looked brighter here than in most places because there were no competing lights. Henbane was a dark spot on the globe seen from space.

Black flakes like falling ash scattered across the moon as bats swirled through the sky. They spilled out of Old Scratch on summer nights and swooped through the valley to feed, their presence as familiar and comforting as the bugs and frogs that sang me to sleep. Dad once spent a month working a construction job in Little Rock, sleeping in a hotel, and when he came home, the nighttime sounds were deafening to his unaccustomed ears. The hotel room had been too quiet at first for him to sleep, but in time he'd gotten used to the absence of night music. I wondered if it would be the same for me when I left Henbane, if all the little pieces of home would so quickly be forgotten.

I had deer steaks and gravy in the skillet when Dad walked in Friday night with a book under his arm. Even though it wasn't quite summertime, his skin was already dark from working outdoors every day.

"That deer smells like heaven after a week of McDonald's," he said, grinning and pulling me into a hug. He let go and handed me the book. "I know you been wanting this one."

Song of Solomon, its pages brown and swollen as if it had been dropped in a bathtub. "Thanks, Dad."

"So you're all done with school, right? How was the last day?" he asked, flipping through a week's worth of junk mail on the counter.

"Fine. Nothing new." I laid the food out on the table and poured glasses of tea while Dad pulled his boots off and set them by the back door.

We sliced our steaks in silence. The venison was tough. Birdie had taught me how to make it several years back, though her recipe involved soaking it in milk for twenty-four hours, and I never managed to start a meal that far in advance.

"Have you talked to Uncle Crete?" I asked.

"Yep. He seems to think you're coming to work for him."

"So? What do you think? Maybe I could finally get my own phone. And I could save some money for college." I thought surely I'd hook him on that one.

"You don't need a cellphone. And you'll get scholarships."

"Dad."

"I didn't say no." He pulled a piece of gristle out of his mouth and set it on the edge of his plate while I waited for him to continue. "But there's gonna be some rules."

I smiled. This was going better than I'd hoped. I was already following the long list of rules he'd created for when I stayed home alone. A few more couldn't be that bad. And with him gone, he'd never know when I bent the more ridiculous ones. "Go on," I said in my most dramatic voice.

"I'm being serious here," he said. "No working after dark. No walking home alone through the woods after dark. No socializing with your uncle's pals over there." I thought of Becky Castle with her crusty hair.

No temptation to break that rule. "And you're gonna save most of your paycheck."

"Sure," I said. "Is that it?"

His knife and fork stopped moving and he was quiet for a moment, a strange look crossing his face. He stumbled around whatever he was trying to say. "Crete'll be looking out for you . . . but you need to use your best judgment. You don't know what kind of folks you might run into up there, and . . . you just need to mind your business and do your work and stay out of anything that don't concern you. And if anything makes you uncomfortable, let me know. I can give him some reason you gotta quit."

"What're you talking about?" I asked. I could tell he wasn't joking around, but I couldn't imagine what had him worried. "I'll be renting canoes and selling worms. It's not exactly dangerous."

His left eyebrow curled down like it did when he was about to lose his patience. "I want you to take in what I said, and I want you to agree to it."

"Sure," I said. "But you don't have to worry about me. I'm really good at taking care of myself."

"I know," he said softly, looking down at his plate. As though he regretted that fact.

CHAPTER 2

Lila

I was used to moving around. All my stuff fit in the same ugly brown suitcase I'd had since I was twelve, when my parents died and I had to leave the farm where I'd grown up, north of Cedar Falls. I'd switched foster homes seven times in six years, and sometimes I didn't even unpack. But this move was different. I was leaving Iowa, and I wouldn't be coming back.

My social worker, who'd been telling me from day one that teenagers rarely got adopted, had tried to prepare me for aging out of the system. I was actually looking forward to it until it happened to my foster sister, Crystal. She was a year older and we'd shared a bedroom at the Humphries' house. My parents wouldn't have approved of Crystal, who was always ditching school and talking back, but the two of us had something that bonded us together: No one wanted to keep us for very long, not even people like the Humphries, who took in disabled kids and crack babies.

Crystal said we got moved around so much because we were pretty and had big boobs, that foster moms didn't want us tempting their husbands and sons, but in Crystal's case it might also have had something to do with her habit of setting things on fire. She was partly right about me. It wasn't my fault if my foster fathers or brothers had roving eyes, if they looked at me inappropriately. I never purposely flirted with them, though I did sometimes flirt with their friends or neighbors. I might have even slept with one or two. And gotten caught. (Cue suitcase.) The social worker called it a problem with impulse control. I'd done something else, too, after my parents died, something worse. I didn't know for sure if it was in my file, but if it was, I couldn't blame them for passing me around like a hot potato.

Crystal had lightened the mood at the Humphries' house, always mocking our foster mother's obsession with modesty. Mrs. Humphries bought us sports bras to mash down our breasts, even insisting we wear them to sleep. Crystal would jump up and down on her bed, topless, waving around the Bible Mrs. Humphries had given her and quoting the crazy mom from the *Carrie* movie: *I can see your dirty pillows!* It always cracked us up.

When Crystal turned eighteen, she dropped out of school and moved from Cedar Falls to Des Moines to work at a strip club. She wrote me a letter and invited me to join her, and I thought about it. Then I didn't get any more letters. Six months later, I learned that Crystal had died of an overdose. The social worker gave me a moment to let the news sink in, then launched into her scared-straight routine, pushing up the sleeves of her blue blazer, the one she'd been wearing since I met her in 1986, when giant shoulder pads were in style.

What have you done to prepare yourself, to keep from ending up like her? she asked, her eyes bulging. *All these years I've been trying to get through to you. You're too busy moping about your old life to plan for a new one. Your old life is gone, and you'll never get it back!* She was so worked up, she was yelling. Little drops of spit flew out of her mouth. I wanted to punch her in the face. I curled my fingers into a fist.

She tossed a stack of pamphlets at me. *You have nothing. NOTH-ING. Nobody's going to take care of you but you. YOUR PARENTS WOULD WANT SOMETHING GOOD FOR YOU. Figure it out. You're running out of time.*

I wondered if she said the same thing to everyone—to Crystal, whose parents were still alive and, to my knowledge, didn't give a rat's ass what became of her. I didn't need the social worker to tell me what my mom and stepdad would've wanted. I was their only child, and they'd been overinvolved in everything I did. My mom was my Daisy Scout troop leader. My stepdad had hollered encouragement from the sidelines of my Pee Wee soccer games. They had continued to waste money on piano lessons year after year, refusing to acknowledge defeat. My mom was a teacher, and I'd actually done really well in school before everything fell apart. I knew my parents would want me to do something with my life. If they hadn't died, maybe I would have found some sense of direction. Maybe, if they were still with me, I'd be a completely different person. I had no way of knowing.

That night, I flipped through the pamphlets the social worker had given me. Community college, trade school, cosmetology school. They all cost money, and I'd already missed the cutoff for financial aid, so there was no point in applying until the next semester. I had a part-time job at IHOP, but my pay wouldn't be enough to cover rent and expenses when I moved out on my own. I set aside the army and navy recruitment brochures as my last resort and opened the one remaining pamphlet. It advertised an employment agency specializing in live-in positions where room and board were included. Nannies, housekeepers, laborers, companions for the elderly. I didn't want to do any of those things for the long term, but in the short term it would be a good way to save up money until I figured out what I *did* want to do.

Their office was in Des Moines, in a half-empty strip mall, and I had to take the bus. A guy with a long, snaking ponytail plucked me from the waiting room ahead of two middle-aged women who had been there longer. He asked a lot of personal questions that didn't seem relevant, but I answered them anyway. *Now we just need a photo*, he said when we finished the application. All I had in my purse was a picture of me and Crystal at the pool. I'd been carrying it around in my address book since she left. I asked the guy if he could photocopy it so I could have the original back, and he assured me he could crop it down to a head shot. A month later I received a contract in the mail, signed it, and sent it back. I'd agreed to two years on a southern Missouri farm in a tiny town called Henbane.

The social worker drove me to the Greyhound station and wished me luck. Mrs. Humphries had insisted I take the Bible she'd given me, and I left it on the floor of the social worker's car. My suitcase was swallowed up in the belly of the bus, and I climbed on board.

The bus ride from Des Moines to Springfield took fifteen hours, including a layover in Kansas City. An old man named Judd picked me up at the bus station, explaining that my sponsor, Mr. Dane, was sorry he couldn't be there himself but would take me to breakfast in the morning. Judd wrestled my suitcase into the back of his truck and didn't say much the rest of the way to Henbane, except for some aggravated muttering when he switched between two country stations to find both playing "Achy Breaky Heart."

We drove for over two hours, turning onto increasingly rough and winding roads, and it occurred to me that I'd never be able to find my way back. Finally, we reached a dirt path that cut through fields of churned earth specked with rows and rows of seedlings. Judd parked the truck in front of a concrete-block garage, and we stepped out into the humid evening air. Low green mountains rose beyond the fields, and I could smell the nearby river: wet rocks and moss and mud. When I accepted the job, I'd imagined—hoped—that this farm might be something like my parents' farm. It wasn't. Everything was unnervingly distorted, like my reflection in the bus station bathroom, the warped mirror and flickering fluorescents making me question if this was how I really looked—raccoon-eyed, sallow, scared; if the real me no longer matched the version in my head.

I had to remind myself I was only one state south on the map. How different could it be? But the hills were too steep, the sky too blue. Even the dirt was wrong, rocky and red and alien. It was a place where you'd have to watch your footing, be careful what you touched. It made me miss the flat, welcoming expanses of home: the black dirt and whispering corn, the big white farmhouse I'd grown up in, and the lush square of lawn that surrounded it. Here in Henbane, the few clumps of grass sprouting at the edge of the garage were parched and prickly, a warning to bare feet.

Regardless of my first impression, there was no going back to Iowa, nothing to go back to, so there wasn't much point in whining about it. A handful of machine sheds surrounded the garage, and behind them, halfway up the hill, sat a small cottage. My new home, I guessed. Judd grabbed my suitcase, but instead of heading up the hill to the house, he opened a door on the side of the garage and shoved my luggage inside. "You'll be staying in here," he mumbled. With a nod, he got back in his truck and left. I felt a flicker of disappointment, but I tamped it down. I'd learned from my time in foster care that you never knew whether a place would be cozy or hostile or filled with creepy Precious Moments figurines until you stepped inside.

It was dark in the garage, and musty, like it had been closed up for a while. A narrow bed sat under the one window, piled with faded quilts. In one corner was a kitchen counter with a hot plate and tiny refrigerator. In another corner was a makeshift bathroom with a toilet, sink, and stall shower, blocked off from the rest of the garage by flowered sheets that hung from the ceiling. The only furniture aside from the bed was a dresser with the varnish peeling off. I opened the drawers and found them half-full of someone else's abandoned clothes.

The garage, with its concrete floor and exposed rafters and gritty film of dust, wasn't exactly charming, but there was one thing I liked about it: It was mine. A room all to myself, something I hadn't had since I left my parents' house. I turned on the little lamp and opened the window to the racket of insects; as I listened, the noise sorted itself into distinct whining rhythms like sirens, intensifying, fading, intensifying, the sound of a thousand alarms. With nothing else to do, I got ready for bed and lay down on top of the quilts, sweating. This was it. My new life would start in the morning. I swore to myself that I wouldn't do anything to screw it up.

I woke early and was showered and dressed when Mr. Dane banged on the door. He was nearly as tall as the doorway and broad-chested, casually dressed in jeans and a gray T-shirt. I'd thought the farm's owner would be older, but he didn't look over thirty-five. His hair was slicked back, just beginning to recede at the temples, and his wide grin revealed lower teeth splayed and overlapping like a hand of cards.

"Mornin'," he drawled, reaching out to shake my hand. "Good to finally meet you. I'm Crete."

"Lila," I said. "Obviously."

He was handsome in a rugged way, with strong features and intense blue eyes. The bridge of his nose had a bump at the top and angled to one side, then the other, as though it had been broken more than once.

"Glad to see you made it here safely. How's breakfast sound?"

"Sounds good," I said. "I'm starving." I followed him out to his truck, a heavy-duty model with a double axle and a shotgun rack in the rear window. He opened the door for me and offered his hand to help me climb up into the cab.

The air-conditioning roared at full blast when he started the engine, and he quickly apologized and turned it down a notch. "So are you comfortable enough in the garage?" he asked. "I'm fixing to get a window unit put in there so you don't roast to death. I'll have Judd get right on that."

"Thanks," I said. "That'd be great."

"Well, you just let me know if there's anything else you need. I want you to feel at home here."

I smiled at him and he smiled back. I hadn't had many expectations of my new boss—I'd learned that expectations weren't terribly useful—but it was a relief to find he was reasonably normal, as far as first impressions went. It was a quick ride to Dane's, a rustic, tin-roofed cabin that sat across the road from the river.

"Dane's?" I said. "This is yours, too?"

"Yeah. Not much to look at," Crete said, parking the truck, "but we do all right."

Two gas pumps sat out front, and various hand-painted signs listed the offerings within: Breakfast. Canoe rental. Shower. Bait. We stepped inside, the plank floors creaking, and I smelled bacon and burnt coffee. The restaurant occupied most of the right side of the building, and I saw Judd in the cramped kitchen scrambling eggs. Crete gave me a tour while we waited for our food, rattling off more details than I could keep track of. His family had built the store in the 1920s, and his dad had passed it on to him. They sold camping and fishing equipment, groceries, firewood, and an assortment of jams and vegetables canned fresh from the farm. The outdoor shower cost two dollars for tourists but was free to locals who had just come off the river. Blue laws ordained that certain items couldn't be sold on Sundays, he explained, but that was ignored unless a preacher or member of law enforcement happened to be in the store. Certain people would come in to buy a bottle of White Lightning, a homemade grain alcohol, but it had to be kept out of sight in unlabeled bottles because, technically, it was illegal to sell alcohol in grocery or convenience stores.

"We won't need you over at the farm full-time," he said. "I thought if it was okay with you, we might have you help out over here a bit. We get real busy when tourist season hits, lots of folks wanting to float the river."

"Sure," I said, trying to sound enthusiastic. "Whatever needs doing." We sat at a picnic table on the outdoor patio to eat, the morning sun glaring in our eyes. I could see a rickety old school bus and a couple of boat trailers out behind the main building, and a large metal shed. Beyond that, nothing but woods.

"I don't mean to throw too much at you at once," he said, studying my face. "But once you get used to it, I think you're gonna like it here."

I doubted I'd ever like Henbane, but that didn't really matter. My contract was for two years. I could make do for that long. And when I was done, I'd have enough saved to move someplace and start over on my own. Hopefully enough to start taking classes, figure out what I wanted to do.

"More coffee?" His hand skimmed mine as he reached for my mug.

"Sure, thanks." I brushed toast crumbs from my lips and glanced up to see him looking at me. I didn't look away and neither did he.

"Damn," he murmured, shaking his head. "I don't mean to stare, it's just . . . You're a beautiful girl, you know it? Pictures don't do justice."

He flashed a confident smile and got up to fetch the coffee. It was wholly unprofessional, I knew, for my boss to talk about my looks, but nothing at Dane's was really what you'd call professional. And part of me, the part that always acted without thinking, couldn't help liking what he'd said.

CHAPTER 3

Lucy

Summer had officially arrived, even if the calendar said otherwise: School was out, it was hot, and I had set out the first jar of sun tea. Bess and I had a few days free before starting our jobs, and we spent one of them floating down the North Fork. We stopped to swim at Blind Hollow and paddled our canoe into the dark chill of the old moonshiner's cave as far as we dared without flashlights. It was a Thursday and traffic on the river was sparse, mostly fishermen looking for walleye and small-mouth bass. We ate lunch on a pebbled shoal and napped for a while in the sun. When Gabby picked us up that evening, we were sunburned and sore, and by the time I reported to work Monday morning, the skin on my face and shoulders had started to peel.

I walked into Crete's office at the back of the store, and he got up from his desk to give me a bear hug, lifting me off the ground just like he did when I was little. "Glad you're finally here, kid," he said.

"Me, too," I said. "Thanks for talking Dad into it."

"Honey, I could talk your dad into anything. Just don't tell him I said so." He winked. "So, you ready for your first day?"

"You bet."

There was a sharp knock, and I turned around to see Daniel Cole standing in the doorway. My breath caught in my throat.

"Sorry to interrupt," Daniel said to Crete. "Judd said to tell you the boat's ready."

"Thanks," Crete said. "Lucy, you know Daniel? He just started last week."

They both turned to me, and I hoped my sunburn masked the sudden blush that heated my face. Daniel had graduated from Henbane High the previous year. He'd never spoken to me at school, though he'd given me a pensive half-smile the few times our eyes met in the hall—not ignoring or avoiding me, like most people did. He was always alone when I saw him, but it didn't seem to bother him, not belonging to any particular group, and I admired him for that.

Everybody knew that Daniel's mom took food stamps and his dad and three older brothers were in prison. But I knew him another way. He occupied a line in my book of lists, kiss number four from the time I played spin the bottle. The first three were classmates who never paid any attention to me at school, and one of them was so embarrassed to be kissing me that he only pecked me on the cheek. Daniel had been sitting outside the circle the entire time, not participating, but when the bottle pointed in his direction, he grudgingly came forward and slid his hand along my jaw, gazing down at me with a grim expression before leaning in. It was awkward at first, but almost immediately something shifted, and for the first time in my admittedly brief experience with boys, I felt a kiss beyond the reach of lips; it spread through me, warming, loosening, and my insides fluttered, *thwap thwap thwap*, like a deck of cards collapsing in a dovetail shuffle. I'd clutched his shirt to pull him closer. Everyone laughed when he gently—firmly—pushed me away, but I was too stunned to care what they thought. Daniel disappeared from the party without speaking to me, and I tormented myself for weeks afterward, embellishing his name in my notebook, replaying the kiss in my mind, scrawling a self-conscious list of reasons he didn't like me.

I tried to appear uninterested. It didn't help that he was even better-looking than I remembered, with his dark chocolate eyes and shaggy hair and tautly muscled arms. He watched me with what looked like amusement, and I remembered to speak.

"Hi," I said. "I'm Lucy."

"Hi." He smiled and extended his hand. "I remember you."

My stomach knotted. I shook his hand with an extra-firm grip, like my dad taught me, but Daniel was stronger, nearly cracking my knuckles, sending nervous aftershocks through my body.

"Well, we better get busy," Crete said.

Daniel headed out, and we followed him until he disappeared into the boathouse. Crete's truck was parked out back, a boat trailer hitched to it. "Get on in," he said.

We climbed into the cab. "Where're we going?"

"I thought for your first day, we'd start with something easy." He grinned. "How about some fishing?"

"That doesn't sound like work," I said. "Not that I'm complaining."

He laughed and held a finger up to his lips. "Don't tell your dad. And put on some sunscreen. All that skin peeling off makes you look like a goddamn leper."

We fished until lunchtime, not catching anything worth keeping, and then headed back to Dane's for hamburgers. Crete set me up at the front register, and I spent most of the afternoon staring out the window, hoping to catch sight of Daniel. Crete drove me home after work, telling me that he'd be gone the next day and Judd would be in charge. I ran straight into the house to called Bess, and we spent a good hour discussing the way Daniel's hair hung down in his eyes (sexy), and the fullness of his lips (not *too* full), and the dimple that appeared in his cheek when he smiled (also sexy).

Bess complained that no hot guys ever came into the Laundromat. She'd spent her first day, and probably would spend every day after that, watching granny panties and overalls swirl around in the machines.

There was no mention of Cheri on the Springfield nightly news. Her murder was no longer the top story, and more and more time had started to creep in between updates. I wondered how long it would take her to fade into legend, just like my mother.

The next morning at work, I found Judd in the kitchen and asked him what I should be doing. "I don't know," he said after asking me to repeat myself. A knife trembled in his liver-spotted hands as he sliced a sandwich into crooked halves. "Go watch Debbie work the register."

"I already know how to do the register," I said, extra loud so he could hear me. He had to be getting too old to work, but he'd shown no interest in retiring from his position as assistant manager. "I can help you. Need me to make sandwiches?"

"Nah, just packing lunch for the new kid. He'll be doing some cleanup out on the property today."

The new kid. Daniel. "Why don't I go help with that? If you don't really need me around here. I'll just make an extra lunch for myself." I grabbed the jar of peanut butter.

Judd looked uncertain. "Ain't easy work, I expect. Don't know if Crete'd want you out there."

"He told me to do whatever you said. To make myself useful." I spread jelly on bread and rummaged around for paper sacks.

Judd sighed. "I suppose it'll get done quicker with two."

I finished packing the lunches, and Daniel walked up to the counter, nodding hello. "Lucy's coming along," Judd said. Daniel nodded again, his expression unchanged, and the three of us headed out to the parking lot and piled into Judd's truck. I held my arms in my lap to keep from brushing elbows with Daniel—up close, he smelled like Ivory soap and line-dried laundry—and began to second-guess my impulsive decision. As much as I wanted to be near him, he made me nervous. We'd never had a real conversation, had never spoken about the game of spin the bottle. How could spending the day alone with him be anything but awkward and uncomfortable?

I was also starting to wonder what exactly I'd volunteered for. Crete's property contained an abandoned homestead, thickets of impenetrable brush, and a scrap-metal graveyard littered with car parts and appliances. I hated to guess which of those things I'd be cleaning up.

We bumped along the dirt road that led toward Crete's house, and Judd turned off on another, narrower road, just two tire tracks with weeds growing in between. The path cut through a stand of cedars and descended into a valley where the Danes first settled in Ozark County. Dad used to tell me bedtime stories about the old homestead, stories passed down from his parents and grandparents. How Emily Dane, upon finding a blacksnake in the chicken coop, cut open the snake to retrieve the stolen eggs and place them back under the hens. How, when the well was dug, John Dane lowered an ax handle on a rope to check the water, and the underground current was so strong he had to let go.

What was left of the homestead now was a cluster of tin-roofed outbuildings in various states of decomposition, a collapsed barn, a root cellar with its crumbled steps leading into the earth, and the stone foundation and chimneys of the main house. Walnut trees had sprouted in the spaces between the buildings, and blackberry brambles tangled in the field. Judd pulled up behind the barn and parked in front of a single-wide trailer that looked out of place among the ruins but every bit as forsaken.

"All right," he said, handing me a key. "Crete's selling this trailer and needs to get it cleared out. Everything goes. Should be trash bags and whatnot inside."

"Since when did he have somebody living out here?" I asked. The last time I could remember visiting the homestead was sixth grade, when Bess and I had come berry picking. There hadn't been a trailer then.

Judd shrugged and fiddled with his hearing aid. "I dunno, some friend of his."

Daniel and I got out of the truck. "When're you coming back?" I asked.

"'Round quitting time," Judd said, not elaborating on when that might be. Then he was gone and Daniel and I were alone in the valley, the hills rising up around us and the sun bearing down. We stared at each other.

Daniel spoke first. "It's a little spooky out here," he said, surveying the abandoned buildings.

"My grandparents thought the house over there was haunted," I said. "There'd be knocking at the door odd times of the day or night. But when they went to answer it, no one was ever there."

"Thanks," he said, grinning. "That makes me feel better." He started walking toward the trailer.

"It wasn't really haunted," I said, catching up to him. "When they opened up the old kitchen fireplace that'd been bricked in, they found a poker hanging on a hook. If the wind came down the chimney just right, it'd knock against the wall."

"Real ghosts don't need to knock, I guess," he said. We reached the trailer and he motioned for me to go first.

I climbed the steps and twisted the key in the lock. The door swung inward, releasing a wave of putrid heat.

"Whoa," Daniel said. "Smells like something crawled in and died." He pushed past me, and we waded through trash to reach the nearest window. It was covered with heavy drapes that had been nailed to the wall at the top and bottom so they couldn't be opened. With a bit of effort, Daniel ripped the drapes down, illuminating the living room. A cracked vinyl sofa sat against the wall. Across from that, a TV balanced on a stack of cinder blocks. There was no other furniture. I wrenched the window open and sucked in fresh air.

To the left of the living area was a tiny kitchenette where a dark puddle spread out like a shadow from the base of the fridge. A narrow hallway led to a bathroom and bedroom, both strewn with beer cans, food wrappers, and dirty clothes, and one empty room with the carpet cut away.

Daniel found the cleaning supplies on the kitchen counter. "All right," he said. "How about we bag everything up, toss it out, then scrub the place down as best we can."

"No amount of scrubbing'll fix this carpet," I said.

"Yeah, probably not." He handed me a pair of gloves, and I started filling my trash bag. As I worked my way around the room, I uncovered a stack of *Teen Pussy* magazines, which told me all I needed to know about the trailer's former tenant. I'd found a *Playboy* once in my dad's closet and was struck by how fake it all looked—the boobs, the blond hair, the poses, the ridiculous ice cream parlor backdrop. But I'd never seen anything like *Teen Pussy*. The models looked startlingly real, like girls you might see at school. Textbooks and pom-poms and stuffed animals lay scattered in the background to give the illusion that the girls were posing in their own bedrooms. Then it occurred to me that maybe they were. I looked more closely at their expressions. Daniel stood up to stretch, and I quickly chucked the magazines in the trash, not wanting him to see me with them.

We finished the living room without saying much. It was quiet, just the rustle of our work and the wind lisping through the window screen. I wished we had a radio. Or a fan. Or gas masks. Or that Daniel and I could have a normal conversation. I couldn't glance at him without reliving our kiss, and I was starting to think maybe we should acknowledge it and move on. Laugh it off. Start over and get to know each other. Surely he was thinking about it, too. Unless the encounter hadn't been as memorable for him as it was for me. In that case, it was better not to bring it up, to let my insecurity fester in silence.

"You hungry yet?" Daniel asked.

My watch showed just after eleven. I didn't feel like eating, but I was ready to get out of the trailer for a while. "Sure," I said.

The air outside was fresh and cedar-scented. We carried our lunches over to the foundation of the main house and sat in the shade. I watched him eat his peanut-butter-and-jelly sandwich in four bites.

"So this was your grandparents' place?" he asked, wiping his mouth with his hand.

"They were the last ones to live out here before my grandpa built the house we live in now."

"Such a lonely feeling out here," he said. "Something about abandoned places, I guess. I'd hate to live in that trailer, looking out at these empty buildings every day."

"I don't think they spent much time looking out the window. Not with the curtains nailed shut."

"True. I've never seen anything like that."

He tore open the mini bag of Doritos I'd packed in his lunch sack and bit a huge chunk out of his apple. I watched him eat in silence as long as I could stand it.

"You said you remembered me."

"Yeah," he said, taking a moment to chew and swallow. "From

school. I used to see you on my way to first period. You were always helping that friend of yours with her locker."

A lump rose in my throat. Few people referred to Cheri as my friend. It was always "that _____ girl." Fill in the blank: *poor, retarded, dead*.

"I'm sorry about what happened. She seemed like a nice kid."

"She was," I said.

Daniel stood up, observing my uneaten lunch without comment. "I guess we should get back to work." We made our way back to the trailer, grasshoppers zinging through the weeds in front of us. I should've been relieved that he didn't remember the night at the bonfire, but I wasn't. I tried to think of an explanation that had nothing to do with me. Maybe he had kissed so many girls that their faces blurred together after a while. I didn't really believe that, though. I'd never seen him with a girl at school.

"Hey," he said. "Let's rock-paper-scissors to see who gets to clean the fridge." I lost, with the fleeting consolation of his hand closing over my fist. *Paper covers rock.*

I was in no hurry to get to the kitchen, so I started on the empty back room instead. It was dark, but I didn't want to bother asking Daniel to help with the curtains if I wouldn't be in there long. The carpet had been torn out, and the exposed plywood floor was blotched with stains. There wasn't much trash to pick up, just a few candy wrappers and cigarette butts, and then I moved on to the closet. It looked like it had already been cleared, but when I swept my hand across the top shelf, I felt something crammed into the corner. I pulled down a wad of twisted bedding and heard the clink of metal against the bare floor. I knelt to find a thin silver chain with a charm attached. My spine prickled as I held up the necklace for a better look. A blue butterfly dangled from the chain, a familiar chip missing from its left wing. I recognized the necklace because it was mine. I'd given it to Cheri a couple years back when I cleaned out my jewelry box. It was nothing special, a trinket I'd won at the school carnival, but Cheri had loved it. She wore it every day, up until she disappeared.

I clutched the necklace in my palm and sank to the floor, my heart thudding. Had she been here, in this trailer, in this room? Or was it merely a coincidence? She could have lost the necklace or given it away. Maybe I was wrong and the necklace wasn't even mine. Surely there were others; the butterfly charm was cheap—maybe they all had chipped wings. "Tell me," I whispered to the dark room. I knew Cheri's bones lay sealed in the earth, that weeds covered her grave, but I was quiet, and I listened. *Tell me what happened to you*. If she persisted somehow, in some form, within the membrane of this world or the next, she gave no sign. My head throbbed, pressure building inside my skull. I waited until I could no longer stare at the stains on the floor, and I retreated to the bathroom, shutting the door behind me.

"Hey," Daniel said, tapping on the bathroom door. "You've been in there a while. You do know that's not a working bathroom, right?"

He was trying to be funny. "I'm fine," I lied, rubbing my eyes and sliding down from the counter. "Just finishing up."

He pushed the door open a crack. "Need some help? I'm about done out here. Except for the kitchen, I mean. Still saving that for you."

"I'm good," I said, turning my back to the door and shoving it closed with my foot. I pulled out the vanity drawers and dumped their meager contents—Band-Aid wrappers, cotton swabs, crumpled toothpaste tubes. Things Cheri might or might not have used. I peeled a stiff towel from the tub, a pair of socks. Had she showered in here? Changed clothes? In the year she was missing, she'd been living somewhere, doing those everyday things. An entire year, hundreds of days, and on any one of those days I could have found her alive and brought her home. I hadn't looked hard enough. No one had.

I didn't want to talk to Daniel, but I couldn't hide out in the bathroom all day, so I dragged my trash bag past him to the kitchen and started clearing the cabinets.

"Whoa," he said. "You okay? You get something in your eyes?"

I looked away from him. "I'm allergic to mold."

"Maybe you should go outside for a minute, take a break."

I ignored him, brushing mouse droppings from the shelves. I couldn't take a break. If I left the trailer, I wouldn't want to come back. It would be better to finish early and start walking, meet Judd partway. After a minute, Daniel gave up on waiting for a response and unscrewed the lid from a bottle of bleach. He doused the sink and counters and started to scrub.

Dad called after dinner to ask how work was going, and I kept my answers as vague as possible. I'd promised to tell him if anything at my new job made me uncomfortable, but I couldn't tell him about the necklace any more than I could tell him I'd spent the day alone with Daniel. I didn't want him to get worried and make me quit.

I spent the rest of the evening on the phone, letting Bess distract me with questions. She was irritated that I didn't sound more excited about working with Daniel, but any thoughts of him had been pushed to the back of my mind. I wanted to tell her about the necklace, but I couldn't bring myself to do it. She'd never fully understood my friendship with Cheri and barely tolerated my continued interest in her. I tried to go to bed, but no amount of singing frogs could lull me to sleep with the necklace hiding under my mattress, so I started a new list on the reverse side of "What Happened to Cheri."

1. Coincidence. Someone else had the exact same necklace. With the exact same chip.

2. Cheri lost the necklace or gave it to someone else. No connection to the trailer.

3. She stayed in the trailer sometime during the year she was missing. For how long? Alone? If not, who was she with?

I didn't scratch out number one, but I didn't believe it. Number two wasn't likely, either, because Cheri had loved that necklace and wasn't careless with her things. I had no way of knowing what had really happened. She'd been in the trailer or she hadn't. Either way, she was gone, and no list would bring her back.

CHAPTER 4

Lila

Ransome Crowley, the field supervisor, lived in the cottage up the hill from the garage, the cottage I'd assumed was mine. She had the posture and skin of someone much older than her fifty years, which she attributed, without bitterness, to a lifetime of hard work and hand-rolled cigarettes. She was so scrawny, I thought at first that she must be seriously ill. That was before I saw how she worked the rows, heaving rocks and yanking weeds with ruthless authority, her gray hair knotted in a heavy bun at the base of her skull.

"I work the fields three seasons, put up the canning and preserves," she said, shaking dirt out of her stiff canvas gloves. "Wintertime I do my quilting, sometimes go up to my sister's place in Blue Eye. Job don't pay much, but I live here for free." She gestured at the drab cinder-block cottage. "And Crete, he leaves me be for the most part, long as the work gets done. Don't like to get his hands too dirty."

"You run this whole farm yourself?" It was small in comparison to my parents' acres of corn and soybeans, but a lot of work for one person.

"Oh, he hires on a bit at planting and harvest, when we need bodies. But most of it's me. What else am I gonna do? Got no man around to wait on."

She didn't look me in the eye when she talked, and she asked no questions about where I'd come from, how I'd ended up here. The gloves she'd given me were curled into the shape of someone else's hands, and I flexed my fingers to loosen them.

"Have there been others like me?" I asked, wondering why he'd chosen now to hire long-term help. Maybe he thought Ransome was getting too old to handle it on her own.

"Like you?" She directed her gaze down a row of spiraling vines. "I wouldn't say so. Not exactly. No."

We spent the morning together weeding, Ransome watching closely to ensure that I could distinguish good plants from bad. During her frequent smoke breaks, she talked about the vegetables: the difference between pole beans and bush beans, the best tomatoes to eat raw and the best ones to make into sauce, the right time to pick zucchini. My shirt was soaked through with sweat by the time we stopped for lunch, and my legs and back ached from all the squatting and kneeling. Ransome rolled out a tarp under the tree that shaded the garage. I sat down and watched as she spread out the contents of her cooler. Chunks of ham. Boiled eggs. A crumbled biscuit. A jar of murky tea.

We sat together in the shade, the breeze warm as breath on my damp skin. Birds chirped and whistled in the field, and I could hear Ransome working the ham with her dentures. "Didn't you bring anything?" she asked finally.

I shook my head. "He said meals were included."

Ransome groaned. Apparently, Crete hadn't mentioned anything to her about feeding me.

"He probably meant at the restaurant. Out here, you gotta bring something."

"Sorry," I said. "I haven't had a chance to go shopping."

She spread her napkin out in front of me and weighted it down with an egg and a slab of ham. She handed me the plastic container that had held the eggs and filled it with tea, spilling some over the side and down my arm. Translucent slivers of ice floated at the top. I took a sip and quickly drained the cup.

"This is really good."

"I mash up mint leaves in the bottom," she said, not looking at me. "And plenty of sugar."

"Thanks for the food."

She shrugged, scanning the hills, where large patches of shadow spilled over the treetops as clouds slid by. A hawk drifted in broad circles high above us, its wings outstretched and motionless as the currents kept it aloft. "Gotta eat to work," she said.

I spent the next few days working in the fields. Ransome shared her meals with me, claiming she was too busy to drive me into town to go grocery shopping. She must have complained about feeding me, though, because Judd stopped by the garage on the third day with a sack full of food. I was disappointed when I dumped it out on my bed and found only prepackaged snacks—crackers, Slim Jims, peanuts—nothing I could make a real meal out of. Later that afternoon, Crete's truck rumbled down the road, kicking up dust. He tapped the horn and dangled his deeply tanned arm out the window, slapping the door like it was a horse's flank. "Hey there," he hollered, smiling. "Ready to get trained on the dinner rush?"

I was helping Ransome maneuver a wheelbarrow full of rocks to the end of the row so we could dump it. "Go on," she muttered, shooing me away. "I'll finish up." I scrubbed my hands and splashed water on my face at the outdoor spigot, drying off with a flannel rag Ransome had draped over the handle. I hoped that I looked halfway presentable.

"You about wore out?" Crete asked as I climbed into the cab of the pickup. "I promise this'll be an easy shift, and you can get back home and rest."

"I can't remember the last time I sweated so much," I said. "Mind if I turn up the air?"

He chuckled. "By all means."

We parked out front, and he guided me through the store by my elbow. "Gabby," he said, flagging down a girl with frizzy blond hair who looked about my age. She wore frayed cutoffs and a white T-shirt with DANE'S GENERAL STORE ironed onto it in shiny black letters. "This is Lila, the lovely new waitress I told you about. Take good care of her, you hear?" He gave my arm a little squeeze and left me with her.

"Hi there," she said. "I heard you were up here the other day. I must've just missed you." She had a warm, genuine smile and a smattering of freckles across her nose and cheeks. "I'm Gabby."

"Lila," I said. "I guess you already knew that."

"That's such a pretty name," she said. "Now, where is it you're from, exactly? Crete didn't say."

"Iowa."

"Iowa! I knew you weren't from anywhere around here. I could tell by looking. Whereabouts in Iowa?"

"Uh . . . northern?" There was no point in explaining where I was from. She wouldn't have heard of Waverly, the little farming town where I'd grown up, or Decorah, where I'd stayed with a cousin after my parents died. Probably not Cedar Falls, either, where I'd exhausted the supply of foster homes. Possibly she'd heard of Des Moines, but I wasn't from Des Moines, not in any way that mattered. I'd boarded a bus there, was all.

She smiled and I smiled back. "We'll have a shirt ready for you next time. Now, let's hurry up with kitchen training so you can get on to waiting tables. That's where the money is."

The dinner menu was simple—greasy burgers and sandwiches slathered with mayonnaise. Judd showed me how to work the grill. Gabby had me shadow her as she waited tables. The indoor dining space held only ten people, including the two stools at the counter, but the outdoor patio was twice as big. We served Mountain Dew and Pepsi and sweet tea in plastic cups and brought out the sandwiches on red trays with little bags of potato chips.

Gabby knew everyone who came in, and most of them smiled and chatted with her. Nobody smiled at me. They stared like I was on display at the zoo. One table of inbred-looking assholes with Billy Ray Cyrus haircuts knocked their drinks on the floor and laughed while I cleaned up their mess. I wanted to kick in their teeth, but I was determined not to let anything get to me. The social worker had been right. I had nothing to fall back on. I couldn't afford to screw up. I concentrated on the lousy tips left on the tables and did my best not to look pissed. It was six-thirty and the slow stream of customers had dried up when a burly guy in a ball cap walked toward the counter where Gabby and I were wiping down ketchup bottles. His clothes were streaked with grime, like he'd been tuning up a car or handling livestock, and I felt a familiar pang, my weakness for a good-looking workingman. Without reading any weird Freudian crap into it, I knew it probably had something to do with my grandpa and stepdad being farmers and my mom always telling me that a man with clean nails hides his dirt on the inside.

"Why don't you take this one?" Gabby murmured. "Carl's a good tipper."

"Hello, sir," I said, stepping around the counter and grabbing a menu. "Would you like to dine inside or outside?"

His laugh was husky and soft as he studied me, half-delighted, half-confused, as though I were some mythical creature he had heard about but wasn't sure existed. I felt my face flush as Gabby laughed, too.

"No need to treat him so fancy," she said. "He's Crete's baby brother. Comes every day at the same time, sits on that stool there, eats two burgers with pickles, and drinks his tea extra sweet. You barely need to talk to him."

"You're a sweetheart, Gabs," he said, taking off his hat and ruffling his flattened hair. "Carl Dane. And you are?"

"Lila." He enveloped my hand with his, which was warm and calloused, and pumped it up and down.

"She's from *Iowa*," Gabby said, as if it were equivalent to Oz.

He was tall and sturdy and blue-eyed like Crete, but Carl's nose was straight and his smile more boyish. I guessed he was in his early twenties, quite a bit younger than his brother, not too much older than me.

"Glad to meet you," Carl said, releasing my hand but still staring, amused.

I stepped into the kitchen to give Judd the ticket and pour a glass of tea. When I came back out, Carl had a newspaper folded in front of him but wasn't reading it. I set the drink down and started to walk away. "Hey," he said. "How you like Henbane so far?"

It took me a moment to think of something good to say. "It's really green," I said finally.

He grinned. "True. You been downtown yet? Crete let you out?"

"I just got here, really. I've only been here and at the farm."

"Huh," he said. "Well, you really ought to check out town, then, when you get a chance."

"Yeah," I said, chewing my lip. "I will. I need to get some groceries." He looked like he wanted to keep talking, but I grabbed a rag and made myself busy cleaning tables until Judd called the order up. I served Carl's food and carried the last of the dirty trays to the kitchen, squeezing past Judd as he left for the night. I'd started to scrape the contents of the trays into the trash when I realized just how hungry I was. We'd been too busy earlier for meal breaks, and I didn't feel like fixing anything now that we were so close to closing. Plenty of times at IHOP, I'd snatched bites of food while busing tables—kids were always leaving pancakes untouched or stacking bacon and sausage to the side in finicky piles. I picked up a half-eaten burger and took a bite from the clean side. The door swung open, and Carl walked in as I stood eating out of the bus tub.

He stopped and stared, and I burned with embarrassment, my mouth stuffed full. "I was just gonna get some more pickles," he said, reaching toward the cooler. I turned back to the sink and ran water until I heard the door swing closed. I hoped he wasn't going to tell Crete I was eating the trash. It wasn't like I was stealing; it was just going to be thrown out anyway. I made sure I was alone, and I took another bite.

I cleaned everything I could think of in the kitchen, hoping Carl would be gone by the time I came out. But he wasn't. "Anything else you need me to do, Gabby?" I asked.

"No," she said, not bothering to check my work. "You did great. You can go on home. Now hurry up so I can leave," she told Carl, slouching on the counter next to him.

"I need to start coming in earlier," Carl said, one burger still on his plate, "so I can actually finish my food."

I hung up my apron and left the two of them to their friendly bickering, mentally calculating the tips in my pocket. The air outside was slightly less stifling than it had been inside. Crete's truck wasn't in the parking lot, and I wasn't sure if I should wait for him or start walking. It wasn't too far to the farm, maybe a few miles, but I was worn out. I could see the river edged by a wide, rocky beach on the other side of the road and wondered how it would feel to wade in, sink down into the clear, cool water, and let it bear my weight.

"Hey."

Carl stood next to me, close enough that I could smell the sweat and dust that covered him. He held out a paper sack.

"What's that?"

"I . . . It's a burger."

I glared at him.

"Look, I didn't mean to embarrass you—"

"I'm not embarrassed."

"Gabby figured you ate before your shift. She said next time—"

"You told her? Are you trying to get me fired?"

"No, I . . . I just thought you might be hungry."

"Not anymore." I walked over to one of the benches in front of the store and sat down. My feet hurt. Actually, my whole body hurt.

Carl came over and leaned against the wall next to me. "Look, I'm sorry," he said.

I could tell that he meant it. And really, he didn't have anything to be sorry for. He'd only been trying to help me out. "It's okay," I said. "No big deal. It's just been a long day." I took off my shoes and checked for blisters.

"I can give you a ride if you want. I'm heading over to Crete's."

"Thanks," I said. "I think I'll just wait."

"Okay." He stuck his hands in his pockets. "Guess I'll see you to-morrow." He started toward his truck, then turned around. "I didn't mean that in a weird stalker sort of way, just that I always eat here, and . . . I'll stop talking now." He grinned, and I couldn't help smiling back at him.

Just then Crete pulled up and stepped out of his truck. "Sorry I'm late," he said to me. "Hope you weren't waiting too long."

"Your brother was keeping me company," I said, putting my shoes back on.

Crete patted Carl on the back and slung his arm around his shoulders. The resemblance between the two was more obvious when they were standing side by side. They had the same dark brows, strong jawline, and slightly cleft chin. Crete was an inch or two taller and slightly heavier.

"So you met Carl. He's a good kid. Perfectly harmless," Crete said, and Carl rolled his eyes. "You still up for shooting some pool, little brother?"

"You bet," Carl said.

"I'll just take Lila home and meet you up at Bell's in a few."

Carl looked at me. "Maybe she'd like to come along."

Crete answered for me. "Some other time. Poor thing's barely had time to blink since she got here, she's probably beat. Let's give her a chance to settle in."

I *was* exhausted, and week one probably wasn't a good time to start disagreeing with my boss. But it would've been fun to go out with the Dane brothers. They were an interesting pair. It was obvious Crete was the dominant one, older and more assured, though there was genuine affection between them.

Carl shrugged. "I think you just don't want her to see how bad I beat you."

"You wish, kid." Crete shook his head and chuckled.

"I am pretty tired," I said.

Crete drove me back to the garage and made sure I got safely inside before leaving. I fell into bed without even brushing my teeth.

CHAPTER 5

Lucy

The next day at work, I couldn't stop thinking about Cheri. Uncle Crete was back, and he spent the morning showing me how to handle the paperwork for canoe rentals. He didn't say anything about the trailer, and I had no idea if Judd had told him I'd been out there. I wanted to talk to him about it, tell him my suspicions, but something made me hold back. I didn't know for sure whether Cheri had set foot in that trailer. I had a necklace, plus what I'd always been told was an overactive imagination. So far, that was all.

Uncle Crete and I ate lunch together on the patio, and then he stepped out for a while, leaving me at the register. I had trouble keeping my eyes open during the afternoon lull, and I was reminded of all the times I'd napped behind the counter when I was little and Crete was babysitting me. I used to make him sing "Old Dan Tucker" over and over, and he sang it at the top of his lungs every time and danced a little jig to make me laugh.

Arleigh Snell pulled me out of my reverie when she came in for a can of Skoal, the last thing she needed after losing most of her lower lip to cancer. She now had a permanent grimace and kept her chew in her upper lip, which was neither easy nor attractive. We were related by a marriage of cousins, and every time she saw me, she had to work her way through the family tree trying to figure it out.

I rushed Arleigh through the tangled mess of Juniors and Buddys who filled every branch of the family and rang up the tobacco. I had just shut the register when Daniel appeared, holding the door for Arleigh. He wore a fresh white T-shirt and faded jeans, and my pulse instinctively ratcheted up a few notches as he approached the counter.

"Hey," I said, trying to sound normal. "If you're looking for my uncle, he's not here."

"Nope," he said. "Just need to pay for my gas."

"Oh." I rang him up and waited for him to leave, but his hands lingered on the counter.

"You seemed a bit off after lunch yesterday," he said. "Everything okay?"

"Yeah." I forced a smile.

"Not trying to pry," he said, leaning closer. His fresh-laundry scent was tempered with sweat. "It's just . . . you had this look on your face."

I shrugged. "I wasn't feeling very well, I guess."

"Doing better today?"

I nodded. "I better get back to work."

He stared at me, hesitating. I wanted him to stare hard enough to see what was wrong without me having to say it. "Maybe we can talk more later," he said, gesturing to the empty store. "When you're not so busy."

"Sure," I said. *Maybe later.* It was one of those vague commitments you didn't follow up on. The door closed behind him with a jingle of the bell, and I was alone again. I tidied up the counter and neatly stacked the day's rental receipts. There was nothing else to do, so I thought I'd save Uncle Crete some time and file the paperwork for him. I used to help with the filing all the time when I was little, in exchange for an ice cream bar.

I walked into his office and tugged on one of the file drawers, but it wouldn't budge. I tried the others; they were all locked. I stepped around his desk and rolled the chair out of the way, figuring I'd find the key in a drawer, but the desk was locked up, too. Apparently, filing would not be one of my duties. I dropped the papers in his in-box. Then, as I shoved the chair back into position, it caught on the edge of the rug, wrinkling it up under the desk. I knelt to straighten the rug and saw the outline of a safe built into the floor. It wasn't so unusual that he had a safe—most stores probably did—but I hadn't known about it. For some reason, seeing it hidden there for the first time gave me the feeling of pins and needles, as though my whole body had been asleep and was just now waking up.

As I thought more about it, I knew I had to go back to the trailer. Maybe I'd missed something that would tell me for sure whether Cheri had been there. But I didn't want to go alone. When I finally told Bess about everything I had seen in the trailer—the magazines, the stained floor, the necklace—she agreed to drive out with me and take a look. She told her mom she was spending the night with me, and Gabby let her take the car. I had to lie to Gabby, promising we'd be home before dark and lock the doors, which was impossible because our doors didn't have working locks. I'd never worried about unlocked doors, and neither had Gabby before Cheri's body was found. My dad believed shotguns worked better than deadbolts, so he kept our guns loaded on a rack in the hallway. I'd heard him and Birdie talking on the porch one evening, and Birdie, too, scoffed at locking doors. She gave the same warning she always gave when I was little, after reading "The Three Little Pigs": *If the wolf wants in, he'll find a way.*

"I feel like we should be wearing all black," Bess said as we headed down Toad Holler Road with the headlights off. It was two in the morning, and we were fueled by nerves and Mountain Dew.

"It wouldn't matter," I said. "If anyone's out there, they'll see the car. But probably the only person out there'd be Uncle Crete."

"We should at least think of something to say if we get caught."

"We'll say we were going to meet up with some boys. Crete won't like it, but he'll probably believe it."

"Won't he tell your dad?"

"I don't think so," I said. "Remember in sixth grade, when you talked me into skipping school to watch that stupid *Days of Our Lives* wedding episode with you, and then I was too chicken to forge a note?" I'd called my uncle, bawling, scared my dad would find out. Crete was way more open-minded than my dad when it came to following rules, and it didn't hurt that he hated to see me cry. He had come right over and written the note, laughing as he expertly copied my dad's signature. *Dry those tears, sweetheart,* he'd said, squeezing my hand. *What Carl don't know won't hurt him.*

"Back to something more interesting," Bess said, digging around in the console for a lighter. "Are you coming down to the river on Friday?" She'd been bugging me all night about a party I knew my dad wouldn't want me to go to. A bunch of guys we barely knew from school would be there, some of them now graduated or dropped out.

"If I can," I said.

"Tell your dad you're staying the night with me."

"And your mom's letting you go?"

"Texas blackout bingo down in Mountain Home. She'll be out late."

"Fine," I said. I didn't have anything better to do. It might at least take my mind off Cheri.

"You'll have fun, I swear," Bess said. "So where do you think we should ditch the car?" We were on the dirt road approaching the turn-off to the homestead.

"Might as well drive right on up to the trailer," I said. "It's hidden from the road."

The moon cast the ruins in silhouette, featureless shadows hunched on the sloping hill. We drove around the dark outline of the barn and parked. This was where the trailer had been. But it was gone. In its place was a rectangle of bare earth edged with weeds, like the imprint of a grave. My heart seized and I scrambled out of the car, Bess behind me. When I got closer, I could see tracks where the trailer had been hauled out. Uncle Crete hadn't wasted any time.

"Well, where is it?" Bess asked, waving her flashlight in my face. "Let's hurry it up. This place is creepy."

"We're too late," I said, gesturing to the void. "It's gone." I took the flashlight and kicked through the weeds along the perimeter, looking for anything that might've been left behind. Barred owls called to each other in the trees, a conversation of unanswered questions. *Who-cooks-for-you? Who-cooks-for-you-all?*

"Sorry, Luce," Bess said, catching up to me. "We better get out of here."

She took my hand and pulled me back to the car, away from the trailer's footprint. I wondered how long it would take before saplings and briars and weeds filled it in. Another piece of Cheri swallowed up and gone. Disappointment rooted in my stomach.

Bess peeled out and didn't slow down until we were back on my road, creeping past Birdie's house before turning on the headlights and lighting a cigarette. "Hey," she said, glancing over at me. "You should look happier that nobody caught us. And you still have the necklace, right? That's something."

"It doesn't prove anything," I mumbled.

"Well, what exactly did you think we'd find? Some body part the killer left behind?"

"You think she was *killed* there?" I said.

Bess sucked so hard on her cigarette that I could hear it crackling in the dark. "I dunno, maybe. She had to get chopped up somewhere." She shrugged and dropped her cigarette butt into an empty Mountain Dew can.

She was right. Cheri wasn't killed where her body was found, and it had to have happened somewhere. I just didn't want to think it had happened on my uncle's land.

We slept in my bed with the fan blowing on us, Bess murmuring incomprehensible words whenever she changed position. I didn't sleep well. My brain was churning. I was thinking about the stains on the floor of the empty bedroom, trying to remember exactly what they'd looked like. I wondered if Daniel had been there when the trailer was hauled away. Maybe he knew where it went.

I was making breakfast when Bess came downstairs the next morn-ing. "Can I just move in with you?" she asked, pulling a pitcher of apple juice out of the fridge. "I love waking up and not smelling cat piss."

"I wish," I said, grinning. "But I'm pretty sure our parents wouldn't go for it." I handed her a plate of pancakes.

"What the hell?" Bess laughed. I'd made the pancakes into shapes, like Birdie used to do when she watched me on the weekends. Birdie never made anything cutesy like a rabbit or a snowman; her pancake shapes were practical at best. A cross. A shovel.

"They're baby possums," I said, pointing with the spatula.

"Are those chocolate-chip eyes? That's just creepy." Bess flooded her plate with syrup. "So when should I pick you up Friday night?"

I sat down at the table to eat with her. "I dunno. I'll call you after my dad gets back." I'd forgotten about the party. I knew Dad would let me spend the night with Bess—unaware of our plan to sneak down to the river—but it was hardly worth the risk of getting caught, since I doubted that there would be anyone at the party I cared to see besides Bess.

CHAPTER 6

Lila

Carl started coming to the restaurant earlier in the evening and sticking around until closing. Sometimes Crete showed up to eat with him, but usually he was alone, and every time I came by to refill his tea, he'd try to start a conversation. He gave up pretty quickly on asking personal questions when I repeated the same vague answers, and instead he started telling me about everybody who came in. Darrell, the crippled guy with the comb-over, supposedly was left as a baby on the steps of the old rooming house and taken in by the owner, but everyone knew he was really the owner's illegitimate son. Jacob Deary, the redhead with the pockmarked skin, had been caught screwing his neighbor's horse. Apparently, no one in Henbane could keep a secret. Their dirty laundry flapped around out in the open for all to see.

It was nice to have one familiar face at the counter every night, especially since the rest of the customers continued to whisper and stare. One guy started muttering prayers whenever I came near him. There were a couple of greasy-haired ladies who didn't want me touching their trays, and Gabby had to serve them. She apologized like crazy, but there was nothing she could do about it. I considered spitting in their burgers, but every time I had a thought like that, I reminded myself that I couldn't afford to get fired. I had nowhere else to go.

Crete arranged for Carl to drive me home when he couldn't do it himself. "Seems like you're working a lot of hours," Carl said one evening as we pulled up to the garage. "Days at the farm, nights at Dane's? You getting along all right?"

"It'll even out," I said. Crete had promised the winter was slow as molasses and I'd have more time off, but I didn't really mind working. I had nothing else to do, and it kept me too busy to think about other things. I slept so hard I didn't remember my dreams, and I liked it that way.

"I've noticed some folks at the restaurant not treating you right," he said.

"They're not quite as friendly as I expected small-town people to be."

"It just takes folks around here a while to warm up to strangers," he said. "Don't let it get to you."

"It didn't take you long," I said.

He glanced at me sideways and looked away. "You never felt like a stranger to me."

Ransome treated me well enough, though she didn't seem to have any interest in getting to know me better. She never asked any questions about my past, and that was fine by me. Crete came out to see us in the field some mornings before work, and Ransome always had a worried look when he showed up. I got the feeling he wasn't normally so hands-on at the farm, at least not before I started working there. He took pains to make sure I was getting settled in. He stocked my fridge one night while I was at Dane's, and set up a little oscillating fan. He hadn't come through with the air conditioner he'd promised, though, and it was getting hotter by the day. Nights weren't much better; the air was so humid, it felt stifling even when the temperature dropped.

One night after work, when I'd been in Henbane about a month, I got in Crete's truck, turned the air on high, and stuck my face right in the vent. Crete laughed at me. "Still ain't used to the weather?"

"Tell me you're not hot, too," I said. "It's like walking around inside a sponge."

He rubbed his hand over his stubble. I liked how he always looked like he needed a shave but never actually had a beard. "Well," he said, raising an eyebrow. "There's one way to fix that. Wanna go for a swim?"

"In the river?" I asked. I'd been eyeing it every day when I left Dane's, though I hadn't taken a dip. The rivers I'd swum in back in Iowa were brown and murky, but the North Fork was perfectly clear, and you could see all the way to the bottom. "I'd love to. But I don't have a suit."

"Hell," he said, grinning, "you don't need one. It's hot enough to jump in in our clothes."

"Let's do it," I said. It would be the first truly impulsive thing I'd done since I got to Henbane, and I considered that pretty good.

He drove us out to a quiet spot on the river not far from his house and opened up a cooler on the tailgate. He cracked open a can of Budweiser and dug a second one out of the ice. "I know you're not twenty-one," he said, weighing the can in his hand. "But you're old enough to vote, so I figure you can handle a beer."

He opened it for me, and I licked the foam that bubbled out. We sat together on the tailgate, sipping our drinks. The river was calm and flat on our side and made a shushing noise on the far side where it slid over the rocks. Trees crowded the opposite bank, thick with fireflies and the unceasing insect songs, which I was starting to get used to. Crete set down his beer and pulled his shirt off over his head, and I couldn't help admiring his chest, the bands of muscle tapering to his waist. He caught me looking at him and gave me a crooked smile. "Okay with you if I get down to my skivvies?"

I blushed in the darkness and nodded, remembering how I'd felt that first day when he called me beautiful. He hadn't said anything like that since, though I did notice him watching me at times. He was charming and friendly, but for the most part, he kept things business-like. He was my boss, after all. He stripped to his boxers and stepped to the water's edge. "You coming?" he asked.

I hopped down from the tailgate and unzipped my shorts, stepping out of them as they fell. I left my T-shirt on and tentatively stuck one foot in the water. "Yikes!" I said. "That's cold."

He laughed. "That's the point, right?" He walked out toward the current and sank underwater, then popped back up and shook himself like a dog. "Whoo!" he hollered. "Come on in."

I tiptoed into the water, squealing as it inched up my body. When I was waist-deep, I dove under and came up with a gasp. We bobbed around in the water for a few minutes, and then I had to get out.

"Not hot anymore?" he asked.

"N-no," I stuttered, my teeth on the verge of chattering.

"Hey," he said, sloshing out after me. "I've got something that'll warm you right back up." He rummaged around inside the cab and came back with a sleeping bag, a bottle of Jack Daniel's, and two plastic cups. "Can you spread this out?" he asked, handing me the sleeping bag. I unzipped it and laid it out in the truck bed. Crete climbed up to sit next to me and handed me a cup, tapping it against his. "Cheers."

I choked down several gulps as quickly as I could to get it over with. It tasted awful. I'd never had whiskey straight before, only once with Coke, in a much smaller glass. The sound of the river was soothing, and we leaned back to watch the stars for a while. My shirt stuck to me like papier-mâché, and the breeze made me shiver. I folded the bottom of the sleeping bag up over my feet.

"Still chilly? Do you mind?" He carefully slid his arm around me, and my body tensed involuntarily. I was suddenly aware of several things at once: the warmth that spread through my belly as the whiskey worked its magic, a heaviness fogging my head, the intense brightness of stars against the dark, the unexpected arousal at his touch. "Beautiful night," Crete said, and I leaned in to him, allowed myself to relax against his bare chest. I tried to remind myself that he was my boss, that I should not be so close to him, but my head filled with static. I was increasingly distracted by the sensation of his skin against mine, the heat where our bodies met. I swallowed the rest of my drink and felt it burn all the way down. I dropped my empty cup and noticed that his was mostly full.

"Here," he said. "Do you want to take this off? It's just making you colder." He helped me remove my wet shirt, and there we were in our underwear, eye to eye. There was an unspoken agreement in the way we looked at each other. He wanted to cross the line, and I wanted him to cross it. I wasn't sure in that moment if it was Crete I wanted or just the physical release, and I didn't care. He pulled me gently onto his lap and I wrapped my legs around him, felt him pressing against my damp underwear. Our lips touched and heat flowed through me. He wasn't a good kisser, unfortunately, shoving his tongue in my mouth like he wanted to choke me. I started to feel dizzy, and as he unhooked my bra, I thought I might be sick. I pulled away from him.

"I don't feel good," I said. "Maybe I drank too fast." We sat quietly for a few minutes, his hand resting on my knee. My head was spinning.

"Let's get you home," he said.

"I'm sorry," I said, fumbling to clasp my bra and feeling around for my shirt.

"Hey, it's okay," he said. "It's my fault. I shouldn't have given you so much." He helped me into the cab and rolled down the window in case I got sick. The bumpy road made me feel worse, and I closed my eyes, resting my cheek on the door and letting my hair drift out the window in the night air. Crete squeezed my hand as we drove.

Back at the garage, he half-carried me inside and laid me down on the bed. "You gonna be all right?" he asked, pushing my hair out of my face. I nodded. I was so tired. He sat down next to me and traced his fingers along my back, but sickness had dampened any desire, and his touch made me feel like throwing up.

"I think I just need to sleep," I mumbled.

"I'll stay awhile," he said. "Keep an eye on you." He continued to stroke my hair, and I didn't have the energy to tell him to stop. He spoke in a low, soothing voice as I drifted off, and his words began to slip away, no longer making sense.

I woke up the next morning in my nightgown, which I didn't recall putting on. My head was ringing and I'd overslept. The alarm on my clock had been turned off, and I found a note from Crete on the dresser: *Told Ransome you're taking the morning off.*

I showered and dressed and nibbled on some crackers in bed, trying to recall everything that had happened the night before. I'd agreed to go swimming, which wasn't so bad, but things had quickly gone downhill from there. I was beginning to think I wasn't so different from an alcoholic. I couldn't let myself make one small, impulsive decision, because that was guaranteed to lead to a whole six-pack of bad decisions, some likely to end in regret. I was fairly certain that I hadn't slept with my boss—I had no memory of things going that far. In the agonizingly bright light of day, I knew what a mistake it would have been to screw the guy I was contractually bound to for two years. It was incredible luck that I'd gotten sick when I did, because nothing else would have stopped me from going through with it. Crete probably felt the same way, like he'd dodged a bullet. We'd just gotten carried away.

I had a little speech ready for when he came to drive me to Dane's, but I figured I'd give him a chance to go first. Then I could agree with what he said and get on with my day. When I first got in the truck, he asked how I was feeling, and we had a little laugh about my low tolerance for alcohol. I thanked him for helping me home and waited for him to launch into the reasons why the previous night shouldn't have happened. But he didn't.

"I was thinking you might like to come over to my place after work tonight," he said. "We could have a real dinner."

I squirmed, not sure how to start my speech. It didn't dovetail easily with what he'd just said. "I don't know," I said. "I'm still not feeling very well."

He smiled at me. "Tomorrow, then. I'll pick you up after work."

"Maybe . . . maybe it's not the best idea," I said softly.

He was quiet for a minute, chewing on a toothpick. "I thought we had a good time last night," he said, his eyes on the road. "Sure seemed like it."

"No, I did, I had a . . . It was fun," I said. "I was just thinking it over, the whole employee/employer thing. I don't want to . . . cause any problems."

"Nothing wrong with having a little fun," he said. "You worried I'd fire you over it?"

"I don't want to mess things up. I do that sometimes, and I really want to keep this job."

"You don't need to worry about your job," he said.

"Still, I think it's best if we don't. You know. We can just . . . keep it professional."

He nodded without looking at me. "If that's the way you want it."

CHAPTER 7

Lucy

Over the next couple of days, float season started to pick up. The constant stream of customers kept me busy, and every once in a while, I caught sight of tourists posing for pictures across the street, in front of Cheri's tree. One guy came in to ask me which tree it was, the one where they'd found "that retarded girl's parts." A filthy pink ribbon dangled from the lowest branch, all that was left of the memorial. Crete wasn't around, and when I tried his office door, it was locked. I wondered which of his friends had lived in the trailer, how well he knew them.

I walked home through the woods after work on Friday, picked a few strawberries from the garden, and ate them hot from the sun. Then I lay down on the couch to rest for a few minutes. It wasn't completely dark when I woke up, but the crick in my neck told me hours had passed. The answering machine was beeping and someone was knocking at the door. I got to my feet just as Bess let herself in.

"You didn't call," she said.

"Sorry," I said, rubbing sleep from my eyes. "I just woke up." I punched the button on the answering machine, and we listened to a message from Dad, sorry he couldn't make it back until the next morning. There was a problem with his truck. "I'm still tired," I said to Bess. "I think I might stay in tonight."

"Uh-uh," Bess said. "Your dad's gone, that's a free pass. And I'm not going by myself. Let's get you dressed."

"Can't I just wear what I have on? It's gonna be dark out anyway."

She eyed my Dane's shirt and cutoffs critically. "No." I followed her upstairs, and she began flipping through my closet, as if something new might magically appear amid the shorts and T-shirts I wore every day. "These look like your dad's old shirts," she said disdainfully. "Don't you have anything dressy? I knew I should've brought some of my clothes." She wore a pair of shorts tight enough to prohibit sitting and a low-cut tank top with sequins along the neckline. "Hey, how about this?" She pulled out the very last thing in my closet, a gauzy white dress I'd sewn in home ec and never worn.

"I can't wear that to the river."

"Sure you can." She held it out until I shucked off my work clothes and slipped the dress over my head. "Now makeup," she said, sitting me down at Grandma Dane's vanity table. I didn't bother to protest. She dumped out her purse and plucked a stubby little eyeliner pencil and a tube of Maybelline mascara out of the mess. I tried not to flinch while she worked. "Lip gloss," she said, handing me a tube.

"It's too sparkly."

She groaned, cupped my chin in her palm, and slathered the gloss on my lips. It smelled sweet and tasted bitter. "Damn," Bess said when she was done. "You should let me fix you up more often."

"Thanks," I said. "You look good, too."

"No Gypsy witch like you." She smirked. "Here, take your hair down." She pulled out the ponytail holder and spread my hair over my shoulders, dragging the brush through it one section at a time. "You're freaking my mom out, you know."

"What do you mean?"

"She was going on about you the other day: *It's like she grew into her skin*. Lila's. I mean, you always looked like her, I guess, but Mom said it's weird how, all of a sudden, now that your hair's so long, and with the boobs and everything . . . She said sometimes when you open your mouth, she thinks Lila's voice'll come out. Like Lila's haunting her somehow. Then she lit a big fat doobie and locked herself in her room."

I rolled my eyes. "Should I get a haircut before she has a mental breakdown?"

"No, it's perfect," Bess said, setting down the brush and smiling at me in the mirror. "Now you just need a black cat and a broom."

Fireflies strobed all around us as we followed the narrow path to the river. I regretted letting Bess take my hair down, because it was hotter than a wool scarf and sticking to my skin. Bottles of Boone's Farm clinked together in Bess's backpack, and I carried an old quilt for us to sit on.

We heard voices and music and the hiss of a driftwood fire as we neared the clearing. I recognized a few faces around the bonfire, but no one I much cared to talk to. Bess grabbed my wrist and pulled me around the circle toward the shore, where two of the Petree brothers sat in the shadows taking turns with a one-hitter. Smoke hung in the damp air. "Did you know they'd be here?" I whispered. Jamie and Gage were too old to be hanging around high school parties. Jamie, who was nearly thirty, had always given me the creeps. He was a dealer with long stringy hair and a goatee and a habit of staring at people to the point of discomfort.

"I just want to talk to Gage," she said. "Only for a minute, please?" I knew what that meant. She wanted to see if he was between girl-friends, in which case he'd take her back until he found a new one. Not that he was any prize. He was four or five years older than us, and I'd never known him to hold an honest job.

"Hey, guys," Gage said. "Glad you could make it."

Jamie, as usual, just stared. I spread the quilt out far enough from him that I couldn't make out his face in the dark. Bess sat down next to Gage and held the tiny pipe to her lips as the lighter flared. She handed the pipe to me, and I passed it to Jamie without taking a hit, careful not to let our fingers touch. When the pipe finished its second circuit, Bess and Gage moved from courtship to foreplay, Jamie watching them with hooded eyes. I wouldn't forgive Bess easily for tricking me into this awkward double date. I twisted around to see if anyone new had shown up by the bonfire, and when I turned back, Jamie was beside me, blowing smoke in my face.

"Cheri," he said, inches from my ear. "Friend of yours, correct?"

I rearranged myself to get farther away from him without letting on how uncomfortable he made me. "Yeah," I said. "She was."

"She sure was a sweet thing, weren't she, though?" He brushed his hair back from his face and brought his hand down disturbingly close to mine. Fever radiated from his body.

"Did you know her?" I asked. He could've mentioned Cheri simply because she was a popular topic of conversation, but I was thinking of the trailer and the kind of people who might have hung out there. It wasn't a stretch to picture Jamie ogling *Teen Pussy*.

"Yeah," he said, packing the pipe and sucking it to ash. "Showed me her room one time when I was there to see her mom. Weren't hardly nothing in it. Had this doll made of socks knotted up."

I wondered if he'd been there to sell drugs or get laid, but I didn't ask. Could've been both; he was known to barter. He unscrewed a bottle of Wild Turkey between his legs and took a long swig. I glanced over at Bess, all but straddling Gage, and knew I'd be walking home alone, cursing the stupid too-small sandals she'd made me wear.

Jamie's gravelly voice pulled me back to him. "The strange thing was, I saw her once after she disappeared. Last summer."

"What?" I said. "Where'd you see her?"

He leaned in, filling what was left of my personal space with his shadows and angles and heat. "It was the middle of the night. I was out on the river, and I heard splashing, heavy breathing. Up like a ghost she come, wet and shining in the moon, tearing through the shallows like the devil's on her heels."

"Where on the river?" I snapped.

He was close enough that I could see his eyes, bloodshot, unfocused. He wavered for a moment, mesmerized, like he'd forgotten what we were talking about.

"Where was Cheri?" I prompted.

He blinked hard. "Can't say, exactly," he said. "Upstream."

I wondered if she could've been running toward town, looking for help. Maybe Jamie could've saved her if he'd done something.

"You didn't try to help her?" I said.

"I thought she was a ghost," he whispered. "She looked right through me, kept going. I thought maybe I'd imagined it."

"*Bullshit,*" I said. But I wondered if it was possible, if he was so far gone that he no longer knew what was real, couldn't rely on his brain to make the distinction. I tried to sound nicer. "Have you told anyone else?"

"Yeah," he said, "a few people, right after it happened. They had a good laugh." He paused to take another drink.

"Why'd you tell me?"

"You're different, you know?" His hand traced the outline of my hair, my body, not touching but wanting to. Longing softened his voice. "You're like her. Lila." I pushed away, stood up. Jamie gaped up at me, and I wondered if he, like Gabby, looked at me and saw my mother. He couldn't have been more than a kid when she'd left, but somehow, in that mystical way of hers, she'd impressed herself upon him. How unfair that she lingered in Jamie Petree's burned-out skull, while I hadn't been able to conjure her up in a lifetime of trying.

Bess didn't come after me, probably didn't even notice I was gone. I pried my sandals off at the water's edge and waded in until the river reached the hem of my dress. Dampness wicked up the thin fabric and I shivered, letting the chill displace all other sensation. Jamie's smoke lingered on my skin and hair, and I lowered myself deeper into the current, splashing water over my bare arms. Had I not been wearing the ridiculous white dress, I would've plunged below the surface to remove any trace of his smell.

"Going for a swim?"

I recognized Daniel's voice and mashed down the little quiver of excitement it caused. There was no chance this time of fate and an empty bottle forcing us to make out by the bonfire, though some small part of me held out hope for that very thing. I turned around to face him. "I was just getting out."

"So maybe you have a few minutes to talk. If you're not in a hurry to get back to the party." A teasing smirk.

"I don't think anybody's missing me," I said.

"You're wrong there. I don't know what you did to Jamie, but he's rocking back and forth like a mental patient."

"Funny," I said. I sat down cross-legged on the rocky beach, and he sat next to me, facing the water. "What were you doing, spying from the bushes?"

"Sort of," he admitted. "You've gotta watch out for that guy."

The muffled sounds of the party blended into the rush of water, the swell of insects. I wanted to sit in the dark with Daniel, not talking, until everyone else went home.

"So," he said. "Are you gonna tell me what happened the other day at the trailer?"

I hadn't thought he'd bring it up again. "Nothing happened," I said. "I told you I wasn't feeling well. And the place was just creepy. You said so yourself."

"There's more," he said.

"Why are you so worried about it?"

"Because," he said, his voice low and calm, unlike mine. "You came out of that back room a different person. You shut down. I know we don't know each other very well. I can't tell what you're thinking. It's like, when you talk to me, there's some other conversation going on in your head, and I'm not part of it. But when you came down the hallway, it was there, clear on your face. You were scared. You didn't have time to hide it, or it was just too big to hide."

How do you decide to trust someone you barely know? It was hard not to be swayed by unreliable portents. His earnest brown eyes. His clean, safe smell, which somehow managed to be sultry. Birdie had taught me a thousand ways to divine unknowable answers, mostly passed down through folk wisdom—watching animals, splitting seeds, examining bones. She also relied heavily on the Bible and the Farmer's Almanac. *But if all else fails, trust your gut,* she'd told me. *The way it hollows out when things aren't right, when you're about to take a bad turn.* I wasn't sure I could trust Daniel. But no pit grew in my stomach. And whether it was wise or not, I *wanted* to trust him. So I took a chance.

"It's Cheri," I said. "We know she was alive, she was staying some-where. I think she was in that trailer sometime after she disappeared." I stopped short of suggesting she was killed there.

His expression didn't change. "What makes you think that?"

If I'd made a mistake in trusting him, I was about to make things worse. "I found something of hers," I said. "In that back room. And the way the curtains were nailed shut, the carpet ripped out . . . I thought if she was there, there'd be some kind of evidence. I could figure out what happened to her. But when I went back, the trailer was gone."

"Yeah." He sighed. "I helped haul it out. It never occurred to me that Cheri . . ."

"Did my uncle know where they were taking it—who he sold it to?"

"He said the deal didn't pan out. So he sold it for scrap."

My throat tightened. "It'll get torn to pieces."

He rested his hand on my shoulder, and I couldn't help cataloging it along with the other times he'd touched me—his reluctant fingertips on my cheek when we'd kissed; the bone-cracking handshake at Dane's; the brush of his palm in rock-paper-scissors; now this protec-tive, almost paternal grip of my collarbone—none of them sufficient in duration or intent.

"Have you said anything to Crete?"

"No," I said. "If he knew anything about Cheri, he'd have said so. I'd ask him about the trailer, but Judd said something about a friend living there, and I don't want to sound like I'm accusing anybody with-out knowing more."

His hand slipped down my arm and away. "I don't see you as the sort to let things lie. But that'd probably be the smart thing to do."

"The smart thing's not always right," I said.

Daniel was quiet for a minute. "How about Cheri's mom, you talk to her?"

"No. Cops questioned her up and down. She didn't tell them anything. I doubt she'd say anything to me." I rubbed one foot on the other to dislodge the sharp pebbles pressed into my skin.

"Couldn't hurt to try."

"Didn't you say a minute ago that I'd be stupid to get involved?"

A crooked smile. "I never said that. I was only thinking it's a lot to take on by yourself. You could use some help."

"I've got Bess," I said, standing up and trying to spot my sandals along the dark shore.

"I dunno, she looked kinda busy to me." I gave him my best not-funny face, which just made his smile bigger. "At least let me drive you home. I'd hate to see you walk all that way barefoot."

No one noticed us leaving together. Daniel's truck was held together by rust and primer, and I was surprised it started after a few feeble coughs. Wind funneled through the cab, snarling my hair. We talked a little bit about school, how he'd been taking night classes at the technical college in Springfield but hoped to have enough money saved up to go full-time in the fall. He asked if I was looking forward to senior year, and I said I was looking forward to it being over.

Birdie's house was dark when we drove past, but that didn't mean she wasn't up, watching. Daniel parked in the yard with the engine running. "Thanks for the ride," I said, making no move to exit the truck. We weren't on a date, but I felt like if we sat there long enough, he might get the idea to lean over and kiss me. I was dying to know if the first time was a fluke, if I'd been wasting so much energy feeling anxious about him when the true ingredient to a full-body swoon was something as simple as liquor. I wasn't opposed to making the first move myself, but so far, Daniel had given no indication that he wanted more than friendship. And I refused to throw myself at someone who wasn't interested. I didn't know how Bess could stand it, laying herself out for Gage time and again while he continually saw other girls.

Daniel looked at the darkened house, the rotting gingerbread trim, and toyed with his key chain as though he might turn off the truck. "Can I walk you to the door, or will your dad come out with a shotgun?"

"He would if he were home," I said, returning his smile. We got out and spent another awkward minute staring at each other on the front porch, serenaded by a chorus of coyotes and whip-poor-wills in the hills behind the house.

"Well, good night," I said, finally acknowledging that he had no immediate plans to conduct the necessary research to determine whether a kiss would turn my legs to jelly. I stuck out my hand.

He took it in his, not crushing it like he had at Dane's, not letting it go. "I know it wasn't easy, earlier, for you to tell me those things. About Cheri and all." He examined my hand in his, contemplating the confluence of lines as though preparing to read my fortune. "I said I knew you from school, but we met before, at the river. Spin the bottle. I figured you didn't remember or were too embarrassed to bring it up. But as I recall, it wasn't half-bad." He grinned. "Actually, I think you kinda liked it." He released his grip and stepped off the porch. "So, anyway, just wanted to get that out in the open."

His truck sputtered down the road as I watched from the living room window, tipsy from our prolonged handshake, which could almost legitimately be classified as hand-holding. Sure, he'd been teasing me, at least a little, but he remembered. I didn't have many friends, didn't confide in anyone except Bess, and had never had a boyfriend, but I'd let Daniel right in, based on no more than a gut feeling and the fact that he'd offered to help with Cheri. He hadn't assumed, as most people did, that it was pointless, that the trail was cold. And as always, when I thought of Cheri, I thought of my mom; as I approached her age at the time of her disappearance, I realized how young she truly was. Cheri and Lila, two lost girls, bookends with a lifetime of mysteries between them. And then it occurred to me: If it was possible to find one, why not the other? It couldn't hurt to ask around. Someone out there might know what happened to my mother. It might not be too late to find out.

I was tired and beyond ready to take off the white dress, which I looked forward to tearing into dust rags. As I reached up to close the window shade, I saw a lone figure on the road, moving slowly, a bent silhouette. Birdie on her night patrol.

CHAPTER 8

Lila

Crete was waiting for me at the garage a few days later when Carl dropped me off after work, and seeing him there made me nervous. He joked around with Carl like he always did, like everything was fine, but it wasn't. Things had been tense between us since I brushed him off, and he'd barely spoken to me. No more friendly conversation. No more mention of installing AC. I figured he wasn't used to getting turned down, that he was pissed or embarrassed, but sooner or later he'd get over it.

"Hey," he said when Carl's truck pulled away. "It's payday." He handed me an envelope.

"Thanks," I said, opening it up. Instead of a check, there was cash. And not much. I knew room and board were being deducted from my pay, but how much could it possibly cost to put me up in the crap-hole garage? "Where's the rest of it?"

"I was thinking it might be best if I put the money straight into a savings account, so you don't have to mess with it. I know you're wanting to save it all anyhow, and you don't have much in the way of expenses. That pocket money there should cover whatever you need."

"Thanks, but I'd rather handle it myself," I said. "I could go into town and set up an account."

He sighed. "Sorry," he said. "I think it's best this way."

"Well, I don't. It's my money, and it's not up to you what I do with it."

"Contract says otherwise," he said. "Guess you didn't read the fine print."

I was so angry I was shaking. I stood there mute and watched him get back in his truck. "*Asshole!*" The word tore out of my throat as he disappeared down the road. I knew he was trying to get back at me, to show me he was in control, but he was taking it too far. He couldn't keep my money. The problem was, I didn't know what to do about it. I paced around the garage, working it over in my head.

Crete didn't come around the next day. Ransome told me he'd gone to Arkansas on business, but he'd left a new work schedule. I would have Thursdays off. When she spread out the tarp at lunchtime and sat to one side to make room for me, I told her I needed to rest. I ate crackers and beef jerky alone in the garage. Ransome was staking tomato plants on the far side of the field when I came out, but she'd left a plastic cup of tea outside my door. I brushed ants from the rim and drank.

I practically jumped on Carl when he came into the restaurant that night, and he couldn't have looked happier to have my attention. I'd been worried he'd have to work on Thursday, and he did, but he assured me his hours could be rearranged. He'd have plenty of time to drive me to town, though he wouldn't hear of dropping me off. He insisted that he'd take me to eat at the bakery and help with my errands. *You'll need somebody to show you where everything is,* he said. I'd gone through the slender phone book and written down the address of the grocery store and the one attorney who had an ad in the yellow pages. They were on the same street, one block apart.

He showed up at my door the next morning freshly scrubbed and reeking of Old Spice. "You look nice today," he said, holding the door of the truck open for me. He was obviously delusional. I hadn't bothered to fix myself up in the least. My hair was wet, my eyes shadowed from lack of sleep. "I shouldn't say that," he corrected, smiling. "You look nice every day."

His sweetness was almost unbearable after the crappy couple of days I'd had, and I couldn't look at him. I stared down at my lap. I was wearing a yellow sundress I'd borrowed from Crystal and never given back.

"Hey, are you doing okay?" he asked. From the corner of my eye, I saw his hand move toward me and then pull back. "Feeling homesick?"

He always seemed to think homesickness was the worst problem you could have. I shook my head. I missed the memory of home, but home as I remembered it no longer existed. The most important pieces of my former life were dead and buried, and I couldn't reclaim them by going back. "I'm fine," I said. We drove down the blacktop, and I watched the lush greenery flow by.

"I hope those guys at the restaurant aren't getting you down," he said.

I didn't want to talk about any of the things that were really bothering me, most notably his brother. So I nodded. "They're jerks."

Carl cleared his throat. "The one with the beard? I . . . heard him say something the other night."

I didn't know which one he was talking about. I was pretty sure they all had some kind of facial hair and were equally offensive.

"I'm fixing to have a talk with Joe Bill Sump," he said gruffly. "I'm gonna clear things up a bit. Don't you worry about him."

Joe Bill? That was probably the worst name I'd ever heard. I had to smile a little at the thought of Carl sticking up for me.

We reached the city limits of Henbane, population 707. The welcome sign was peppered with holes, as if someone had blasted it with a shotgun. A two-story limestone courthouse dominated the tree-lined town square, and shops surrounded it on three sides. Henbane was the county seat, Carl explained, the biggest town in Ozark County. I imagined the entire population would fit on the courthouse lawn.

The Donut Hole was no different from Dane's in that everyone stared at me and the food was greasy. Carl insisted on paying, and I let him, since I didn't have much cash. After breakfast, we crossed the square to the attorney's office. I didn't want to tell Carl I was seeing a lawyer because I was afraid he'd mention it to Crete, but there was no way to hide it from him. So I told him I had some legal questions about my parents' estate.

"I'll go in with you," he said. "I've known Ray Walker since I was a kid."

He said the same thing about everyone we saw. It seemed that, aside from me, not a single new person had entered his life, they all had always been there. "If you don't mind," I said, "I'd feel more comfortable alone. I don't talk much . . . about my parents."

"Oh," he said. "I'm sorry. Sure. I'll wait right out here. Take your time." He sat down on a bench outside the office. "Just holler if you need me."

I stepped inside the aggressively air-conditioned entryway and erupted in goose bumps. The secretary spoke briefly to Mr. Walker on the phone and then rose to open the door to his office. He looked momentarily stunned when he saw me—shocked to see an unfamiliar face, I assumed—and then quickly regained his composure.

"Please come in," he said. He was tall and angular, wearing a white dress shirt with rolled-up sleeves and a tie with the knot loosened. His graying hair was combed to the side with pomade, and his eyes were pale and piercing. He stared at me expectantly.

"Hi," I said. "I'm Lila Petrovich."

"I know who you are," he said, reaching out to shake my hand. "I expect the whole town knows by now. I'm Ray Walker. Let's have a seat, shall we?"

I followed him around the billiard table that dominated the room. He sat behind a polished mahogany desk, and I sat across from him.

"What brings you here?" he asked.

While I tried to decide what to say, he poured two cups of coffee and slid one across the desk to me. "If I tell you something, do you have to keep it to yourself?" I asked. If he knew Carl, he probably knew Crete, and I didn't want the conversation getting back to my employer.

"Well," he said, stirring sugar into his coffee, "I do abide by the attorney-client privilege, if that's what you're asking."

That didn't ease my fears, but I didn't have much of a choice. "I have some questions about a contract, and I wondered if you could look at it for me."

He laughed, and it turned into a cough that went on for a minute until he cleared his throat. "Would this be a contract with Crete Dane?"

I nodded.

"Then I imagine your contract is pretty well binding."

The room suddenly felt too small. "Did you write it?"

"Lord, no." He chuckled. "He retains what you might call a more *prestigious* firm in Springfield. Lucky for you, I suppose. No conflict of interest."

"So you could help me."

"Possibly. I would need a retainer, and I would need to see a copy of the contract."

I didn't have either of those things. "How much is the retainer?"

He wrote a number on a notepad and showed it to me. I fidgeted in my seat. "Do you have a payment plan?"

He stared at me as though trying to gauge something with no standard of measurement. He took a swallow from his mug and sighed. "Do you have any money at all?"

"Yeah," I said. "I mean, not very much. That's partly why I'm here. If you could just give me some advice—"

He held out a hand to stop me. "I am a country lawyer, madam. I have accepted chickens in settlement of a debt, and I am certain we can work something out. But I must insist on a small percentage of cash up front. Bonnie can explain the terms on your way out, and you can come back and see me when you have the means to move forward."

"Thank you," I said, standing to leave.

"Aren't you worried he'll find out you've been here?"

His words froze me. "Should I be?"

"I won't say anything, of course," he said. "Neither will Bonnie; her job depends on it. But other people may have seen you come in. And people talk. Now, I'm on his bad side already, but if I were you, I'd think long and hard about which side of Crete Dane you want to be on."

"It's too late, I think," I said.

Mr. Walker swirled his coffee cup. "I figured," he said.

I knew exactly what I wanted from the grocery store. My grandma's dumplings were the ultimate comfort food, cheap and easy, requiring few ingredients. Carl pushed the cart and helped me find what I needed. He greeted everyone he saw with a friendly hello, not bothered by the fact that most of them openly stared at us. As we neared the cash register, an Amazonian blonde grabbed his wrist and screeched like an annoying bird. They started talking, and she ignored me completely after an initial dark glare in my direction. I drifted toward the magazine rack and caught sight of a man in an apron shaking a little boy by the collar. I moved closer and saw that the man was holding a candy bar. The boy looked up, terrified, and I smiled at him. I'd been caught stealing candy years before at a Kmart in Cedar Falls, but the manager had mercy and let me go.

"Please," I said, stepping forward and digging in my pocket. "I'll pay for it." I offered a handful of change, and the grocer stared up at me, slack-jawed, slowly rising to full height. "Here," I said, smiling to encourage him. He glanced down at my palm long enough to pluck the proper coins. He loosened his grip on the boy, who snatched the candy bar and ran.

"How's it going, Junior?" Carl asked, coming up beside me with the cart. "Looks like you just met Lila. She's new in town."

"So I see." Junior snapped out of his trance and squeezed behind the register to ring me up.

"Sorry about that woman back there," Carl said to me. "She's an old friend from school, and she has a way of cornering you."

"It's okay," I said. Had he thought I'd be jealous? *Was* I jealous? Junior bagged up my groceries and took my money. I didn't have much left over.

"Do you have any pans I could borrow?" I asked Carl on the way back to the truck. He'd insisted on carrying my two small bags.

"Sure I do," he said. "You can come on over and use whatever you need."

"I don't want to intrude," I said. "There's a stove burner at my place, I just need something to cook in."

"Come on. It'd be a favor to me," he said. "I'd love to taste whatever it is you're making. I haven't had home cooking in a good long while."

It didn't take much for him to convince me. I was in no hurry to get back to the garage, and I wanted to see where he lived. I noted the decline of roads as civilization receded behind us. The two-lane highway out of town had been cut through stone, cliffs rising on either side as we passed through naked layers of earth. Once we hit blacktop, the road—or its makers—had been humbled. Instead of blasting through the landscape to make its own way, it followed the rolling ridge, traveling along its spine, the world falling away from its flanks. Then we turned onto dirt and drove and drove through woods edged with barbed wire. The trees gave way to pasture on the left, and we passed a small frame house with a close-cropped yard and irises blooming beside the steps. A tiny old lady in overalls stood out front with a watering can, watching us pass. Her dog barked but didn't move from her side. Carl waved, and the woman nodded. "That's Birdie," he said. "The midwife."

A few minutes later, we pulled up to his house, plain except for the decorative trim along the porch. A forgotten garden filled the side yard, a few random blooms showing through the weeds. "This is it," he said, grabbing the grocery bags. "Come on in."

I'd expected a spare bachelor's kitchen but instead found it well stocked, the pots and pans and utensils worn to a dark patina. When Carl excused himself to tidy up the other rooms—he hadn't been expecting company, he said—I sneaked glances at the framed cross-stitch sampler on the wall, the patterned dishes in the china cabinet. An unmistakable photo of Carl and Crete as boys, the older boy's arm locked protectively around his much smaller brother's shoulder. Beside the kitchen door, pen marks broke their height into increments, the highest one well above my head. They had grown up here.

"What can I help you with?" Carl asked when he returned.

I didn't want any help. Dumplings were the one thing I remembered how to make from Grandma's recipes, and I'd made them in every foster home that had allowed me to cook. I wanted to mix and measure and sink my hands into the dough and let the ritual kneading and shaping return me to my mom's kitchen. "You can keep me company," I said, "as long as you don't get in the way."

He leaned against the counter and chatted while I worked. When the dumplings were ready, we ate them at the dining room table, Carl complimenting my cooking repeatedly and finishing off the portion I'd planned to save for lunch the next day. After dinner, we moved to the porch swing with sweating glasses of iced tea.

"I've been meaning to ask, how'd it go with Ray?" Carl asked.

"Fine," I said.

"I don't want to pry," he said. "I know whatever happened with your family must be painful. I can see it on your face when I bring it up. So I'll try my best not to."

I looked around the peaceful yard and out to the hills. There was no indication in the unbroken expanse of green that other people existed. A pair of birds cried in the trees, and it sounded like they were arguing. "We lived on a farm," I said finally. "Me, my mom and stepdad, and my grandma. My stepdad was great, always treated me like his own kid. I never met my real dad, and my mom didn't talk about him. My grandma told me once that he was a visiting professor from some other country—she wasn't sure which one. My mom met him in grad school at the University of Northern Iowa, and they split up before I was born. My mom taught English at the high school in Waverly, and my stepdad ran the farm. They were driving into town to get a carryout pizza for dinner—we did that on the weekends sometimes. There was a combine in the road, and they didn't see it in time. They smashed into it and flipped over. Not too long after that, my grandma passed away, and I got stuck in foster care. I was twelve."

I'd told the condensed version of my life story so many times over the years that I could recite it without emotion. When I said the words out loud, they felt like they belonged to someone else. *Thank God you weren't with them,* the neighbors had said. *You're so lucky nothing happened to you.* As if I could go on like before.

"I'm so sorry," Carl said. He took my hand and I let him. I sipped the tea he'd made. It didn't compare to Ransome's.

"What about your family?" I asked. "Is there anyone besides your brother?"

"I've got cousins all over the county," he said. "My dad was quite a bit older than my mother, and he passed on. My mom's still living, but we had to put her in a home."

"What kind of home?" I asked, sliding my hand out of his.

Carl looked uncomfortable. "Well, she . . . she gets confused. She jumped out of the upstairs window once, broke her leg. At the time my dad told me she fell. He planted those bushes all around the house in case she tried again. She'd get real depressed, lay in bed, wouldn't talk to anyone but Dad. She wasn't doing good without him here keeping an eye on her."

"So you sent her away?"

"If there'd been any other way, I'd have kept her here with me. But I'm just not home enough to take care of her."

We rocked in the swing, the porch floor warm under my bare feet.

"Your brother," I said. "You guys are pretty close?"

"Yeah," Carl said. "Always have been, ever since we were kids. He was ten when I was born, and he sort of took care of me. I really look up to him, you know? The way he runs the business and all that. I mean, we've fought here and there, had our differences, but you could hardly ask for a better brother."

"Would you mind not telling him about the lawyer?" I asked. "I just . . . Like you said, my parents . . . I don't like to talk about it. It's better not to bring it up."

There was more to the story, things I didn't want to tell Carl. When my parents died, I'd expected to stay in Waverly with my stepdad's extended family, but one by one they'd bowed out: not enough room, not enough money, not willing to take responsibility for a soon-to-be teenager. I'd grown up around these people, eaten Sunday dinners with them. They looked genuinely sorry when they turned me away, but I could also sense their relief, because I had never been blood to them. As much as my stepdad made me feel like I belonged, his family thought of me as my mother's child, not one of their own, and it was a hurtful thing to realize.

Finally, a second or third cousin of my mother's, a guy I barely knew, was tracked down in Decorah and pressured into taking me. He sat me down at his tiny kitchen table and explained the burden I'd put on him. My parents' farm would be sold to pay debts, and when everything was sorted out, there would be very little left to take care of me. I would need to earn my keep. That first night as I slept on the foldout couch, he slid his hand under the blanket and over the planes of my body. The second night he peeled back the bedding, and I slashed him with a kitchen knife. Part of me was terrified by what I'd done—his high-pitched scream, the blood soaking through my nightgown, the increasingly dark detours my life was taking. Another part of me couldn't help thinking that the scar would be impressive. I never got a chance to see it. The third night I slept in a temporary shelter in the care of family services.

CHAPTER 9

Lucy

Dad was home when I got back from work Saturday evening. He'd spent the day fishing out at Rockbridge and surprised me by frying up a dinner of trout and hush puppies without my help. Bess stopped by while I was washing the dishes and sweet-talked me into forgiving her. I made her recite back to me all the things she was now forbidden to do: fix my hair, pick out my clothes, take me anywhere near the Petrees. We made a batch of molasses cookies and sat on the porch talking until Dad came out to enforce curfew and drive Bess home. Bess was almost as disappointed as I was when I told her nothing romantic had happened between me and Daniel on Friday night. She didn't say any-thing about her night with Gage, and I didn't ask.

The next time I saw Daniel at Dane's, he offered to go with me to visit Cheri's mom. There was no mention of our spin-the-bottle conversa-tion, but it felt good to no longer be hiding anything. Exposing our shared secret seemed to have dissipated the tension between us, and talking to him felt normal now, like talking to a friend.

He picked me up after work so we could drive to see Mrs. Stoddard together. I'd brought along the last of the molasses cookies in an at-tempt to give my visit legitimacy. I figured once Mrs. Stoddard invited us in and we were eating, I'd casually start asking questions.

There was a conversion van parked in front of the trailer when we pulled up, and a scrawny boy, four or five years old, stood in the dirt yard throwing rocks at a pile of animal droppings. He watched as we approached, blond hair hanging down in his eyes.

"You better not go in," the boy said. "He'll kick your ass. He said stay-right-here-don't-move."

"Oh," I said, wondering who *he* was. "Okay. Can we wait out here with you, then?"

He shrugged and resumed throwing rocks. We watched him in si-lence, shifting back and forth uncomfortably as we waited for whoever was inside to finish up whatever he was doing. Flies swarmed around the droppings and then buzzed away briefly when a rock came near.

"Yeah!" the boy cried. "Got you, little fucker."

Daniel and I exchanged looks. "You got a fly?" he said to the little boy. "Way to go. They're fast."

"Hey," I said, opening the bag. "You want a cookie?" The kid eyed me warily and then eyed the cookie. He snatched it out of my hand and wolfed it down. I handed him another one.

A scraggle-haired man in a flannel shirt and Dickies stumbled out of the trailer, snorted, and spat on the ground. He looked up and saw us all watching him, and his eyes locked on mine before turning to the boy. "What's that?" he growled. "Where'd you get that?"

The boy stood frozen, the cookie inches from his lips, as the man walked up and slapped it to the ground. "Don't take shit from strangers," he said, grabbing the boy's arm and dragging him toward the van.

"I'm sorry," I said. "It was just a cookie, I didn't think—" Daniel put his hand on my shoulder, and I stopped talking. "Who was that?" I asked as the van tore out of the yard.

"I don't know. Haven't seen him around Henbane."

We waited a minute and then knocked at the door. Doris Stoddard appeared in a ratty housecoat. "I don't go to church, and I ain't buying no Avon," she said.

"Hi, Mrs. Stoddard," I said. "It's Lucy Dane, Cheri's friend? From down the road?"

She narrowed her eyes, appearing to have some recognition. "Why're you here?"

"I baked these for you," I said, holding up the bag. She took it, pulled out a cookie, and made a sour face. Not a fan of molasses, apparently. A Rottweiler sauntered up next to her, and she tossed him first the cookie, then the entire bag, which he proceeded to tear apart. So much for my plan.

"I thought maybe we could talk a minute," I said. "About Cheri."

She grunted. "That girl was nothing but trouble when she was here, and now she's dead, I got her goddamn ghost hanging on. I ain't got nothing else to say."

"Please," I said. "I think I might have some information about where she was staying when she was gone, and I just wanted to ask you a couple questions. See if Cheri'd been hanging around anyone new before she disappeared."

Mrs. Stoddard's face blanched. "How would you know anything about where she was?"

I hesitated, not knowing how much to say. She looked at once angry and afraid. "I found something of hers."

She gazed at me for a long moment, then moved to shut the door. "I got appointments coming."

"You said her ghost is here," Daniel said loudly, stepping in front of me. "That true?"

I didn't know what he was doing, but he'd succeeded in getting Mrs. Stoddard's attention. She paused, pressed her lips together, and nodded.

"You want to get rid of it?" Daniel said. "I can help. I can get you something."

Mrs. Stoddard angled forward to better examine Daniel's face. "I know you," she said, her voice hushed. "Your mama's the medicine woman, up Crenshaw Ridge. I thought she'd quit after all that trouble with the Walker girl."

Daniel's stance was commanding and assured, his expression calm. He wasn't bluffing. "She does a little work here and there," he said. "You'd have to keep quiet about it."

She nodded vigorously. "'Course." I could see in her eyes how badly she wanted this, believed it.

"Surely you know this sort of thing's expensive. But she'll do it for free if you talk to Lucy. Tell her everything you know."

"Fine," she said. "I'll talk once the ghost is gone."

"So," I said. Daniel and I were meandering along the riverbank, cooling our feet in the shallows. "Your mom gets rid of spirits. She sounds like more of a witch than my mom."

He smiled wryly. "Not exactly. She's into herbs and that sort of thing."

A cottonmouth slid into the water and rode the current away from us. "What was Mrs. Stoddard talking about, the trouble with the Walker girl? Did she mean Janessa?"

"Yeah, do you know her?" he asked, rolling a stone in his palm.

"I know *of* her. She went to school with my dad, and he's friends with her uncle Ray. She's one of the few people I know of who left Henbane and didn't come back. How did she get your mom in trouble?"

"Back when it happened, her dad was the mayor and Ray was a lawyer—not yet a judge, like he is now, but they had a lot of influence. Janessa was home from college for summer break, and she came to see my mom." Daniel looked away from me, across to the far bank of the river, where a tree leaned low enough to wet its leaves. "Janessa couldn't sleep. At least that's what she said at first. She'd heard that my mom could help with things like that. So Mom gave her some valerian root to make tea. Janessa left, but she came back a few days later. She said the tea wasn't working, and she started bawling, and Mom knew something else was wrong. My mom's pretty good at getting people to open up—you'll see when you meet her—and after a while, she got Janessa calmed down and asked her what was really going on, why it was she couldn't sleep in the first place."

"What was it?"

"Promise you won't repeat any of this, even to Bess?"

"I won't," I said.

Daniel threw the stone he'd been holding, and it flitted across the surface of the water one, two, three beats before sinking. "Her parents had found out that she'd dropped out of school in the middle of the semester, and they were furious. They'd always expected her to go to law school after college and then come back home and work with her uncle Ray. Her dad was making all kinds of threats about cutting her off if she didn't go back to school, and her mom was so disappointed that she wouldn't even speak to her. They didn't want anybody to find out, because it would be an embarrassment to the whole Walker family. But Janessa didn't want to go back to school, and she didn't want to stay in Henbane, either."

"Why did she drop out in the first place?" I asked.

"That's the crazy part. She was going out a lot, meeting guys her parents would have hated. They'd blamed her for screwing things up with Carl—your dad—and she was getting him out of her system, dating guys who were nothing like him. Nothing serious; she was just having fun.

"Then one night a guy gave her a drink that made her feel all sick and dizzy. When she asked him to take her home, he carried her out to the alley and laid her down in the back of a van. She was confused and barely conscious by that point, but she said she caught sight of a guy with a ball cap pulled low over his eyes and a bushy beard covering half his face. The guy started arguing with her date, and she swore to my mom that the guy was holding a pair of handcuffs. She heard the bearded guy say something like 'I ain't messing with no mayor's daughter.' The next thing she remembered was waking up in some bushes behind a liquor store. She got back to her apartment and locked herself in, and after that, she was so scared to leave that she stopped going to class. When school got out, she came back home. But she didn't feel any safer in Henbane, because whoever that guy was, the one who knew she was the mayor's daughter—she was scared she might run into him. She was suspicious of everybody."

"Wow," I said. "That does sound crazy. Like something from a TV show."

"Yeah. Mom believed her, though. There wasn't any reason to make up a story like that, and she could tell Janessa was really scared. The poor girl was so worked up about it that she was having trouble eating and sleeping. She asked Mom for something stronger than the tea to help settle her nerves, but Mom didn't have anything more to give her. She tried to convince Janessa to talk to her parents or go see a doctor. But Janessa must have found something stronger somewhere else, because whatever she took that day nearly killed her. I don't know what she told her parents, but the Walkers came after my mom. They threatened to prosecute her and run her out of town, even though they couldn't prove anything."

"So that's why your mom practices under the radar now."

"Pretty much."

"And that's why Janessa never moved back here?"

"I guess. Her parents whisked her away somewhere, and she's barely been back since."

I'd seen pictures of Janessa in my dad's old yearbook, with her poufy eighties hair and wide smile—student council, volleyball captain, fall harvest queen. It was hard to believe a girl like that could get herself into such a mess. But there was always so much we didn't know about people, lurking right below the surface where we couldn't see it. I'd pored over old photo albums, trying to locate despair in the corners of my mother's smile, depression in the set of her shoulders as she held me gleefully suspended in the air. Anything to indicate she was about to kill herself. Abandon me. But there was nothing so obvious as to be visible. In the pictures, she was madly in love with me and my dad. If the pictures said anything, it was that she was happier and more beautiful than anyone in Henbane had a right to be.

Cheri's pictures were more telling. In her ninth-grade photo, you could see the shadow of a bruise on her cheek. A wariness in her eyes. A tentative smile coaxed by the photographer, a stranger who had no idea that the portrait would later end up on the front page of hundreds of newspapers. And in the hollow of Cheri's throat, for the world to see, the blue butterfly, the symbol of our friendship.

I thought about what Mrs. Stoddard had said about being haunted by Cheri's ghost. If I didn't find out what had happened to her, she would always be drifting somewhere in the ether, a life that never quite materialized. She would haunt me in a quiet, ghostless way, the knowledge that in life I had neglected to save her, and in death failed to bring her peace. I would have preferred to see her ghost, in the way that I'd always hoped to be visited by my mother's. But ghosts never came when you wanted them to, and I didn't know how to stop wanting.

The next weekend Dad was meeting some friends at Bell's, so he gave me a ride to Bess's. She and her mom usually cooked a big meal on Saturday nights, and then Bess and I would watch a movie while Gabby went out to play bingo. It was one of the few vices she had left, and she clung to it like a religion.

Bess and I sat on the porch with a tick-covered hound dog, tending barbecued chicken on the grill while Gabby made potato salad in the kitchen. Clouds darkened the sky, and a cool breeze picked up ahead of the storm, rattling wind chimes in the trees around the trailer.

"Gage still hasn't called me back," Bess said, parting the dog's fur to remove a swollen tick.

"Sorry," I said. I could tell she wasn't surprised. Lightning threaded through the clouds, and I counted to ten before I heard the muted grumble of thunder.

"So what's going on with you and Daniel?" Bess asked, pinching my arm.

"We're friends."

Bess groaned. "You're not trying hard enough."

"I'm not trying at all."

Gabby hollered at us to bring in the chicken, and we got inside before the first drops of rain tapped the trailer. Throughout dinner, I'd look up and catch Gabby staring at me with a troubled expression. When I asked her if the possums were doing okay, she nodded absently. After we finished eating, we put our dinner plates on the floor for the various cats to fight over, and Gabby excused herself while Bess and I dug in to the blackberry pie. We were sprawled on the couch trying to decide what movie to watch when Gabby reappeared, lugging a cardboard box. She set it at my feet.

"This is for you," she said, her face puckered like she might start crying. "Some of your mom's things, just some clothes and such. I was thinking they might fit you now. Your dad had me take it all way back when. I think it hurt him too much to have it around. I saved it for you, though, most of it."

"Thanks," I said. I hadn't known there was anything left besides the photo albums. My mom hadn't had much to begin with.

"I just— I look at you now, and it's eerie, almost, like I'm seeing *her*." A few tears broke through.

"God, are you going through menopause?" Bess said. She turned to me. "I swear, if she's not high, she's crying."

"I gotta get to bingo," Gabby said, wiping her nose and heading for the door.

"Good luck," I said. We heard the car start up and drive off in the rain.

"I really think she's losing it," Bess said. "You know what she told me? She said that box had been sitting in the same spot on her closet shelf for years, and then the other day, for no reason, it fell off and spilled all over the floor." She nudged the box with her foot. "You gonna open it?"

I shook my head. "Just pick a movie. I don't care which one." I didn't want to open the box in front of her, in front of anyone.

"What's that?" Dad asked when he came to pick me up. He smelled like beer and smoke, but he wasn't drunk.

"Just some clothes," I said, climbing into the truck with the box on my lap.

"We're gonna have a problem if you start dressing like Bess," he warned. A deer stepped into the beam of our headlights then, and he swerved around it, tires crunching gravel in the ditch and diverting his attention away from me and the contents of the box.

CHAPTER 10

Lila

A week had passed since I made dumplings at Carl's house, and I'd started to look forward to him showing up at Dane's every night for dinner. It was the one part of the day I could count on not to suck. I found myself smiling when I thought about him, and I felt a little silly about it, but I didn't care. Unfortunately, things weren't getting any better with his brother. Crete had me doing split shifts at the restaurant and working at the farm in between. Maybe he thought if he worked me hard enough, I'd change my mind about sleeping with him. I didn't know. He was holding a grudge longer than I'd expected. His bad mood put Ransome on edge, and she crabbed at my every little mistake.

"Cheer up, darlin'!" Gabby said when I showed up for my shift. "It's fixing to be ninety degrees today, and we'll surely die of heatstroke before we have to serve a single plate of food."

I couldn't help but smile. Gabby was the closest thing I'd had to a girlfriend since Crystal. "You're happy today," I said.

"Well, yeah. I'm seeing somebody new. I love the honeymoon phase, before they start farting in bed."

"Wow," I said. "Hope it lasts."

When Carl came in for dinner, he was carrying a bouquet of lilies tied with a ribbon. Gabby clamped her hand over her mouth, trying to keep all her comments stuffed inside.

"Hi," he said, holding the flowers out to me. "These made me think of you."

His gesture was sweet, but it made me feel a little sad. The last man to give me flowers had been my stepdad, after a piano recital in which I'd butchered "Für Elise." I'd kept the roses on my dresser long after they dried, and packed them up when the house was sold, impractical as it was to move dead flowers. My cousin must have thrown them away, as I'd been sent to foster care with what fit in my suitcase and never saw any of my other belongings again.

Carl sat at the counter until closing time, when Gabby told me not to worry about finishing the side work. "Enjoy yourselves, lovebirds!" she called after us as we left Dane's.

"I hope you don't mind if I don't take you straight home," Carl said. He was beaming like a child trying to keep a secret. "I wanted to take you someplace special tonight."

I was tired but in no hurry to get back to the garage. And I wanted to be with him more than I wanted to sleep. "I'd like that," I said, cradling the flowers in my lap. I rested my head against the seat as we drove, and had nearly drifted off when he stopped the truck in a sweeping valley rimmed with trees.

"This is my old family home," he said proudly. "Dad built our house on Toad Holler Road before he and Mom married, but my grandparents lived over here until they passed on. Me and Crete used to play out here all the time when we were kids."

He led me around the homestead, nostalgic about the sagging buildings and rotting landmarks. He told stories about his relatives, some dull, some unbelievable. His grandfather briefly served as mayor when the real mayor died from an untreated snakebite. His grandmother's cream pies were the pride of the First Baptist bake sale. I remembered barely listening as my grandma repeated family stories I'd heard a hundred times, thinking I'd hear them a hundred more. Now they were fuzzy and disjointed, and I wished I'd paid more attention.

At the end of the tour, Carl led me to the main house, where a quilt covered the plank floor in front of an old stone fireplace. The roof was gone, but portions of the walls remained, and it was at once spooky and beautiful.

"I don't mean to scare you with this setup," he said, gesturing at the quilt. "I just wanted you to see this place as I remember it, get a sense of who I am. I thought we could lie here and watch the stars and get to know each other better."

He lit candles in the fireplace, and it took me a moment to realize what he was trying to say. That he hadn't brought me out here to take advantage of me. The thought hadn't crossed my mind. Not for a second had I worried about being alone with Carl.

We lay side by side, talking and listening to the rise of night sounds as the sky settled into full darkness. After a while, the haze of the Milky Way was visible against the black. Carl propped himself on his elbow. "What do you want most in this world?" he asked.

I didn't need time to consider an answer; I'd spent years thinking about it. "I want to have a family again."

He nodded soberly. "Family's the most important thing," he said. "Your blood, your kin." Which, for him, included Crete. I couldn't forget that.

"What do you want?" I asked.

His expression softened, and a smile lit his face as he got up from the floor. "To dance with you." He pulled me to my feet and twirled me around, nearly knocking me down. "Sorry." He chuckled. "That went smoother in my head."

I put my arms around his neck—as far as I could reach, anyway—and he drew me close and swayed the way you do at junior high dances. His embrace was warm, protective, and I leaned in to him. There was something about him that made me feel safe, at ease, and I hadn't felt that way in a very long time. Later, as we lay there talking, I leaned over him, my hair falling in his face, and stole the first kiss. I expected it to be sweet and gentle, like him, and it was, but I could feel him holding back. I kissed him again, harder, and he began to let go. We couldn't get close enough to each other. Our kisses deepened, and the heat between us grew, but he made no move to take it further. This wasn't how it had been with other men, and I was starting to feel frustrated. I *knew* he wanted me. Then an overwhelming sense of clarity cut through the fog of desire. This was my choice. He wanted it to be up to me. I pulled away from him and stripped off my clothes, standing naked in the starlight in the ruins of the house. His gaze drifted over my body and came back to meet my eyes. He looked at me like there was nothing else in the world worth seeing. He held out his hand and I went to him. I knew there would be no regrets.

On the way home, Carl told me he'd taken work on a construction project in Arkansas that would keep him away for a month. The news snapped me out of my dreamy state. I wasn't sure I could deal with Crete without Carl there. Without meaning to, I'd become dependent on his presence, a bright spot in my day, an antidote to his brother.

"Do you ever think of leaving this place behind for good?" I asked. "We could just keep driving. Not go back." It sounded a little desperate, asking him to run away with me, but I didn't care. Dread weighed me down as we neared the garage.

"I like the part about being with you." He squeezed my hand. "But my life's here in Henbane, my family, the land. I can't leave all that, ditch my job."

"I could go with you to Little Rock."

He smiled. "I wish you could. But I don't think Crete would appreciate me stealing you away at the busiest time of the year."

"I can't picture him getting mad at you," I said. "You always put him in a good mood."

"Not all the time," he said. "I can tell you, you don't wanna see him ticked off. It's not pretty." He parked in front of the garage and kissed me. "I'm sorry I have to run off right after . . . you know. I wish I didn't have to. I'd rather be here with you."

I nodded, biting my lip.

"Hey," he said, tucking my hair behind my ear. "Don't worry. I'll be back before you know it."

I wanted to tell Carl what Crete was doing, how he was holding back my pay and acting cold, but I wasn't sure how to bring it up. Something gnawed at me—the thought that between the two of us, he might choose his brother. No matter how he felt about me, I wasn't blood. I wasn't the one he had loved for his entire life.

When I walked into work the next morning, Gabby took one look at me and knew something had changed. "Looks like somebody had a late night," she said.

I tried not to smile. "Yeah."

"How was it? What'd you guys do?"

"We talked and . . . stuff. It was nice."

"*How* nice?" She wiggled her eyebrows.

"Gabby!"

"Sweetie, your face don't hide *nothin'*." She shook her head. "You're lucky. Single guys like that are in short supply around here—good-looking, hardworking, from a decent family, got him some land. He don't have money, like Crete, with the store and all that, but still. Don't know how he made it this long without getting snatched up."

"I know he's had serious girlfriends," I said. "We talked about it last night."

"Yeah, lots of girls've tried to latch on to Carl, like ticks on a coon dog. Then you show up, don't even *try* . . ." She laughed a little, stacking the menus she had just wiped off. "You kinda lit him up, you know? I could see it that very first day." She lowered her voice. "I think you should know, it's got some folks talking. They're just bitter, hear? Jealous. Don't want to admit you're good for him, maybe you and Carl got some things in common. They been saying you put some kinda spell on him to get him wrapped around your finger. You know, like a witch." Gabby lowered her gaze as though embarrassed to be telling me.

"They think I'm a *witch*? For real? They really believe in that stuff?"

Gabby nodded, biting her lip. "Some do. I think most are just talking, you know, trying to make you look bad. But some of 'em, the older ones, they believe it. There's lots of superstition 'round here. They don't trust strangers."

I laughed. "That's great. If I were a witch, I'd zap myself the hell out of here. No offense."

Gabby was relieved I wasn't upset. "Don't pay it any mind. Most of 'em wish they were in your shoes, half as pretty as you and seeing Carl.

He's in deep, you know. I haven't seen him like that with anybody since his high school girlfriend, Janessa Walker. He tell you about her?"

"Is she the one that cheated on him?"

Gabby nodded emphatically. "They were practically engaged. Till she went and slept with Crete."

"Really? He didn't say who the other guy was. Ouch."

"I know," she said. "I mean, Crete's a charmer and all that, but with ten years between him and Carl, it was the first time they really fought over a girl. Crete told everybody; he was bragging about it. It was quite the scandal around town, Crete being so much older and her being a Walker. Everybody was on Carl's side, even the Walkers—they'd been ready to welcome him into the family, and they were all embarrassed. Carl was pretty heartbroken over it, smashed Crete's nose in a fight and didn't want anything more to do with Janessa."

A customer walked up, an old guy with a cane, and Gabby hurried over to help him, addressing him by name like she did practically everyone who came in the door. Janessa's story made me nervous. What would Carl think if he knew what had happened between me and Crete? I hadn't slept with his brother; I'd had a lapse of judgment that thankfully hadn't gone very far, and I'd straightened it out with Crete afterward the best I could. And Carl and I hadn't been involved at the time. But I was well aware of how bad it could look and how Crete could spin it if he wanted to, especially since he was already pissed at me. Work didn't distract me from my worries, though thoughts of the previous night kept seeping in. I'd been with plenty of other guys— boys from school, foster brothers' friends, a cook from IHOP in the walk-in freezer—and never once had I thought it was serious. With Carl, I wasn't so sure. With him, in the ruins of the old house, nothing around us for miles but trees and stars and wind, I felt something I'd never felt before.

"Do you want to go out after work?" Gabby asked as we sponged the counters. "Figured you might be lonely since loverboy's gone."

"I'm kind of tired," I said. "Crete's probably coming to pick me up anyway."

"I can give you a ride," she said. "I have to pass that way to get to the tavern. And maybe on the way, I can convince you to come with me." She pinched my arm playfully. "Lemme call Crete for you, tell him you got a new chauffeur."

Gabby's hatchback was a mess, discarded lottery tickets and empty pop cans littering the seats and floor. She told me more about herself as she drove. I'd thought she was fresh out of high school, like me, but she was twenty-two, and in all those years, she had never spent a night away from Henbane. She had a little camper at an RV park by the river where fishermen stayed, and she got to live there for free in exchange for managing the place.

"Tomorrow night," Gabby said, popping a cassette into the stereo, "I'm going to a party at Old Scratch, if you wanna come. It's this creepy old cave out in the woods."

"A party in a cave?"

"C'mon, they don't have cave parties in Iowa?"

"Um, not that I know of."

"Old Scratch isn't pretty like Bridal Cave or Meramec, those tourist ones with the little trains you ride through. You go in too far, there's bat shit two feet deep. Passages every which way. People get lost in there every once in a while, fall down a hole and can't get out. A guy from the conservation department drowned in there a long while back. But there's a big open room right inside called the auditorium. Cool place for a party."

"Sounds like fun," I lied. It sounded scary. The sun was down by the time Gabby dropped me off at the garage, and I went straight to bed. I dreamed of a cave, a big dark mouth swallowing me up, and someone pounding on the wall of the cave, trying to get me out. The pounding went on until I was no longer dreaming; the sound was real, someone knocking at the door. When I stumbled across the room, half-awake, to see who was there, the door wouldn't open. I switched on the lamp, and that was when I saw the window had been boarded shut.

Lucy

It was a long ride to Daniel's, east along Ridge Road, which curved and dipped like a roller coaster. The handful of houses in Crenshaw Ridge were spliced into the hillside with sloping shale yards. The bare planks of his mother's house blended into the surrounding trees. A narrow porch spanned the width of the house, with firewood stacked to the eaves on either side. Near the front door sat two rocking chairs, each occupied by dozing cats.

Daniel's mother was waiting for us in the kitchen, a crooked room that had been tacked onto the back of the house. The wall behind the kitchen table was lined with shelves, and on the shelves sat a hundred or so old canning jars filled with seeds, dried herbs, wild mushrooms, feathers, moss, roots, tree bark, and plenty of things I couldn't distinguish through the glass. Mrs. Cole came forward and took my hand in hers, a soft smile on her face. Her dark hair was streaked with gray, and her bangs were uneven, as if she'd cut them herself.

"Glad to meet you," she said. "I'm Sarah. Go on and sit. I made sassafras tea." I could smell the roots boiling in a kettle on the stove, a sweet, earthy smell like root beer. Sarah smacked an ice tray on the counter to loosen the cubes and parceled them into three mugs, then spooned in sugar and poured the tea. She sat down across from me and Daniel.

"I've got everything ready for Mrs. Stoddard," Sarah said, stirring her tea with a tarnished spoon. "I wrote the directions down, just be sure and follow 'em right close."

"Okay," I said.

She nodded and sipped her tea. "Daniel, fetch a box, would you, from the shed? Get this all packed up for Lucy?" She waited until he left the room and we were alone. "I was right about you," she said, her gaze moving over my hair, my eyes, my hands. "I told your mama, and lucky for you, she listened."

"You knew her?"

"Yep. That's why I made Daniel bring you here today, wanted to see you in the flesh. Make sure. But I knew then, when you were a speck in the womb, and I knew when my boy started talking about you. I can sense things."

I wasn't following. "Were you and Lila friends? I'm sorry, I just never heard my dad mention you."

"No. She came to me, looking for help, like people do. Friend of hers brought her. She was pregnant and thinking it over."

Thinking it over? My dad had always told me how much my mother wanted a baby, wanted *me*. But then, what else could he have said?

Sarah's hands gripped mine. "Don't be pained, child," she said. "She had a bad feeling, wasn't sure who the daddy was. I told her you were good, I could feel it through the skin."

"She's not talking you to death, is she?" Daniel grinned at me, striding into the room and setting down the box. "Mom, I told you not to scare her off."

Sarah released my hands, laughing softly, and I sank back into my chair, stunned. "Just girl talk," she said. "I didn't get much of that, raising boys."

Different scenarios ticked through my mind on the way home. I knew my mom and dad were married when they had me, but I didn't know the actual date—it had never seemed strange to me that there was no mention of their anniversary, no marking of the day. An anniversary was hardly something to celebrate alone. I'd spent my life believing the fairy tale that had been woven for me: love at first sight, whirlwind romance, elopement, me. I wasn't bothered to learn it might have happened in a different order, that she might have been pregnant when they got married. But I'd never entertained the notions that my mother had been with someone else—or that Carl wasn't my father. If she'd been with another man in the narrow margin between arriving in Henbane and meeting my dad, I'd never heard about it. Even in the ridiculous stories of her enthralling various men, no one ever claimed she'd cared for anyone but Carl Dane.

Maybe Sarah had made the whole thing up. That was the problem with secondhand accounts. You could believe them or not, but you could never be sure they were true. It didn't seem possible that I could belong to someone else. I looked like my mother, but I had Dane features, too. My height. The slight dent in my chin. The second toe a little longer than the first. Things I had to admit might not stand up to questioning.

When Daniel dropped me off, I asked if his mother had ever mentioned mine. "Not until I told her I was working with you. She said Lila Dane was the most beautiful woman to ever set foot in Ozark County. That beauty could be a curse." He smiled apologetically. "She didn't say anything to upset you, did she? She just kind of rambles sometimes. Doesn't mean anything by it."

If she hadn't told my mother's story to Daniel, she might not have told anyone. But she had mentioned a friend bringing Lila to the house. Aside from my father and Birdie, Gabby was my mother's only friend.

When I got home, I pulled out the box Gabby had given me. I'd been saving it for the last few days, but I couldn't wait any longer. I opened it. At the top of the box was a dress with an empire waist and a pleated skirt. A maternity dress. I had worn it with her. I recognized the next dress, the green sheath she wore in the photograph that sat atop our TV. In the picture, she stood with my father's arm around her, a lily in her hair. Ray Walker had taken the picture with Dad's camera. It was their wedding day. I wondered if I'd been with her that day, too, and whether she knew it. She was happy in that picture, it radiated out from the frame. I pulled off my T-shirt and slipped the dress over my head, the soft, musty fabric floating over my body. Then I let down my hair and draped it over my shoulder the way Mom's hair fell in the picture. The image in the mirror was uncanny, and for a moment I tried to imagine myself as her. A young bride with a child on the way, her mind filled with paint colors and garden plots and nursery furniture.

Beneath the clothing were some papers. I found a little notebook with sketches of plants and their descriptions. On the back cover were pencil outlines of two hands, one inside the other. I touched the larger one. *My mother's*, I thought. The small one had to be mine. I pressed my hand to the notebook, trying to make it fit, but it eclipsed the other hands entirely, my fingers long enough to curl around the edges.

A door slammed downstairs and Dad called my name. I walked to the top of the stairs and looked down to where he stood gripping the banister. He stared with bewilderment that prickled into anger. "Where'd you get that?"

The dress. I held the fabric away from my body to distance myself, feeling guilty, sick to my stomach, as though I'd done something unforgivable. "Gabby," I said softly.

He turned wordlessly and left me there on the stairs. Back in my room, I lay on the bed, surrounded by my mother's things, and let tears seep down into my hair. Dad rarely spoke of her anymore, keeping all his memories to himself. It wasn't fair to me. My image of her was warped and incomplete, relying on what others told me. Especially Gabby. She'd always kept up the fairy tale, indulging me, her guilt at being here in my mother's absence still raw beneath the surface. I knew her stories well, but I was ready for her to tell me more. I wanted everything, good and bad. I needed all of Gabby's pieces of my mother to make her whole and real.

Gabby was asleep in the lawn chair with her feet up and her head tilted back. She twitched as a fly buzzed around her face. "Gabby," I said, shaking her foot, "I need to talk to you." She moved her head from side to side as though disagreeing with something in her dream. "Gabby," I said, louder, and she opened her eyes and lurched backward in her chair.

"Jesus!" she said, sucking in breath.

"Sorry," I said, brushing lint off the dress. Lila's dress. "Didn't mean to scare you. It fits, sort of. Maybe a little short. She was shorter than me, though, right? My mother?"

Gabby nodded and pulled a cigarette out of the pack on her lap. Her hands trembled as she lit it. "Yeah, few inches, maybe." She cleared her throat and took a deep drag.

I leaned against the railing. The wind chimes clinked halfheartedly. "I was out in Crenshaw Ridge today, and Sarah Cole told me she knew my mother. That a friend brought her in for an abortion."

Gabby's face flushed. We were quiet, smoke dulling the air between us.

"It wasn't like that," Gabby murmured finally, flicking ash.

I squatted down next to her. "I need to know what happened, Gabby. I'm not a kid anymore. I'm almost as old as she was when she had me."

Gabby snorted. "Hardly. What she went through, growing up, it ages you. She was nineteen going on a hundred."

"Then tell me," I begged. "Tell me everything. All I have of her is what I'm told. You don't think that's hard?"

"She didn't want an abortion," Gabby said. "Not really. She was worried something was wrong with the baby . . . with you. Had a bad feeling. I took her to Sarah because she sees things, knows things. I knew she'd tell your mom everything was fine. And if she didn't, well, Sarah's known to be right about those things. She's the one who told Ray Walker's wife their baby wouldn't make it."

"Sarah told me Mom wasn't sure of the father. My father."

Gabby paused. "It's plain as day who your father is."

"Why'd she think it was somebody else?"

Gabby rubbed her eyes with her palms. "Maybe Sarah heard wrong, because your mom never said anything of the sort to me. Though I guess that's not the kind of thing you go around telling people. In the time I knew her, she only ever talked about your daddy."

"Do you think it could've happened before she came here?"

She tapped another cigarette out of the pack but didn't light it. "Timing-wise, I guess it's possible. But I don't know. And it doesn't matter, so you might as well leave it be."

"She kept a secret that big from Dad."

"Oh, no. Don't you go getting high and mighty. We all got secrets. I bet you got some yourself. Some you keep from your dad, for his own good." She eyed me sharply. "She had her secrets, all right, but they were part of her past. Once she married your dad, it was like her life started over. Things were good for a while there, just think on that."

Neither of us spoke, ruminating on the fact that the good hadn't lasted, that something had changed at the end. I'd asked Gabby a thousand times why she thought my mother left; I believed now that she hadn't been lying when she claimed not to know the real reason. She and my mother had been friends, but they hadn't shared everything. Gabby was right that we all had secrets, secrets that would hurt other people or expose us in ways we didn't want to be exposed. I couldn't fault my mother for that.

CHAPTER 12

Lila

The hammering ceased, and I ran back across the room to try the door again. I heard the rattle of a key in a lock, and the door swung open. Crete stood in the doorway, his expression cold and blank.

"I don't get you," he said quietly.

I cringed away from him, confused, my mind quickly shaking off the veil of sleep to make sense of what was happening.

"After all I done for you, you can barely look in my direction. Can't bother yourself to be grateful for the opportunities I give you. Then I let my brother drive you around, and you can't keep yourself from fucking him. He thinks he's in love, ain't that something? Maybe you are some kinda witch, making fools outta men."

My heart was a caged bird bent on escape. He couldn't have known what happened between me and Carl at the homestead. Surely Carl wouldn't have told him. I backed away and he stepped inside, closing the door. His anger vibrated like a taut wire, intensifying with each step he took toward me. My back touched the counter in the makeshift kitchen, and I couldn't go any farther.

Crete's hand pressed against my throat, the weight of his body driving my spine into the sharp edge of the counter, and tears blurred my vision. He ran his grizzled face along my cheek, stubble grating my skin. "Did you like fucking my brother, you little cunt? Huh?" Though I knew the countertop was bare, my hands scrabbled blindly on either side, seeking a weapon. I thought of Carl and Gabby and Ransome, the only ones who would notice if I disappeared. What would he tell them? That I had run off? Carl would be hurt, maybe, but in time he'd forget. It would be like I'd never existed.

"Let's see who you like better," he said, pushing up my nightshirt. I clawed at him and he wrenched my hands away viciously. I felt the heat of his mouth on my breasts, my nipples, the awful wet probing of his tongue on my breast, and then he bit down, hard, breaking the skin. I screamed and he clamped down on my windpipe. My hands were now free and pushing against him to no effect. He brought his mouth to mine, forcing a kiss, and I tasted blood. I tried to twist myself away from him, but he was too strong. His free hand worked between my thighs, snagged my underwear. There was a soft thud as his pants fell to the floor. He squeezed my throat with both hands as he entered me, and pain radiated through my body. The anger and fear began to dissolve along with my consciousness, and I drifted away from the weight of him, dissipating, like smoke into darkness.

I lay cocooned in my bed for unknown hours, my head buzzing, nerves jangling with the fear that Crete would burst in at any moment. I had no plan, no idea what I would do when he returned, and the harder I tried to organize my thoughts, the more they jumped around like live wires. My throat was swollen and bruised, my back raw where it had scraped against the counter. The bite on my breast pulsed, tender to the touch. Thirst finally drove me to the bathroom, where I guzzled water from the tap and used the toilet, wincing at the sting of scraped flesh. Dots of dried blood stained one side of my shirt. I dabbed at my wounds with a damp washcloth, my eye on the door the whole time, waiting.

I didn't know how long I sat watching the door, tensed for any sound or movement. Finally, the constant stress of being on alert wore me down enough that I could think beyond the moment. I showered, changed into clean clothes, and assessed the security of my prison. The window glass smashed easily with my suitcase, but the board beyond it must have been reinforced, because it wouldn't budge. The door was locked from the outside, and I couldn't get through the concrete-block walls. I was trapped.

Packets of crackers and raisins and beef jerky sat on the kitchen counter, and a bottle of aspirin that I knew Crete wouldn't have left for me. It must have been Ransome. She was in on this, partly if not completely. It hurt to know she was involved, but it gave me a flicker of hope. There was a tiny possibility I could convince her to help me—and in time, Carl would return. Crete couldn't keep me hidden from him forever. Carl wouldn't accept the explanations Crete would come up with. I told myself he'd come looking for me.

Two days passed. I had nothing to do but think about what Crete had done to me, my pain and soreness a constant reminder. I alternated between anger and tears, burning the lamp at all times, even while I slept, because the room was too dark without it. It was night-time when I heard a rattle, keys turning, locks releasing, and my body tensed. My instinct was to hide, but there was nowhere to go. The door opened and closed, and Ransome stood just inside, ready to dart back out if necessary.

"No point trying nothing," she said, resigned, apologetic. "You won't get far."

"I know," I said, my voice hoarse.

She moved toward me, a bag in one arm, and I wondered if I could knock her down, make it out the door. If I could get across the field, slip away into the woods . . . I'd spent hours dissecting what to do when this moment came, yet somehow I couldn't will my body off the bed. I felt weak, exhausted, not in charge of my own limbs. And I didn't know what waited outside.

Ransome stopped a few feet in front of me and set down the bag. "You okay?"

I laughed, a dry laugh that sounded more like a sob. Her eye twitched, and she knelt down to my level, keeping her distance—wary, perhaps, that I was faking my helplessness. She pulled a square green tin from the bag. "I brought some ointment. Works on udders, thought it might work . . . you know." My breast. She'd been in the room that first night as I slept. Had she noticed the blood on my shirt? Lifted it to see the wound? Maybe Crete had told her.

"Thank you." I closed my eyes and laid my head back down.

"You know why he brung you here, don't you?" She waited for me to open my eyes before continuing. Her lips were pressed together in a flat line, and her gaze flitted away when I looked at her. "It weren't to pull weeds and wait tables. He had men lining up for you right away, but he wanted to ease you into it, take it slow. I saw how he took a shine to you, thought maybe he'd change his mind and let you be. But that's all gone to hell now, and you'll be doing what you came here for. He's gonna start bringing customers for you. Next week."

"Customers?" Nausea spread through me. Surely I was misunderstanding her.

"He says they'll pay top dollar for a girl like you. I told him you needed time to heal up, but he ain't giving you long."

"I won't do it."

She looked down. "He has ways to make you."

"You could help me," I said. "Ransome, please, you could get me out."

"I'm sorry, I am." She shook her head. "I just . . . There ain't much I can do. I need this job and this place, and I ain't got nothing else."

No wonder she hadn't made much effort to get to know me. She'd shared her meals but kept her distance, doing her best not to get involved. Because she'd known what was coming. An exodus of built-up tears wet my face, and she pressed a handkerchief into my palm. She sat stiffly while I cried and blew my nose.

"There was another girl," she said. "Before you. Younger, not much English. Wild as a barn cat. Couldn't let her be seen in the restaurant, so he just kept her out here on the farm. She weren't here long. She wouldn't cooperate, and a man come to get her." Ransome wiped her nose with the back of her hand. "You gotta do what he wants, show him you can behave, do what you're told. You don't want him to have to move you, and that's what he'll do. He's already talking about it, says he's gotta get you outta here before Carl comes back. You gotta change his mind, get him to let you stay. There's worse places, see? The man that took her, that other girl . . . just, there's worse places. This ain't the worst."

I tried to process everything she'd said. As she stood up to leave, her voice lowered to a whisper. "Running ain't wise now, anyhow. He's ready for it. You best bide your time." I pictured traps in the woods, armed men with dogs. Who knew what he had in store for me.

I opened the bag after Ransome left. Canned SpaghettiOs. Apples. And a jar of her tea. I unscrewed the lid and drank it all. Another week trapped in this room, and then . . . Crete would get what he wanted from me. Ransome had hinted that I might have a better chance to run when I'd proved myself trustworthy and cooperative. Who knew how long that would take. Maybe Ransome was right, and there were worse things. But I thought of Crete's attack, and I tried to imagine reliving that shame and fear and disgust and rage every day with other men. How much worse could it get?

I was partly in shock, understanding what was going to happen but not fully believing it. Days passed, and my bruises and scrapes were healing. Everything except the bite. I'd been slathering it with the sticky yellow balm Ransome had brought, but it was still painful and swollen and had begun to ooze pus. The garage was hot, suffocating, and I was so tired. The lightbulb had been flickering, and I couldn't bear to watch it burn out, so I curled up on the quilts and slept.

CHAPTER 13

Lucy

"There's no way I'm letting you go out to the Stoddard place alone," Daniel said. I was helping him lock up the canoes for the night, even though I was off the clock. His voice had taken on a bossy tone that got under my skin. I'd actually *wanted* him to come with me, but I didn't like that he was suddenly telling me what I could and couldn't do. It made me want to do the opposite of everything he said. I wasn't scared to go see Doris Stoddard by myself, despite the guys who sometimes hung around her trailer. Most of them knew who I was and knew my uncle Crete, and that was enough to keep them from bothering me. They either thought I was witchy or that Crete would beat the crap out of them.

"I thought this was something we were doing together. And don't you need a ride?" Daniel prodded. "You've got that big box to carry."

"I could call Bess."

"How'll Bess protect you if something happens?"

"I don't need protection. I'm going to visit my friend's mom. Simple as that."

"Your murdered friend's mom. To get rid of a ghost. You're right, pretty simple."

I hated how he made me smile when I was mad. "What would *you* do to protect me? Blind the bad guys with your pretty smile?"

Within the space of a breath, he grabbed my arms and pinned them behind my back, pressing me against the boat shed so I could feel the tensed muscles of his chest. He looked down at me with an impish grin. "District wrestling champ, junior year." He released me just as quickly, the phantom of his touch lingering on my skin. My insides were giddy with wanting things I shouldn't have.

"Show-off," I said.

"Sorry." He stepped back. "I only resort to force when necessary. Usually the pretty smile's enough."

I rolled my eyes and sighed. "Fine," I said. "You can come."

It was dusk when we reached the trailer. Doris let us in, wearing the same housecoat she'd had on the last time we saw her. A cigarette trembled between her fingers. "You bring it?" she asked.

I held up the box. "It's all here." I'd read Sarah's lengthy instructions, and while I wasn't sure what we were about to do would cleanse the trailer of spirits, it might be enough to convince Doris. I'd asked Daniel whether he believed in this stuff, and he'd shrugged, saying it couldn't hurt.

We began by holding hands in a circle, the three of us, as I recited Sarah's blessing word for word. Then I lit a bundle of sage and walked through the trailer, cleansing each room with smoke and prayers. Cheri's room was stale and dusty, the lightbulb burned out and the mattress on the floor stripped bare. As we left each room, I placed wrinkled green hedge apples in the four corners. I seemed to remember Birdie telling me hedge apples kept away spiders, not ghosts, but maybe they worked for all kinds of pests.

When I finished with the sage, we were supposed to feel a sense of lightness as the spirits left us, set free, but I didn't feel any lifting of the heavy air in the trailer. Sarah's instructions didn't say what to do if I thought it wasn't working, so I retrieved the jar of salt and crumbled leaves and continued. This part of the ritual was meant to keep spirits from returning once they'd been released. They would no longer recognize their earthly home; it would be repellent and unfamiliar and no longer pull them back from the light. It was sad, and cruel, if you believed it, that you could so easily unmoor a being from all it had ever known. We walked the borders of the property, pouring the salt mixture into the earth and repeating the earlier blessing. We lit candles at the end and walked the path in reverse, dripping wax over the salt, circling back to the front of the trailer, where we blew out our flames.

Daniel and I followed Doris back inside, where a lilting breeze lifted the curtains and dissipated the haze of sage smoke. "You feel that?" she said, holding her hands out and looking around. "I can breathe."

I didn't feel anything, but I nodded, packing the remaining supplies back in the box. Doris sank into a recliner, and I perched on the edge of a shredded sofa that I assumed, from the fur and the smell, was the dog's bed. Daniel leaned against the wall. "There's one more thing we have to do, to make sure it sticks," he said. "We'll finish when you've told Lucy what she needs to know."

"Cheri," I said. "Was she hanging around anybody new before she disappeared?"

Doris snorted. "What, you think she got some other friend 'sides you?"

"I thought, maybe, one of the men . . . ?"

Her eyes narrowed and she hunched forward in her seat. The housecoat gapped open between the snaps, revealing glimpses of flesh. "Look. I know you're sitting there blaming me. But you ain't got no idea. She's the one fucked everything up. I was doing what I could. Had three kids to look after, plus one my sister dumped here when she got sent up to Chillicothe on a five-year stretch. I was stitching uniforms at the factory in Mountain Home all day and cleaning the old folks' home at night. I didn't always have somebody to watch the kids. My oldest, Joey, he was real responsible. Had to leave him in charge some of the time, and he did real good. One night he was boiling macaroni for dinner, and Cheri—couldn't get nothing through that kid's thick skull, you tell her the stove's hot, and she'd stick her hand right on it—she grabbed the handle and pulled the boiling water down all over Joey. Burned him pretty good. He'd pushed her outta the way, and she was fine, not a spot on her. I salved the burns when I got home, but they wouldn't heal up, and after a while they started looking worse. Took him to the medicine woman on my day off, and she sent me straightaway to the doctor. I did just like she said, went to the doctor in town, and they still come and took my kids from me. Stuck 'em in foster care, like they get treated any better in there. Well, wouldn't you know they brought Cheri back. The one that caused the whole mess. Said she had special needs, she was still so little and wouldn't stop crying for her mama. And surely I could do better, taking care of just one. I tell you why they brought her back: couldn't handle her. Asking the same dumb questions over and over, doing the same stupid things, pissing her pants and walking around like nothing happened.

"I had to start working from home to watch her; nobody else wanted to do it after what happened, they knew she was trouble. Gave up rights on my other kids, knew I couldn't support 'em no more. Curtis, he got adopted, he was still cute enough, but Joey, all them scars. Nobody took him. Used to write me these letters wanting to come back home, but he don't write no more. Don't know where he is." Doris rubbed her eyes.

"I'm so sorry," I said, but she didn't seem to hear me and went on with her story.

"Cheri was always getting in my way when I was trying to work. Walking in at the wrong time, staring. Grew them big tits when she was ten, that weren't normal. Didn't have sense to wear a bra. She brought it on herself, all that attention. She liked it, too, lemme tell you. Crawl up in their laps while they's waiting, show 'em the pictures she's drawing, retarded little stick things."

I thought of Mr. Girardi, how Cheri's face had glowed when he'd helped her in class, taken her artwork seriously. She'd been starved for any kind of attention, good or bad.

"Was there anyone in particular she talked about, maybe? Anyone she might've wanted to leave with?" I asked.

"Hard to tell. She jabbered all the time, 'specially about that art teacher at school. That's what I told the cops."

"What didn't you tell them?" Daniel asked. I had practically forgotten he was there.

"I ain't ratting nobody out. I ain't got proof of nothing."

"My mother has other spells," Daniel said. "To summon ghosts. Maybe Cheri needs some company."

Doris's face hardened as she looked at him, but there was fear in her eyes. She'd had a taste of what she felt was freedom from Cheri, and she wanted to hold on to it.

"There's one guy," she said, turning back to me. "Prick to do business with, but he was nice to her. He'd make a point of coming by when she was getting home from school. But he never tried nothing on her. They just sat on the steps and talked. Then I got to thinking that's what was strange about him—he didn't try nothing."

"What's his name?"

She laughed. "I don't know his real name. Ain't from here. Drives a van, that's all I know."

"Was he here the other day, right before we stopped by?" Daniel asked.

She looked down at her lap. "Might of been."

Daniel and I exchanged glances. She didn't want to tell us too much, just enough to ensure that the ghost wouldn't come back. She didn't say anything more, so I stood to go. "Thank you," I said.

"Finish up whatever you have to do to keep her away, and then get out of here," she said. "Just let me be."

"Poor Cheri," Daniel said when we were back in the truck. "Growing up with a mother like that."

"Worse than not having one at all," I said. "So what's the last thing we were supposed to do? I didn't see anything else in Sarah's instructions."

He shrugged. "If you think you're haunted, you're haunted. And vice versa. Doesn't matter what we do so long as she believes it."

CHAPTER 14

Ransome

Ransome knew infection when she saw it. When she was a kid living up on the ridge, her dog Beans got in a fight with a coyote and won. He was a scrapper, guarding the chickens like a true working dog, like it was in his blood, and maybe it was—he was five kinds of mutt, maybe more. No doubt that coyote was sorry it bit Beans, if it could be sorry from inside the stew pot, but Ransome was sorrier. The bite was on Beans's hindquarters, and he couldn't quite twist his neck enough to lick it. Ransome and her sister cleaned his wound every night before he jumped up on their bed to sleep, but a wet rag lacks the curative properties of dog tongue, and every morning he'd be right back out rolling in filth, as dogs do.

The bite festered and Beans got sick. His nose dried and scabbed. He slept on the stone slab behind the springhouse, where it was cool and shady all day, his flanks shuddering with each shallow breath. Ransome's mama wasn't one for pets you didn't eat; said when Beans died, another mutt would wander in to freeload in his place. But Daddy gave in to Ransome's begging and got Birdie Snow to come. She was midwifing animals more than people back then, working for a farm vet. She made a poultice for Beans to ease the pain and help draw out the infection, but she thought it might be bad enough that he'd need an antibiotic. Daddy bagged up one of the bantam hens to trade for the medicine. Not likely a fair trade, but Birdie took it and called things even.

Beans got better. Before long, he was back to stealing salt pork off the kitchen counter. But a coyote bite's not a human bite. You'd think a person would be cleaner than an animal, but a human bite's got venom to it. Poison. Maybe because a person's got to think to bite, Ransome guessed, to make a choice. Poison's in the intent. She knew from the beginning that Lila wouldn't be okay, though she told herself she would. She put some of Birdie's salve on the wound, because that would fix most anything.

Ransome walked back up the hill after checking on Lila for the last time. She couldn't sleep, knowing the girl was right down there in the garage, in the dark, waiting on things to come. She thought about the other girl, the wild one, that Crete had sent away. Such a tiny thing, full of piss and vinegar, as her daddy would say. Never let down her guard, never did a single thing Crete asked, but Ransome could hear her crying at night, hoarse, choking on her own snot. She'd been relieved when that girl was gone, and tried not to think about where she went. She thought Crete had given up on that sort of thing, trading in girls. She figured he'd lost money on the first one, and that was his least favorite thing to do.

Then Lila showed up, and Ransome pretended this one was different. She'd come to the farm of her own free will. It was hard to understand why such a comely girl had need to sell herself anyway; in Henbane, a girl that pretty would be married to the car dealer's son. Ransome expected her to dress up in slut clothes and sit around filing her nails while Crete drummed up customers, but that wasn't Lila at all. She took a real interest in the farm, like she really thought that was her job. And heck, maybe she believed it; maybe she was in some kind of denial about the mess she'd gotten herself into.

Ransome wondered what had happened to Lila to make her end up here, in a place like this, but didn't ask. The girl had some sweetness to her, like she hadn't given up on things completely. Sometimes, in the field, she'd look up at the sky with a little smile on her face, and it made Ransome think of herself and her sister when they were kids, playing in the sweet corn, and how glad they were to be out in the sun, how other things didn't much matter, and she wondered if Lila felt that same way. Still, Ransome stood by and let the bad things happen. She showed Lila less care than she'd shown her mutt dog. But she needed the house and the paycheck and didn't know what Crete would do to her if she crossed him. She told herself Lila would get used to her new job, or she'd get sent away, too, and either way Ransome wouldn't have to worry about it.

That last night, the night before the first customer was set to come, she found Lila sweating in her bed. The sheets were soaked, and she blazed with fever. She didn't stir when Ransome pulled up her shirt. Red lines spidered out from the bite, and Ransome couldn't deny anymore that it was infected, that Lila could die if it went untreated. She couldn't let that happen. Part of her job was protecting Crete's assets, and he'd made it clear that Lila was an unmined vein of gold. So she called Crete close to midnight and told him that Lila needed to see the doctor. The phone went mute while he turned things over. It didn't take long. Some folks thought him cold-blooded, but Ransome knew he wasn't all bad. He said he'd see to it first thing.

The next morning she was out weeding before the sun got too high. After a while a truck pulled up to the garage, and she squinted across the field to see if it was Crete or the doctor, but it was an old two-tone Dodge that belonged to Joe Bill Sump. She wiped her face off with a handkerchief and hurried through the rows to see what he wanted. If he had an appointment, it would have to wait. She doubted Lila would let Joe Bill touch her unless she was sedated first, and Ransome wasn't about to drug the girl when she was already so sick.

"Need you to open up early," Joe Bill said, spitting tobacco juice at her feet. "Crete said the girl needs breaking in. Gotta get this done before work."

"You'll have to come back," Ransome said. "She's sick."

"I paid my money," he said. "Now, lemme in or I'll make you."

"I'm gonna call Crete," she said, turning toward the house. "Just need to make sure that's all right with him."

Joe Bill grabbed her shirt and yanked her back, reaching around to feel her pockets for the key.

"Hey!" She heard footsteps quickening on the grit path. Joe Bill shoved her aside, and she nearly lost her balance. "What the hell's going on here?" It was Carl, who'd come from the direction of the woods. She hadn't expected him back for another couple weeks. He gripped the front of Joe Bill's shirt, but he was looking at Ransome. "You okay?"

She didn't know what to say. Lies spilled out like water from a spring, an effortless gush. "He's gone crazy," she said. "He's trying to get to Lila. He attacked her once already, we had to lock her in to keep her safe. Crete's getting the doctor."

"Doctor? She all right?"

"She's a lyin' bitch," Joe Bill spewed, twisting himself out of Carl's grasp.

Ransome bit down on her lip and shook her head. Carl's face darkened, and for a moment he looked just like his brother. He spun around and shoved Joe Bill into the wall. "I told you to leave her alone," he snarled.

"I got every right to be here," Joe Bill said, shoving him back. "You wanna fuck her, you can wait in line."

It happened so fast that it all smeared together in Ransome's brain, leaving only one thing clear: the sharp crack of Joe Bill's skull against the garage after Carl struck him. They stood there staring at the crumpled body. An accident. Had Joe Bill been a few more inches from the garage, his head wouldn't have hit the wall with such force, if at all. Had Joe Bill not been such an asshole, he wouldn't have been punched in the first place. Part of it fell on her, she knew; had she not lied, he wouldn't be dead. Everything that came after hinged on her lie, a door swinging open on a future that hadn't existed until that moment. The lie worked out better for everybody involved, everybody but Joe Bill, though she was hard pressed to find that a bad thing.

She had to work quickly to smooth out the edges. She sent Carl home to get his truck—he'd walked through the woods to surprise Lila—and ran up to the house to call Crete. She told him about the scuffle with Joe Bill and Carl showing up, how she panicked and blamed everything on Sump because she didn't know what to do. Then she explained how Joe Bill needed getting rid of, and Carl was too worked up over Lila to take care of it himself. Crete was quiet for all of one second before he calmly told Ransome her pay would be docked the hundred dollars he wouldn't be getting from Joe Bill now that he was dead, though she'd done the right thing by trying to see if he'd paid up front. (He hadn't.) She kept her mouth shut about that not being fair. If that was all she had to pay for what she'd done, she'd call herself lucky. He gave her a message for Carl—that Crete would handle Joe Bill, and Carl could owe him—and told her everything was scrapped now, to let Lila go, to make sure the girl kept her mouth shut or Ransome would be out on her ass, looking over her shoulder every step of the way.

She ran back to the garage, her joints wobbly and threatening to give, and shook Lila awake. The girl was groggy and unfocused, but Ransome gripped both sides of her head and explained that this was her chance to get out and she had to do everything just right or hellfire would rain down on the both of them, that if they didn't end up dead, they'd be chained in a cellar sucking redneck dick every last miserable minute of their time on earth. She didn't know if that was true, but she sure didn't want it to be.

He's lettin' you go, but you ain't free. You can't tell Carl, can't tell nobody. He'll kill you, understand? Do you hear me? Ransome screamed in Lila's face, begging for some sign that the girl understood, and her eyes flickered and her head moved in Ransome's hands. She was nodding, *yes, yes*, and Ransome hugged her, a crazy, panicked hug, grateful that she'd made it through those first ugly minutes when everything could have caved in on her.

After Carl took Lila home for Birdie Snow to fix up, and Crete doubled Joe Bill over into a bag in the back of the Dodge and drove off, Ransome set out for her swimming hole. It was hidden in the cedars, spring-fed and deep, and she stripped to her drawers and untied her hair and dunked herself in the icy water. She stayed under as long as she could. The cold slowed her down, made her work for the surface. Back in the sunlight, nothing had changed. She was the same as she'd always been, no better. She didn't know why she'd expected any different; she couldn't step out of her own skin. She dressed soaking wet, wrung out her hair, and headed back to work. Her bones ached as the cold let go, and pretty soon she was right back to sweating.

It wasn't long before folks started clucking about Joe Bill being gone. Sump's ex-wife didn't think it was a coincidence that he'd disappeared two days before his child support payment was due, and that, plus the fact that his truck hadn't turned up, left little doubt what had happened. But then some of Sump's pals brought up Lila, said he was planning to pay her a visit the day he went missing. Deputy Swicegood cornered Ransome one Saturday in the cereal aisle at Ralls' and asked if she'd seen Joe Bill at the farm on the day in question. Angie Petree stopped in front of a display of puffed rice and cocked her head to listen. Junior Ralls watched from the meat counter, never taking his hand off the ham he slid back and forth on the slicer. Ransome told Swicegood she and Lila had worked the fields together like any other day. Didn't see a thing.

That so? he sneered. *Didn't see one single thing all day? Not one thing caught your eye? Maybe I saw a snake,* she said, *laying in the dirt. But the next time I looked, it was gone.*

Angie Petree nodded knowingly, and Swicegood grudgingly stepped aside.

CHAPTER 15

Lucy

I worked Fourth of July, a busy day for Dane's, with both locals and out-of-towners swarming the river. Dad was working on the construction of a new Walmart in Branson, but he came home for the holiday weekend and made sure I got back to the house before all the drunks started setting off fireworks. Bess came over, and Dad gave us a bag of blacksnakes and sparklers he'd picked up from a roadside stand. We sat on the porch steps lighting our kiddie fireworks while the muted pops and cracks of more impressive displays echoed through the hills around us.

Dad went back to work on the fifth. I sat on the porch with my journal after he left, watching the breeze work through the hayfield across the road. I was working on a new list: "People Who Knew My Mother." Dad, Crete, Gabby, Birdie, Ray Walker, Ransome Crowley, Sarah Cole. Not a lot to go on, since I'd already talked to Sarah, and since Dad and Crete never said much about her—and I'd mined everything Gabby and Birdie were willing to share, down to favorite songs and foods, which I'd cataloged in "Things I Know About My Mother." That list had dark gouges along the bottom of the page. After my visit with Sarah, I'd written something about Lila not wanting me, then later scratched it out.

I'd always been able to talk to Birdie about Mom, but she told the same stories over and over, her favorite being about my birth. How Mom had hollered curse words during hours of back labor and insisted on scrubbing the nursery floor between contractions. How she'd let out this otherworldly scream when Birdie had dragged me out, sunny side up, and laid me slick and squalling on her chest. Then Mom had started laughing because she'd bet Dad I was a girl and she'd won naming rights. Lucy, after her grandmother Lucille.

Birdie's other favorite story was about my mom showing up on her porch with a plate of squirrel dumplings, which were just about the best thing Birdie had ever eaten. She tried to teach me to make them from my mom's handwritten recipe, but they never turned out right. Finally, I gave up, because Dad refused to eat them.

I wasn't sure how well Ray Walker knew my mom, aside from witnessing the wedding. It would be easy enough to talk to him, though; he had an office down at the courthouse. Then there was Ransome. She'd worked with my mom on Crete's farm, retiring a few years back when emphysema forced her to. I'd seen her plenty of times from afar, a stooped figure in the field when Dad and I drove by, but we'd never shared more than a few words. I knew she was over in Howell County now, at the same nursing home where my grandma Dane had lived out her days.

———

After a lengthy explanation of what to do if it wouldn't start, Daniel let me borrow his truck to visit Ransome at the Riverview Care Center. Riverview had no view of the river. The flat, sallow building horseshoed around a gravel courtyard splotched with clumps of dead grass and potted marigolds. Dad claimed he'd brought me here to see Grandma Dane before she died, but I was too young to remember.

The front door opened into a dim common area where wheelchairbound residents were parked too close to the television. Ransome sat in a folding chair against the wall, her arms resting on her walker. The walker had tennis balls on its feet, to make it easier to slide, and a basket holding an oxygen tank. She wasn't quite seventy, but she looked ancient, mummified, draped with a quilt made of clothing scraps. Her mouth gaped open, drawn down at the corners and flexing, desperate for air despite the tubes delivering oxygen through her nose. Her eyes widened when she saw me, and her chest heaved like a frightened horse's.

"My mind's still good," she rasped as I sat down in the chair next to hers. "Just my body giving up. Ain't lost a lick of sense. They told me you was coming. So I know you're not her. Not a ghost. You're her little girl."

I nodded and tried to smile at her wasted figure. "I'm Lucy."

She stared at me, reaching out and pulling back, like she wanted to touch me but was afraid I might bite. "You remember me at all?" Ransome asked. Every few words were punctuated by a long scraping breath. "You was out to the farm a few times when you was little. I drove you around in the wheelbarrow? Fed you strawberries?"

I shook my head. "No. Sorry."

Her shoulders slumped. "Well. You was little. Don't expect you to remember a thing like that. So what is it you want, then?"

"You worked with my mother," I said.

"Yep. From the time she got here to the day she ran off with your daddy. She didn't work no more after that. Didn't need to, I suppose."

"What was she like?"

"She was pretty, you know that, and sharp. Hardworking. Daydreamer, though. She'd be staring at the sky, pulling weeds, had to stop her before she yanked up the carrots."

"Did she talk to you at all about what it was like leaving home to come here? How she felt about working for Crete or meeting my dad?"

Ransome shifted in her chair. "She didn't talk about home. Didn't seem to miss it. We didn't talk too much, really, about anything other than the work we was doing."

"Oh," I said, trying not to sound disappointed. Ransome was one of the few people who'd been close to my mother, and she wasn't telling me anything I didn't already know. "So she never mentioned a boy from back home? Or anyone else here aside from my dad?"

Ransome's eyes watered, and she sucked in a wheezing breath. "Like I said, she didn't talk about home." She picked at the yarn ties on the quilt. "Why you coming around asking about Lila after all this time, anyhow?"

"She was my mother, and I never got a chance to know her. I was really hoping to find out more about her, get a sense of what her life was like. I want to know why she left. Do you know anything that might be helpful?"

She stared at me for a long, uncomfortable minute, her mouth working like a fish's. "I've had emphysema for a while now," she said, "but it weren't so bad till I come here. I could still get out in my garden. Fill up the hummingbird feeders. Could still smoke, too, even though the doctor told me not to. Now every morning the nurse comes in, I say if you're not gonna gimme a cigarette, gimme a knife so I can slit my goddamn throat. She don't do it. The smoke or the knife. I ain't long for this place, thank the Lord, 'cause I can't stand being stuck indoors, strung up to this cart. I forgot what dirt feels like in my fingers. It's no way to live. So there's not much can happen to me now if I say something. The worst could happen, I'll be put outta my misery."

"What are you talking about?"

"I done things I ain't proud of. But I did what I could to help her, I tried."

"It's okay," I said, my stomach tightening. "Just tell me what happened."

"You know she worked for your uncle."

"Sure. That's why she came here in the first place. For the job."

"Before you knew it, she up and married your dad and quit the farm. Now, Crete and Carl've always been close, but around that time, they had some sort of falling-out. It had something to do with your mother."

"Why? Crete didn't want Dad to marry her? Was he mad that she quit working for him?"

"Some of both, I imagine. Your mother stirred people up in ways you had to see to believe. Weren't her fault, a course. There was something about her, a strange pull. You wanted to get close to her, touch her, smell her, see if she was real. It made people scared of her, too— angry with her for making 'em want her, or because she didn't even notice 'em wanting her. Your uncle, he knew she was something special, and he didn't wanna let her go so easy."

If I'd had any say in the matter, I wouldn't have let her go, either. I waited for Ransome to say something more, but she was staring into a past I couldn't see, images that no longer existed anywhere except in her head.

"Was that all?" I asked. "She got between Crete and my dad?"

"It was an ugly time," Ransome said. "But she came out okay. Better than okay. Husband, baby, house. Couldn't want more than that."

Her vagueness was exasperating. "What ugliness, exactly?"

"A deal was struck. It put a strain on things. Now, I said all I can live with, and I'm doing penance for the rest. In this life and the next, I imagine."

"A deal? If you know what happened, why can't you just tell me?"

She turned her attention to the quilt, running her finger along a seam. Her mouth opened and closed, but no words came out. She was one of the few people who could help me, and she wouldn't. I wanted to throw myself at her feet and beg. I wanted to grab her shriveled body and shake out all the answers, though the look on her face told me how pointless that would be. Suffering had etched itself in the cracks of her weathered skin. It welled in her sunken eyes, gave off a sour smell. She was poisoned by the things she carried inside, things she refused to share. Oddly, her story ended with my mom being happy; she hadn't mentioned the disappearance at all. So maybe whatever troubled Ransome came before and had no bearing on what followed.

"Thank you," I said. I stood to go, and her gnarled fingers brushed my wrist. She emitted a series of internal creaks and rasps before she spoke.

"She liked her tea muddled with mint."

I smiled. The herb bed beside the house was overgrown with mint. I'd tried tearing it out to plant sage and thyme, but mint always grew back and crowded out everything else. As I left Ransome in the place she'd never get out of, a warren of stale, dark rooms, I wondered what she'd done that she felt she deserved such penance.

Work kept me busy. Crete was back from his latest business trip, and I found myself scrutinizing everything he did, each word he spoke. I tried to picture him with my mother. Had he secretly been in love with her? Ransome hadn't made it sound quite like that, but I was skeptical of all my previously held assumptions. Crete stepped up my responsibilities at the store, giving me some accounting, scheduling, and inventory tasks. When he wasn't out at the farm, he spent most of his time in the office with the door closed. I'd started thinking that the next time I found his office empty and unlocked, I would sneak in and check his rental records, see who'd been in the trailer. So far, I hadn't had the chance.

Since I was in charge of scheduling, I made sure that Daniel and I had the same days off. Until I could get into Crete's office, our next best lead in figuring out what happened to Cheri was to find the man in the van, the one Doris had mentioned. Though I had no idea what to do once we did find him. He hadn't exactly been friendly during our first brief meeting. I was hoping Jamie Petree knew him, but I wasn't thrilled with the prospect of asking him for help.

Bess and I talked on the phone most every night, though our jobs kept us from spending as much time together as we usually did in the summer. She told me she'd been seeing someone and wanted to tell me about it in person. To see my face when she said his name, because I just wouldn't believe it. I hoped that her new guy was better than Gage Petree, or at least wasn't worse.

CHAPTER 16

Lila

I was too alarmed by what Ransome had said to feel relieved when Carl scooped me out of bed and carried me to his truck. I grasped that I wasn't supposed to tell Carl what his brother had done to me, and Ransome had made it easier by lying to him herself.

Back at Carl's, I was placed in an upstairs bedroom with white-washed walls and an old iron bed. Light filtered through the trees outside the window and played across the wood floor. I was grateful to be out of the darkness, to know night from day and sense the passing of time. Once I was feeling more alert, I realized the room was too feminine for Carl; it must have been his mother's. There was a dressing table with a large round mirror across from the bed, and I could see myself propped on a pile of feather pillows. I looked like a storybook witch, my eyes ringed with shadows and my dark hair bushy and tangled.

I spent a whole week in bed, Birdie Snow feeding me pills and spreading sticky concoctions on my skin while Carl watched anxiously. I expected to be pressed for details about what had happened, but there were few questions. I got the feeling Carl didn't want to upset me by talking about it, and I was terrified that Crete would come after me if I didn't keep his secret. Though there was no hiding the bruises or the bite, Carl thought Sump was to blame. I didn't know how much he'd told Birdie. She rarely spoke as she tended to me, aside from occasional orders for me to swallow something, lift my nightgown, or hold still.

By the end of that first week at Carl's, my bruises had faded. I was able to get up and move around, though I felt nervous leaving the bedroom by myself, even to use the bathroom across the hall. Carl kept me company as much as he could, but there was someone else I wanted to see. I asked him for Gabby's phone number.

Gabby sounded surprised and happy to hear from me, and it was good to know that I'd been missed. She asked if things had let up on the farm. Crete had told her I was too busy in the fields to work any shifts at the restaurant. I didn't contradict what Crete had said, only added to it with the story Carl and I had agreed on—that I'd come down with something and gotten really sick. She wanted to know how I'd ended up at Carl's, and all I could think to tell her was that he'd been worried about me. She had no problem believing it.

The next morning, Gabby stopped by, and Carl brought her upstairs to see me. She forced a smile and hugged me and didn't say anything about how awful I looked. We sat on the bed, and she filled me in on all the gossip I'd missed. Everybody was talking about Joe Bill

Sump running off to spite his ex-wife, who depended on him for child support. He was a snake-eyed son of a bitch, Gabby said, and she wouldn't miss him at all. He'd never left her a tip in his life. I wondered if people were talking about me, too, but if anyone besides Gabby noticed or cared that I hadn't been around the restaurant, she didn't mention it.

Gabby insisted on coming over every day on her way to work. She would sit on Carl's mother's bed with me and style my hair or paint my nails or insist that I put on some blush. There was a man in the house, after all, and she didn't want me letting myself go. Gabby had been through two new boyfriends since I'd seen her last. She asked me lots of questions about Carl, like how serious were we, and wasn't it romantic that he'd brought me to his house to recuperate.

"Not that romantic," I said. "I'm wearing his mom's ugly-ass nightgown." Gabby laughed, and I laughed, too. For the first time since leaving the garage, I let myself stop worrying that Crete would barge into the house and drag me back. I didn't feel safe—memories of the attack hung over me like storm clouds—but somehow, in the bright bedroom, I felt a little less afraid.

Carl stayed in the house most days, though he left me alone much of the time so I could rest. I heard him downstairs rattling pans in the kitchen and watching TV. I'd asked him why he came back from Arkansas early, and he said there'd been an accident on the job site, and the project was on hold for a day or two. He'd been glad for the unexpected time off, because there was something he wanted to talk to me about. All he'd tell me now, though, was that it could wait. Everything could wait until I was better. I didn't know how long he could put his life on hold for me. He'd been home from work for almost two weeks, and I fretted about what would happen when he had to go back.

Sunday evening, Carl brought two bowls of vegetable soup up to the bedroom so we could eat together, him in the chair and me with a tray on the bed. "Mmm," I said, savoring my first spoonful. "I can tell it's homemade. Is it Birdie's?"

"Now, why do you always assume Birdie made it if it's good? I can cook."

"Sorry," I said.

"I'm just joking." He smiled and patted my leg. "Of course she made it. There's buckets of it in the deep freeze; it'll last us through winter."

I looked down into my bowl, wondering if that was true. Would we be here together in this house, eating Birdie's soup, come winter? I didn't know what was going on with Crete. I didn't know if it was safe to stay, if I even *wanted* to stay.

"And if you're worried about your job, don't be," he said. "Crete's hired a kid to help Ransome out, and he's gonna get somebody on part-time at the restaurant. It'll all sort itself out." A grim look crossed his face, but I might have imagined it, because then he was smiling again and teasing me about how much I'd eaten and did I want seconds. It was a good sign, he said, my appetite improving.

I felt woozy the next morning when Birdie came to check the bite. I closed my eyes every time she removed the bandage, because it nauseated me to think about Crete's mouth on my body, but this time she didn't put a new bandage on. My visible wounds had healed. I talked to her about how I felt weak and dizzy sometimes when I got up for my shower, and she said it was from spending so much time lying around. The more I got up and about, the better I'd feel, and there was no reason for me to be in bed.

When Gabby arrived, Carl left to run a few errands. I was feeling better by then. It was her day off, so I knew she had extra time, and I asked if we could go outside.

"Does Carl approve?" she asked, only partly teasing.

"Birdie does," I said. "She says I need the fresh air, need to get used to using my muscles again."

She helped me up and we started across the room. "Wait," she said. "You can't wear that awful nightgown outdoors. No offense to Mama Dane."

"Are my clothes here?" I asked.

"I don't know," she said, "but Carl got you a few things." She opened the closet and pulled out a simple dress. "It's secondhand, but that's all we've got in town. If he'd been willing to leave you alone long enough, he would've driven down to Mountain Home and bought you some new stuff."

Gabby and I sat on the porch swing for a while, just watching clouds inch by. "Can we walk down the road a little?" I asked.

"Sure, if you're up to it."

We walked slowly, stopping frequently to shake out my secondhand sandals when rocks slipped in between the straps. We hadn't made it far when I noticed something draped over the barbed-wire fence. As we got closer, I could make out the body of a snake, maybe four feet long, its brown skin patterned with diamonds. I pointed it out to Gabby.

"Oh," she said. "That's to make it rain. Old superstition. We had a drought a couple years back, and there was snake jerky hanging all over the place."

The smell reached me, and my head swam. I doubled over and threw up in the road.

"Uh-oh," Gabby said. "We best get you back to the house." She took my arm and led me back, making me lie down in bed even though I no longer felt sick.

"I'm fine," I said. "I think it was just the smell."

"Smell wasn't that bad," she said. "You should tell Birdie. Could be something's still not right."

"I told her I've been feeling weak and dizzy, and she said that's normal. It's usually just in the morning, though."

Gabby stared at me the way people do when you have a spider on you but they haven't figured out a good way to tell you.

"You're sick in the morning."

I nodded. "It doesn't last. I'm starving by lunch."

"Uh-huh. And when was your last period?"

"My period?" I didn't know. It had never been regular.

"Are you *pregnant*?"

It was a ridiculous thing for her to say. "No."

"But it is *possible*. And how do you know you're *not*?"

Time stopped as all the different pieces came together. I'd been lulled into a kind of blissful ignorance during my time at Carl's, had forgotten the pattern my life was following, where it grew shittier at every turn. I'd dreamed of having a new family, but not now, not like this. I could not imagine anything worse at that moment than something growing inside me. I felt too hollow even to summon tears.

We sat there, and after a while I noticed that Gabby was holding my hand. Carl would be back soon, and I would have one more horrible thing I couldn't tell him.

"It'll be okay," she said. "Carl's not like some guys. He won't be mad. He won't think you did it on purpose."

I didn't want to tell her it might not be his. I couldn't bear the thought myself.

CHAPTER 17

Carl

Carl had trouble sleeping. He'd turn out all the lights downstairs and go around to every window and door, looking outside for a minute or two, each view framed a little different but all the same: dark road, dark field, dark hills. Nobody out there, no *thing*, nothing. He didn't know what he expected to see. Joe Bill Sump dragging himself up half-eaten from a hog trough, or his bones all split up like kindling from a long fall down Devil's Throat? Carl didn't know where Crete had taken him, where the body was, if there was anything left of it, but Joe Bill was dead and Carl had killed him. The scene replayed in his dreams on an endless loop, a record stuck on a tuneless refrain. His arm pulling back like a piston and shooting forward to smash the words out of Joe Bill's mouth. The burst of numbness in his knuckles as they struck the jaw with a sharp crack. Joe Bill's head hitting the wall. The sudden absence of Joe Bill despite his body on the ground. Ransome buzzing in his ear, *Get your truck, go!* And then he was running, because there was something more important than Joe Bill, and that was making sure Lila was okay.

The guilt didn't seep in until later, not until she was under his roof and healing and he knew nothing would hurt her, and then he felt sorry that he'd killed Joe Bill, because he hadn't meant for it to happen. He also felt guilty for being glad Joe Bill was gone. How could Carl have gone around every day doing normal things, knowing what Sump had done and what he still might do? Knowing that he somehow could get to Lila? He didn't have to worry about that now, and freed from worry, he had plenty of room for guilt. He could carry that weight. But it made it hard to sleep.

Crete knew how to dispose of a body. He and Carl had learned from their dad and grandpa, growing up. Dad preferred the respectable way of laying a body to rest, digging a proper grave and tamping it down nice and smooth before the family arrived to mourn. But that wasn't always what the job called for. Sometimes measures had to be taken to keep things quiet, hidden. *The spirit's fled*, Dad would say. *Nothing left but a body, and a body without a spirit'll fall apart whether you help it along or not.* Sometimes you did things that disrespected the body, and that was just part of the job. There wasn't any way around it.

So Crete had taken care of things. He'd always been a good big brother, protecting Carl from bullies, dragging him out of the river when he got swept up in the current. He made it clear they were there to help each other, it was what brothers did, and he led by example. Joe Bill was gone and so was his truck, and Crete wouldn't say where. *Better you don't know*, he said. He'd kept Joe Bill's wallet and license plate, and though he didn't say why, Carl knew. So Crete would have something over him if he needed it. He'd always had that seed of distrust in him, even when it came to his brother. *I owe you,* Carl had said, and he meant it. He promised Lila that Sump would never touch her again.

CHAPTER 18

Jamie

Jamie knew the guy in the white van, the one Lucy had seen at Doris Stoddard's—though even if he hadn't, he would have lied and said he did, made up a story, anything to keep her with him, alone and in arm's reach. She'd found Jamie at his fishing spot on the river, and he knew in order to do that, she first would have had to hunt down Gage in whatever hole he was crashing and convince him to give her directions. It was good that she'd gone to some trouble. It meant the information was valuable. Through his years of dealing and bartering, Jamie had developed a knack for knowing how far somebody would go to get something. He could stare right through a person's eyes to the scale that seesawed in the brain, weighing wants and needs, balancing desire against guilt and pride. Lucy had agreed to his terms without argument. He couldn't believe his luck, that by virtue of the very life he led, he had something she needed. People needed him all the time in various sharp-edged ways, but not people like Lucy. Lucy would never stumble over him in some dark corner, press her tits in his face, and beg to blow him for meth.

He'd gotten close to her at the bonfire, as close as he'd ever been, near enough to taste her breath. He'd mentioned Cheri partly to get her attention, but also because he'd been spooked—the memory of it choked him, the rasp of Cheri's breath as she splashed by, looking right past him without seeing, as though *he* were the ghost—and he wanted to share it with Lucy, that feeling of not knowing whether he was real or the world around him was real or if anything was real. He knew Lucy would believe him, that she would somehow understand, because he imagined her privy to that spectral world, the realm of un-knowable things that existed beyond an invisible sieve, and maybe if he tried hard enough, he could break apart into tiny pieces and sift through to the other side.

Lucy had pounced on his story, questioning, prodding, taking it se-riously, like he'd known she would. But he hadn't been prepared for her anger. He hadn't thought to help Cheri as she fled down the river. If anything, he would have asked *her* for help, asked how to get where ghosts go on earth, how to stay and watch and haunt without anyone knowing he was there. He hadn't expected Lucy to get so caught up in Cheri that he wouldn't have the chance to tell her the other, more important story: that he'd met Lucy's mother at Ralls' grocery when he was twelve, and she'd cast a spell on him, held him in thrall all these empty years until Lucy emerged from the void.

Back then, Jamie was the runt of the Petree clan, the scrawniest of all the boys. That was before he got into his present line of work and started benching cinder blocks, before people stopped calling him skinny and started calling him wiry, which was what you called skinny people you didn't want to mess with. He'd tried to sneak out of Ralls' with a Mr. Goodbar stuffed down his pants, but Junior Ralls had grabbed him by the shirt collar, his calloused knuckles scraping the back of Jamie's neck. Jamie played dumb, which wasn't much of an act; as a kid, he often didn't know what people expected of him or how he'd failed to meet their expectations, which he inevitably seemed to do. Junior shook Jamie back and forth, hissing in his face, *Answer me, boy, why you think your white-trash ass can get away with stealing.*

Then an angel appeared, the lights of the dairy cooler bending around her like an aura. She looked right into his eyes, and he saw himself mirrored there, a stupid kid with a candy bar sticking out of the waist of his hand-me-down Wranglers; his mom would never buy him a Mr. Goodbar no matter how hard he begged, because her holy-roller stepfather had whipped her into believing everything good was evil, including chocolate, soda, and birthdays. The woman, Lila, paid for the candy, allowing Junior to pluck the coins from her outstretched palm. Junior let go of Jamie's collar, and Jamie saw the way the grocer gawked at the woman, his mouth gone slack, and he knew Lila's power wasn't in his imagination. It slowly came to him that she was no angel. Angels didn't show so much cleavage or smile at the likes of him. No, she was something else entirely. Long hair gleaming like a blackbird's wings and eyes like a wolf's, sharp and beautiful and full of secrets. He'd jacked off to that image uncountable times. He had run straight home from the grocery store, in fact, and humped the bathroom rug. Later, when he learned her name, he'd moan it in time with the stroke of his hand. *Lila, Liiilaaa.* Savoring the undulation of the tongue, the exotic taste of her name in his mouth.

His mother heard him and thought sure he was possessed. She started telling people that Lila Petrovich, the trampy new waitress at Dane's, was some kind of old-world witch. Beneath that disguise of comely flesh and shiny hair, she was probably covered in hundred-year-old wrinkles and warts. The witch had done something to her boy, had crept close enough to enthrall him, and now he was trapped in her magic, helpless as a fly in molasses. Jamie had believed it, too. Lila had cast a spell to make sure no other woman would ever measure up. And none had, not until Lucy arrived at the bonfire, grown up, blood and flesh warming the shape of his memory, her eyes identical to Lila's save for the way they assessed him. He longed for her to look at him the way Lila had, to take him in, but Lucy's eyes locked him out.

He'd started dreaming of Lila again the night he met Lucy at the river party. She was so real in his dreams, as she always had been, but now she didn't smile and hold out her hand, as she had done so many times in the past. She was trying to tell him something that he couldn't understand, her words rising soundlessly like bubbles underwater. Her eyes, though, were clear as ever, and when he looked into them, he was twelve years old again, and she was saving him from Junior Ralls, his scrawny body flooded with relief.

Lila was the one in his dreams, but when he woke, it was thoughts of Lucy that lingered. He'd been trying to figure out how to see her again ever since the party. Now Lucy had hunted him down, tracked him to this remote fishing spot, and stood before him on the riverbank, her arms crossed over her chest, waiting. She had questions for him, about Cheri and the van, and they had struck a deal. *I'll tell you what I know*, he'd said. *If you kiss me. One kiss. I start it, I finish it.*

CHAPTER 19

Lucy

I was grateful that Jamie was willing to tell me what he knew, even if it was for a price. He moved closer, his stringy hair hanging in his face, and I steeled myself for what was coming. I tried to pretend he was an ordinary guy from school, not a drug dealer a dozen years older than me. It wasn't the wisest choice I'd made, to come here alone without telling anyone, but I didn't want to have to explain myself, the things I was willing to do to get what I wanted. I'd never imagined myself as the sort of person who'd use my body in trade. But I was starting to think you were one kind of person until a situation arose that required you to be something else. It didn't mean that I was on the road to ruin. It just meant that I would do what I had to. You didn't wait for snakes to come out of their den, according to Birdie. You poured the den full of gasoline.

It was only a kiss, I reminded myself. That was all he'd asked, though not all he wanted. I could feel that much in the air between us.

"Just get it over with," I said.

He leaned in, his breath sour. The breeze brushed his long hair against my arms, and I smelled his sweating body, acrid and earthy like burning leaves. He watched me for a long minute, his hand reaching up and smoothing my hair, trailing across my cheekbone. I kept my expression detached, tried not to shudder. His eyes stayed open as he tilted his head, pressed his lips against mine. He pulled back slightly to look at me again, and I thought he was done. It had been nothing, an instant of touching skin. Then his mouth was hard on mine, wet and open. I shrank away from him and he caged his arms around me, locking me in place. I tried to stay calm and focus on why I was doing this. I let my mouth soften and he pushed his way in. He tasted like smoke and liquor and an underlying bitterness I couldn't identify. He loosened his grip and his hands traveled tentatively over my body, barely grazing the sides of my breasts, and then drawing my hips firmly against his. Tendrils of fear curled up my spine. I had placed my trust in a criminal and in my own belief that I could protect myself. He pushed himself against me more insistently, and for the first time, I gave in to thoughts of what would happen if he shoved me to the ground, held me down. I would fight him, of course, but I wasn't sure I would win.

I risked his anger by pulling away, slowly this time, and he opened his eyes, dazed. Before I could say anything, he pressed his cheek to mine and spoke softly into my ear. Had anyone been watching, we might have looked like lovers embracing.

"Name's Emory," he said. "Don't know if that's first or last. Hear he's got a place up on Caney Mountain, but I've never seen it and neither'll you. Dogs'd eat you first. He sells things. Drugs, guns. A friend of mine told me a while back Emory was selling *people*. Girls. You remember Eldon Johnson? Found dead underneath his deer stand, everybody figured he got drunk and fell and broke his neck. Wouldn't be unlike him. I believe your dad laid him to rest in his parents' pasture. Eldon was the one flapping his mouth about Emory."

Jamie nuzzled my hair and inhaled, long and deep, before letting me go. "People think I'm nuts," he said, squinting at me like I hurt his eyes. "But I got enough sense to fear all the right things."

I knew he was referring to Emory, that I should stay away, but I wondered if that was also why he let me go instead of taking what he wanted. If he feared my family would come after him, bury him in an unmarked grave. Or if he still thought there might be something to those witch rumors. My legs trembled but held. I resisted the urge to turn and see if he was watching me walk away. My breathing didn't return to normal until I'd put some distance between us, and even then I could still taste him, his bitterness mingled with fear in my throat.

Daniel's face turned new shades of red when I told him what I'd done. I considered not telling him at all, then settled for a tamer version of the truth, so I wouldn't have to lie outright if it somehow got around that Jamie had kissed me.

"So all I had to do was give him a little peck. Creepy. And kind of sad that he's so starved for affection. But I don't guess anybody would kiss him for free." I sat on my hands to hide their shaking.

Daniel looked about to boil over, like Birdie's old coffee percolator. "Did you even stop and think what he might've done to you? For all we know, he's the one who killed Cheri."

No need to tell Daniel about my moments of doubt on the riverbank, from which I hadn't quite recovered. One of Birdie's sayings came to mind: *If the wolf wants in, he'll find a way.* "If he wanted to hurt me, he'd do it whether I kissed him or not. And he didn't kill Cheri. Whatever else he might be capable of, I don't see him killing her."

Daniel rubbed his hands over his face, as though trying to wipe away his annoyance. "Okay," he said. "I'm not as sure about that as you are, but let's just say Jamie's not involved. So we're thinking if this Emory guy sells girls, he might've taken Cheri and sold her. We still don't know who he sold her to or who killed her. And I doubt that guy's gonna tell us. How the hell does somebody *live* on Caney Mountain, anyway? It's all conservation land up there."

Caney Mountain rose out of the earth just north of Henbane. The park encompassed eight thousand acres of springs, caves, woods, and cliffs. Tourist maps proclaimed it to have the best views in the Ozarks. Bess and I had gone there on our fifth-grade field trip, made the pilgrimage to see Missouri's champion black gum tree, the biggest in the state.

I shrugged. "It'd be a good place to hide."

"Did you ever think it was something like that? With Cheri, I mean? People had all kinds of ideas, everything from satanic sacrifice to voodoo to an affair with the art teacher. But I never heard anybody mention her being sold."

"No," I said. "I kept a list. That wasn't on it."

"It's just hard to believe, in a place like this where everybody knows everybody else's business, there're still secrets."

I might have thought so, too, but I was uncovering more secrets every day. "Do you know how to pick locks?" I asked.

"Excuse me?"

"We're at a dead end here. I have to get into Crete's office, look through his files. We need to know who rented that trailer."

Daniel sighed. "You know my brothers are serving time for robbery?"

I looked away, feeling guilty for having asked.

"We're good at picking locks," he said. "Not so good at getting away with it."

"You don't have to help," I said. "Just teach me how to do it."

He paced a slow circle in the dirt, hands in his pockets. "I can do better," he said, sending up a plume of dust with his shoe. "I know where to find the keys."

A half-moon silvered the parking lot as we crept toward Dane's. A dark night would have been better, but it had to be done before Dad got back to town, and once I knew Daniel had access to the keys, I couldn't get in quick enough.

Daniel ticked off the reasons he'd held back on telling me about the keys: He didn't want me getting into trouble, didn't want to lose his job, didn't want his mom to have to visit all of her kids in jail. Still, he'd insisted on coming along. He used his key to get into the boathouse, where a ring of spare keys was hidden under a floorboard in the supply closet. He didn't know which keys went to what, but he'd once walked in to find Judd returning them to their hiding place after locking the cash drawer in the office for the night.

I waited on the dark side of the building, listening to the scratch and clink of failed keys until Daniel called softly that he'd found the right one. When I scurried over to join him, he stopped me before I could slip inside. "Wait out here," he said, holding on to the bell at the top of the door so it wouldn't make noise. "You can be my lookout." I started to argue, but he pulled the door shut behind him and locked it. He had broken into Dane's without me.

I sat down to wait. It was still hot enough outside to make me sweat. The river beckoned from across the road, gleaming under the moon, and I wondered if I could convince Daniel to take a swim with me when we were done. Cheri's tree hung over the water like it was bending to take a drink. Had her killer admired this same nighttime view when he disposed of her body? No, it had been cold that night, freezing, the air laced with fog. Surely he hadn't taken the view into account.

The beam of a flashlight swept across the gas pumps and startled me to attention. I gave the front door two quick taps and sneaked around the corner to the patio, where a side door led out from the restaurant. We had planned to escape this way if anything went wrong. I hoped Daniel had heard my warning, though I wasn't too worried about it. Most likely the light belonged to a camper wandering around in search of a soda machine. I waited for the flashlight or footsteps to move past me, but they didn't. Then I heard the bell jangle on the front door.

Adrenaline surged through me, making my muscles twitch. I didn't want to risk going back around to the front, so I pressed my face to the little window in the patio door, trying to distinguish shapes among shadows in the dimly lit store. One of the shapes darted toward me, and I stepped aside as Daniel burst out the door and hurriedly shut it behind him. The keys rattled in his hands as he sought the right one and relocked it.

"Let's go!" I hissed. He pulled a folder from under his arm and reached around me, one hand lifting the back of my shirt and the other sliding the folder beneath it, pressing it against my sweating skin.

The door creaked, and there was no time to move. "Hey, now." The unmistakable gruffness of Judd's voice. "What the hell's going on out here?"

Daniel turned around, holding out his arm to keep me behind him.

"Well, well," Judd said. "Past your bedtime, ain't it, Miss Lucy?"

"I was just—"

"I ain't blind," he said, spitting on the ground.

"I'll take Lucy home," Daniel said.

Judd frowned. "Maybe I ought to be the one doing that."

"It's okay, Judd," I said. "I'll get home on my own."

"You supposed to be out in the woods after dark?"

"Straight home. Like a flash." I backed into the darkness, tucking in my shirt to hold the folder in place, hoping Daniel would be able to smooth things over with Judd.

I headed upstairs when I got home, and even though I was alone in the house, I closed my door before opening up the folder. I sat cross-legged on my bed and scanned the first document. It was a lease agreement, but not for the trailer in Henbane, the trailer where Cheri had been. The lease was for an apartment in Springfield. So was the next, then the next. It wasn't surprising to see that my uncle had so many rental properties, because he had his hands in lots of different jars and didn't make a point of telling me about all of them. But when I reached the end of the folder, I hadn't found what I was looking for. The whole point of breaking in to Crete's files for the rental records was to find out who'd rented the trailer, because that person might know what had happened to Cheri. Crete kept records on everything. If he didn't have a rental contract for the trailer, that was telling in itself. I sifted through the pages again, making sure none were stuck together.

There was a knock downstairs, and I knew it was Daniel. I hurried down to let him in. "It's not in there," I said. "Was that the only folder with leases in it?"

He looked distracted. "I don't know. I didn't see another one, but I was in a hurry. So there's nothing on the trailer?"

"No. What's wrong? Did Judd chew you out?"

"It's not that," he said. "I'm not worried about Judd. I . . . I don't think I locked the desk. I remember locking the cabinet, replacing the key, locking the door behind me, but I don't remember the desk."

"Maybe Crete won't notice."

Daniel frowned. "You know him better than me, what do you think?"

"We could go back now and lock it. I need to put this worthless folder back anyway."

"No. Judd might be hanging around. I couldn't put the keys away because he was there, but I need to get them back before someone realizes they're gone. We can't risk using them in the morning to get back into Crete's office and check everything."

I reached out to take his hands. "I'm sorry," I said. We stood there for a minute, not looking at each other. "Do you want to stay?"

He gave me a halfhearted smile, squeezed my hands, and released them. "Nah, Lucy," he said. "Get some rest. I'll see you tomorrow."

I was skittish going in to work the next day and terrified that someone would notice. I'd been up much of the night trying to prepare coherent responses to any questions that might come up. I repeated them until they felt true. Any trace of confidence evaporated when I saw Crete sitting on the bench outside Dane's, watching my approach.

"Sit down a minute," he said. "I need to talk to you." I sat. "Judd called me last night, said he caught you fooling around up here with Daniel."

I had an answer ready. "It's nothing serious," I said. "We're just friends."

"We can get into that later," he said. "What I wanna know is why you were *here*."

"I don't know," I said. "We didn't plan it. I couldn't sleep, I came out for a night swim. He was here."

He stared me down. "So he didn't ask you to meet him. You showed up and here he was?"

I nodded.

"You mighta kept him from robbing the place."

No. No. No. Something had tipped him off. It had to be the drawer, left unlocked, like Daniel had thought.

"The spare keys are missing, and only somebody working the boat-house'd know where I keep 'em. Looks like he got into the office but didn't make it into the safe."

I shook my head, my brain scrambling to catch up and figure out how to fix this.

"That can't be it," I said. "He'd never steal from you. He didn't say anything about it."

"He lied and said he came up here with you. That whole family's full of liars and thieves. I only hired him as a favor to his old man. We grew up together, you know, before he got busted. He thought his youngest was gonna be different, make something of himself."

"He probably just meant we came up here together from the river. We were on the patio. I was with him the whole time."

"I had to fire him, Lucy. And I don't want you around him any-more. You don't need to be messed up with trash like that."

I'd gotten Daniel fired. My stomach churned all day, and when I finally got hold of Daniel on the phone that night, he sounded a thou-sand miles away.

"I'm not mad," he said for the tenth time, though he sounded mad when he said it. "I'm glad you're okay, and I'm glad Crete thinks you had nothing to do with it. It could've turned out a lot worse for me, too. He could've pressed charges."

"But you're still leaving."

He groaned. "Like I said, I need a job to help pay for school, and I won't find anything else around here. Especially if Crete tells every-body I stole from him." He lowered his voice, making it harder for me to hear him. "The last thing I want to do is leave you here alone, with everything that's going on. Once I find a place in Springfield and get some money coming in, I'll be back to visit. I can help you figure things out. But I don't want you stirring up anything while I'm gone, okay?"

"Yeah," I said. I wouldn't be able to tell him what I was doing, be-cause it would only make him worry and nag me. It was easier to let him think I'd wait for him before making another move. Though if he believed that, he didn't know me at all.

"I would've been leaving in another month anyhow," he said. "Even if this hadn't happened."

"I know." It hadn't seemed real, though. His departure had been far away, with infinite possibilities existing in the time between. Any number of things could have changed his course, kept him with me. That was wishful thinking. How could I expect him to give up his plans and stay in Henbane when I couldn't wait to leave myself? And he wouldn't have stayed, even if I'd asked. He would have gone to school, like he was going now. Better, maybe, to get it over with. Better for him to move forward with his life. And for me to move forward with mine. Rule number four, don't let a boy get in the way of rules one through three.

CHAPTER 20

Lila

I'd been staying at Carl's house for three weeks, and he had finally admitted that he wasn't going back to his job in Arkansas. He was looking for something local but hadn't had any luck yet. Now that I was more comfortable moving around the house, we had started eating supper together every night at the dining room table. Tonight he'd heated up some biscuits and deer-sausage gravy that Birdie had brought over at breakfast. I hadn't wanted to eat it the first time I'd seen it puddled on my plate. But like everything else Birdie made, it tasted better than it looked. And I was hungry. Each time nausea swelled in my throat, I thought about the thing in my belly and ate to quiet it.

When I ate, the nausea went away, and I could pretend everything was fine.

After dinner, I took the dishes to the sink to wash them, but Carl told me he would do it later. Now that I was no longer an invalid, I felt uncomfortable with him waiting on me. I wondered, as I did every day, how much longer I could stay here. I couldn't stay forever. We stared at each other, not sure what to do with this moment when I was not quite a houseguest and not quite something more.

"Wanna listen to some music?" he asked.

"Sure," I said. He led me to the living room, and I sat on the sofa while he fiddled with the stereo. All the windows were open, and a box fan pulled in the evening air. Carl sat down next to me and took my hand in his as we listened. The recording was scratchy, the song haunting, a duet with some kind of guitar in the background.

"That was my parents," Carl said when it was over. "They met singing at church. They used to sit out on the porch and sing. Just old mountain songs and such. Dad played banjo."

"It was beautiful," I said. "Are all Ozark songs so fucking tragic?"

He chuckled. "I guess I never thought about it, but yeah. Most of 'em. Love songs, especially."

He put on another album and I felt myself relaxing, almost to the point of falling asleep. I wondered if the tiny creature inside me was already stealing away my energy, strengthening itself against my will.

"Do you like it here?" Carl asked, squeezing my hand.

"Henbane?" He'd asked me that before, and I remembered not wanting to insult his hometown.

"Here," he said. "This house. With me."

"Yeah," I said.

"I want you to stay here."

"You do?"

He nodded. I smiled but didn't answer. If Ransome had been telling the truth, Crete would leave me alone as long as I kept quiet.

Maybe he'd find someone else to exploit, someone who'd consent. I wondered what I'd do if he brought in another ignorant girl like me. Would I be able to stomach knowing what was happening to her and not say a word?

I slept alone in Carl's mother's room—the room I was dangerously close to thinking of as mine. He hadn't made any move to sleep in the room with me, not counting the first night, when I awoke to find him dozing in the chair. Probably he still thought of me as a convalescent, which was just as well because I was in no condition to be intimate with him. I laid my hand below my navel to see if I could feel anything different, but there was no shape, no movement, nothing except my own familiar skin. Maybe it was all in my head, a crazy notion born from Gabby's suggestion. I didn't know for sure that I was pregnant, and there was no sense saying anything to Carl until I knew.

That night my dreams were dark and clouded, full of dead ends and treacherous paths that led me right back where I'd started. I startled awake to a flurry of shadows across the walls and floor. Outside the window, between me and the moon, I saw a torrent of bats. The thought of them spilling from a crack in the earth filled me with unexplained dread.

CHAPTER 21

Lucy

"So he came into Wash-n-Tan a few weeks back with all his collared shirts," Bess said. "You know how he'd been going around all wrinkly since his wife left. You'd think somebody like him could figure out something as simple as an iron. I guess he was just too lazy." She was trying to explain how it was that she came to be fooling around with Vice Principal Sorrel from the junior high, whom I remembered mostly for his sweatiness and fake smile. I was trying to hold my judgment, but it was really, really hard. I kept picturing the yellow stains on the armpits of all his shirts.

"Can we please skip to the part where you discover his redeeming qualities?"

Bess looked embarrassed, and I regretted opening my mouth. "It didn't happen all at once," she said. "Like I was saying, he came in with his shirts and offered extra if I could get 'em done while he waited. Said he needed 'em for some job interviews he had coming up. Normally, my cousin makes me leave all the ironing for him to do, 'cause I fuck it up every time. But I wanted the extra cash, so I told Sorrel I'd do it. He just sat there watching me at first while I loaded up the washer. I mean, he had a magazine, but he wasn't looking at it. He started making small talk, like, he couldn't believe how much I'd grown up since junior high, how were things going for me in high school, what did I think of the teachers, on and on. I got sick of it after a while, so I said, 'Why don't you go ahead and get a tan while you're waiting? So you can look real sharp for your interviews?' Boy, did he think that was a grand idea. I got him all set up in the back room, and he asked me if he had to get naked to get in the thing, and I said, 'Well, you don't have to, but people do, and I wipe down the bed with antiseptic after, so it's safe if you want to do it.'"

I imagined Vice Principal Sorrel getting naked, squeezing his doughy body between the plates of the tanning bed like some messy grilled sandwich.

"I went back up front to the desk, and after a couple minutes I thought I heard something over the racket of the washing machine. I walked toward the tanning room, and the door was cracked open the tiniest bit, and Sorrel was calling my name. Said he was having trouble getting into the bed, could I help him. I was wishing I hadn't agreed to do his shirts, because he was turning out to be a pain, and he was keeping me from watching my soaps, besides. But I figured for the money, I could help squish his fat ass into the tanning bed, it'd only take a minute. Well, I walked in and there he was, sitting naked on the bed with his dick all hard pointing right at me, and he had this sly look on his face, like he was gonna act either embarrassed or sexy, depending on my reaction."

"Bess! What did you do?"

"What do you think I did, jump on for a ride? I said, 'Looks like you're doing just fine,' and I went to close the door. I was thinking how I'd burn his shirts up with the iron, get 'em all brown and crispy and he'd never come back."

"You didn't, though, did you."

She sighed. "No. He started bawling before I even got the door closed, started begging me not to tell anybody what he'd done, that he'd misread me and he did that sometimes and he couldn't seem to help it. I didn't believe him all the way, but he was pretty pathetic, so I couldn't help feeling a little sorry for him." As much as Bess mocked Gabby and her softness for hopeless creatures, she was turning out to be just like her mother in that way, unable to cast aside whatever tooth-less dog or troubled man crossed her path. "I stood there and listened a minute," she continued. "And when he saw I wasn't too freaked out, he calmed down a little, and we kinda started talking."

"What do you talk about after something like that? Was he sitting there naked the whole time?"

Bess laughed. "He laid his pants across his lap. We talked about his wife a little bit at first. He wasn't mad at her for leaving, sounded like he was almost kinda relieved, like he didn't have to keep pretending things were good. He said not to get married without taking a test run first, because he found out too late that her tits were nothing but push-up bras and padding. She was flat as a board and didn't believe in hav-ing sex unless you were trying to make a baby. Then he got all dreamy-eyed and said he didn't mean any disrespect, but my chest was just perfect, he could tell through my shirt, and he hoped he could find himself a girl like me."

"I still can't believe it," I said. "Sorrel? Didn't you feel gross with him talking about your boobs like that?"

"I dunno," she said. "He was kinda growing on me. He's funny, actually, and there was something about seeing the guy who keeps a big whipping paddle in his office at school all naked and backed in a corner. I liked it, I guess." She chewed a hangnail. "He asked if I could deliver the shirts to his house when I got off work. He said he'd pay me in cash and maybe we could talk a bit more."

I was thinking that I would never in a million years go to the vice principal's house after he showed me his penis, but hadn't I met Jamie Petree alone on the river and let him touch me to get what I wanted? Whatever Bess had done, she had her reasons.

"I hate to ask what happened at his house," I said, "because I'm already going to be having nightmares about him naked in the tanning bed. Let me guess, does he have one of those paddles in his bedroom, too?"

Bess's cheeks flushed.

"No!" I said. "I was kidding. Does he really? Did he try to . . . Did he want you to . . . ?"

Bess looked down. "He was playing around with it one time. He thought it'd be funny, and I thought he was just gonna give me a little swat, but it kinda hurt, and I wouldn't let him do it again."

Her tone had shifted, and I could tell she wasn't as confident as she'd been acting. It worried me. "How many times have you been over there?"

She shrugged. "Most days, I guess, the last few weeks. He has cable and air-conditioning, and he always had cigarettes and things for me. It wasn't all sexual." The word *sexual* came out all sticky, like it was hard for her to say. "Sometimes we'd watch movies and stuff. Crank the air and wrap up in blankets and eat a pizza." She was quiet for a moment. "It didn't seem like he was into real sex. . . . He had trouble, you know, getting it up for that. It was mostly other stuff, like he wanted to show me how a guy likes a hand job. He asked if I'd ever gotten off with any of the guys I'd been with, and I hadn't, and he said he wasn't surprised because most of those younger guys don't have a clue what they're doing, they're sticking fingers in everywhere like they're looking for crawdads in a mud hole. So he made a sort of game out of trying to make me come, said maybe I'd reward him when he got it right, maybe I'd let him try some other things."

"Why didn't you tell me any of this before?"

"I dunno. You were busy with Daniel and the whole Cheri thing. I was just having fun, you know. Sometimes it's fun to have a secret. And it *was* fun, Luce. I know it sounds weird, but he made me laugh and he listened to me, and the way he touched me—he knew what he was doing. I couldn't help it, it felt good. I might've been picturing Gage when I shut my eyes, but God help me, Gage Petree flopping around on top of me like he was having a seizure didn't make me feel anything like this."

We sat there on the porch steps, me wondering what exactly Sorrel had done to make her feel so good but not sure I should ask. I was used to Bess moving into unknown territory ahead of me, but she usually made me feel like I was right there with her, sharing every detail.

"Forget about all that stuff," Bess said, flipping her hair out of her face. "That's not the important part. Something happened after I talked to you last. We're not . . . seeing each other anymore. I was over at his place the other night. He was drinking tequila, but I didn't have any because I got sick on it that time at the river, remember?" I nodded. "So he was getting all drunk, and he wanted to fool around, but he wanted to try something different this time. I wondered what it'd be—I was already closing my eyes and thinking about Gage. Well, he went in the bedroom and came out with this old crank telephone. Said he'd hook it up to a battery and put the wires on me, like on my nipples or something, and turn the crank, and it'd feel real good. There was something not quite right about the way he was acting, and the more I thought about it, it didn't sound fun, it sounded like he wanted to fuck-ing electrocute me. Nobody knew where I was. Nobody knew I'd been seeing him. And that's about when I started thinking I needed to get the hell out of there. He was real sweet at first, tried to talk me into staying. Said some girls really liked it, he knew I would, too. When I tried to leave, he got in my way, and his face was all red and twisted to where I couldn't believe I'd ever thought him anything other than ugly, and he said, 'Do I have to tie you down like that retarded girl?' I guess he knew by looking at me that he'd screwed up, because he backed off and sort of laughed and said the whole thing was a joke, he was just kidding. I said, 'Oh, yeah, you got me, but I really do need to get home, I told my mom I was dropping off your ironing.' And I pushed out of there and haven't been back. Obviously."

"Cheri," I said, stunned. "The 'retarded girl.' You think he meant Cheri."

"Who else? I mean, he's obviously into kinky shit, and he likes younger girls. Maybe he's the one who had her in that trailer."

My mind whirled through the possibilities. Did his wife find out? Was that why she left? "Thank God you got out of there," I said. "Who knows what he would've done. Are you worried he'll come after you?"

"I thought he would at first, yeah," she said. "But I think he was waiting to see if I'd tell anybody. Probably figured nobody'd be-lieve me."

"We can't let him go on doing stuff like that," I said. "He can't be working at a school, around kids."

"Then we need to find something to pin him to Cheri, because I can't prove anything we did together. Nobody saw me over there. Prob-ably nobody *would* believe me, my word against his."

I knew she was right. And if he'd been worried that there was any-thing tying him to Cheri's death, he wouldn't have let Bess go.

"Well, I have plenty of free time to work on that. No distractions."

"Hey," she said, squeezing my knee. "It won't take Daniel that long to finish school. He'll come back. They all do."

I got so tired of hearing that. Not everyone returned to Henbane. Not Janessa Walker. Not Birdie's sons. And maybe I wouldn't, either. Maybe I'd see Iowa and keep right on going.

CHAPTER 22

Gabby

Gabby had always loved new things, and it didn't have to be anything big, like driving down to Mountain Home and buying a new pair of sneakers at Shoe Carnival. It could just be something different from the usual, the tiniest change in the everyday. Every single thing in Henbane was always the same, and as her brother Rich used to say, *Ain't nothin' ever good here*. You couldn't see any neighbors from their place, and no neighbors could see them, which reinforced the terrible hopeless feeling that she was all alone, that she could scream her head off and nobody would hear it, nobody would come to see if she was okay. And she wasn't okay, not that anybody asked. They were poor, that was one thing, but being poor wasn't enough to make you miserable. It was who you were poor with. She spent the night with a friend in high school and couldn't believe how good the girl's folks got along in the rickety trailer they lived in. The dad told jokes over dinner—chipped beef on toast, end-of-the-month staple when you were waiting for new food stamps—and the mom asked all of the kids what the best part of their day was. It made Gabby's stomach hurt. When the mom turned to her and asked the best part of *her* day, Gabby lost it. She started bawling, and instead of pretending not to notice, the mom came over and patted her on the arm till the tears let up.

Gabby and her brothers were at the mercy of Dad's belt, and Mom sat there like a deaf mute, not saying or doing anything so long as she wasn't the one getting whipped. Gabby was bitter about that but knew their mom had other burdens to bear—they all heard Dad grunting over her in the next room every night. Her oldest brother wanted something to grunt over, too, and Gabby slept in jeans and a buckled belt in hopes that somebody else in the room would wake up by the time he got where he was going. They chopped their own wood for heat and grew their own food, but they were still cold and hungry. She'd make a game of it where she'd relax all the little bits of her body, starting with her fingers and toes and working in toward the center. She had to make herself limp and draw the hurt and want into a tight core inside, each time adding another layer to that core, so that if somebody came along and cut her open, they'd find inside a shining, perfect pearl, hard as any Willy Wonka jawbreaker.

Whenever something new showed up in the holler, it gave her hope that there was a life other than this one, where other things happened, and she might one day be one of those other people doing those other things. Maybe not something better but at least different and new.

Gabby's mom worked at the sewing factory back then, and the people who'd taken it over needed somebody to watch their cat while they went on Christmas vacation. They were paying twenty bucks for the

week, but nobody wanted to do it on principle, because the new owners weren't locals and had no business taking over the sewing factory.
Mom ended up with the cat because she hadn't said anything either
way. So this fluffy white kitten showed up on their kitchen table Christmas Eve in a brand-new carrier that was cleaner than anything else in
the house. The kitten's name was Clancy, and he was their very first
overnight guest, ever.

The entire Johnson family sat around the table and watched Clancy
strut back and forth. It was obvious right away that this cat was popular
and outgoing. If he'd been a person, he would've been the football
captain who smiled at the outcasts like they were friends, even though
they could never be friends. Gabby had the irrational desire to interview Clancy, to ask him what it was like to sleep in a clean new bed,
and to find out whether he had carpeting in his house. His food came
in cans and smelled better than some things the Johnsons ate. Gabby
wanted desperately to please the cat, to be his favorite.

A couple days into his visit, Clancy had gotten all dusty playing in
the ashes from the woodstove, and Gabby wanted to see his fur shining
white again. She had never before seen a white cat in the holler, and
she didn't want Clancy to start looking like he belonged there, all dull
and ragged like the rest of them. Keeping him clean kept him interesting. So she gave Clancy a bath in the kitchen sink using the special cat
shampoo the owners had sent along, but as it turned out, Clancy didn't
like his bath like she'd thought he would. When Gabby was done, she
wrapped him in a dish towel, planning to carry him to her room and
let him dry on the bed. But Clancy sprang out of her arms and landed
on the woodstove, yowling in pain before quickly bouncing to the
floor. He darted behind the potato bin, and for the rest of his visit,
Clancy wanted nothing to do with Gabby. He hid any time she came
near.

Gabby never came across another cat like Clancy, but she took solace in the various crippled, tick-infested critters that made their way

onto the property. A lame fawn. A coonhound with one eye. An entire litter of kittens dumped in the ditch by the mailbox. They weren't pretty or clean like Clancy, but neither was she. They didn't care how desperate she was for their affection because they were desperate, too.

When Lila appeared at Dane's that first day, Gabby felt that same surge of joy she had felt when Clancy showed up in her kitchen. She'd moved into her own little camper, which at first had been new and exciting and was a definite improvement over living at home. She didn't have to deal with anyone except herself, and she didn't mind being cold or hungry in her own private space. But she had that ache again for something new in her life, and new boyfriends were not enough to soothe it.

Lila couldn't have stood out more if she'd been stuck to a lighted billboard. To Gabby's eye, she was exotic and sophisticated, a fancy magazine cover model who mistakenly ended up waiting tables in a dive, wearing dumpy clothes. Gabby was so glad to have her there, she'd have carried Lila's load at work so long as the girl sat there looking mysterious. But Lila wasn't like that. She was a hard worker, worried about doing a good job. And no matter how worldly—or otherworldly— she appeared, it quickly became clear that she was out of her comfort zone in Henbane.

Gabby felt protective of her, like a mother hen. When Carl Dane walked in, she saw the look in his eyes, like he'd pulled a mermaid up in his net and wasn't sure he'd be allowed to keep it. He was probably the one guy in all of Henbane who Gabby could stand to have looking at Lila that way. She didn't know then if Lila would feel the same way about him but wasn't surprised when she did. Gabby wished some-body would show up to sweep *her* away, so she jumped into the arms of every guy who crossed her path in case he was the one. She didn't get the fairy-tale prince Lila got, but she could never be jealous, with the way things turned out.

When Lila told Gabby she was pregnant, Gabby was happy for her.

She knew Lila hadn't meant to trap Carl—he would've walked into that trap and begged to stay—but she'd secured herself a good man with a house and a job, without even trying. Gabby couldn't get why Lila wasn't happy about it. She just seemed confused. The day after they figured out she was pregnant, Lila told Gabby about the bad feeling she was having. The dark thing in her belly. She wanted to get it out of her. Gabby figured it was some kind of superstition. So she took her friend out to Sarah Cole's, because if anyone could clear up a superstition, it was Sarah. She was sensitive to things, and Gabby had never known her to be wrong.

Sarah wanted to talk to Lila alone, and when Lila walked back out onto the porch not fifteen minutes later, she had her hand low on her belly, and Gabby knew she'd decided to keep the baby.

CHAPTER 23

Lila

Sarah Cole folded up the hem of my shirt to expose my stomach, then sprinkled dried leaves into her palm and crushed them with her fingers. She added a few drops of amber liquid, like olive oil, and rubbed the concoction over my still-flat belly. Her eyes closed, and a smile twitched at the corners of her mouth. We were sitting at her kitchen table, and I wondered momentarily if she was preparing to roast me in the oven like the witch in "Hansel and Gretel."

She wiped her hands on her apron and lit a candle. Mumbling words I couldn't untangle, she dripped wax on a piece of bark and studied it. "I see a scale. She'll bring balance." Sarah examined the bark a while longer. "She's good," she said finally. "You should keep her."

"How can you know that?" I asked. "What does all this mean?" I gestured at the mess she'd made. Leaves and wax meant nothing to me.

"I can't tell you how the truth comes," she said. "It's a gift, and I don't question it."

I wasn't sure I believed her any more than I'd believe a palm reader at a carnival, but I wanted her to be right. "You said 'she.' You think it's a girl?"

"I have a feeling. We can try something if you'd like." She glanced at my hands. "You don't wear a ring?"

I shook my head. She twisted a ring off her own finger and fetched a length of string from a kitchen drawer. Then she looped the string through the ring to make a pendulum that she dangled over my stomach. The ring swung back and forth. Sarah smiled. "I was right, see? Back and forth is a girl. All mine spun in a circle."

The front door rattled, and what sounded like a herd of animals clomped toward the kitchen.

"Ma, look." A cluster of boys burst into the room. "Daniel got a fish."

They noticed me then, and the three older boys stopped and stared. The smallest one—Daniel, I assumed—toddled over with a bucket, showing off his catch. He handed the bucket to Sarah and turned to place his hands on my exposed belly, no doubt imitating what he'd seen his mother do to other women. He smiled up at me, and Sarah gently pulled him away. "Get cleaned up for supper, boys," she said, giving Daniel a quick squeeze. "Take this one with you."

It wasn't how I planned to tell Carl. Not that I had a better plan. He was standing in the bathroom doorway when I got up from the floor, and the look on his face was panicked, like he'd thought I was almost better and now something had gone wrong and he blamed himself. In that moment I wanted to comfort him. "I'm not sick," I said, my hand over my mouth. "I'm pregnant, that's all."

He looked shocked, and we stared at each other in uncomfortable silence. Finally, he pulled me to him, his face in my hair, and held me awhile, and then he left the house. "Don't go anywhere," he said as I watched him from the top of the stairs. "Stay right there."

I lay on the bed and waited. I didn't know what he would do, but Gabby was right, he didn't sound mad. It was almost dusk when he returned, and fireflies hovered at the edge of the yard.

"I'm sorry it took me so long," he said, leading me to the porch swing. "I had to get something first." I sat down and he knelt in front of me, taking my hand. "I wanted to do this a while ago, so I don't want you to think it's just because of the baby. That first night, when I met you at Dane's, it was like I'd been walking in there every night of my life waiting for you to show up, and you finally did. You're the one I've been looking for. Everything about you is different from the other girls here. You don't pretend to be anything you're not. You don't care what anybody thinks of you. And I only care what you think of me. Because I love you. I want to be with you." He smiled up at me. "I was coming to talk to you about it that day at the garage, but . . ."

He cleared his throat. I knew what he was about to do, and I felt like I was slowly suffocating. Air seeped out of my body, and I couldn't coax it back in. Carl let go of my hand and dug in his pocket for the ring, a plain gold band.

"I promise to make a home for you and the baby if you'll just stay with me," he murmured. "Will you marry me?"

Those last four words. They fell like stones dropped in a well, disappearing into the dark. It would be a crazy thing to do, to marry Carl. I was eighteen years old, and I wasn't even sure what I wanted to do with my life. Now I had this other little life putting pressure on all my decisions. There was no doubt by now that I loved Carl. But I didn't know if love outweighed everything else, if it was enough to tip the scale. Because choosing him meant staying in Henbane with Crete.

I paused. I don't know how long. Long enough for him to worry. His fingers curled around the ring.

"Yes," I breathed. I said it like I was trying it out. I wanted to see how it felt, and I knew right away that I meant it. I'd chosen to make a family, a home, with Carl and the baby, and after so many years without roots, I'd found what I'd always been looking for. A place where I was wanted and loved. Relief made me giddy and I stood, pulling him to his feet. "Yes."

"You'll marry me."

"Yes."

An enormous grin broke out on his face, and he whooped like a cowboy. He lifted me down the steps into the yard and danced me around in circles, stopping just long enough to slide the ring on my finger.

I took in the thick night air, the sweet smell of honeysuckle, the chirping of frogs, to impress the moment in the folds of my memory, preserve it like a flower between pages of a book. To remember: This is how it feels to be happy.

CHAPTER 24

Lucy

My next day off, I went down to the courthouse to see Ray Walker. Almost a year ago I'd gone to see him to tell him that Cheri couldn't have run away, that something must have happened to her. I didn't know it for a fact, but it was hard for me to accept that she'd leave without telling me. I thought Ray would spring into action, pull together search teams and investigators and bring her back home. Instead, he'd said that we never knew people as well as we thought we did. That they could surprise us. *It's quite possible that you're right*, he said. *But you can't claim to know.*

Ray looked the same as he had at that last visit: starched shirt, bow tie, slicked-back hair. He plucked a can of Coke from his mini-fridge, cracked it open, and split it between two glasses.

"I need some advice," I said. "And I need you to not tell my dad."

Ray groaned and tilted his glass, waiting for the fizz to die down. "That's never a good way to start things, my dear."

I smiled, because he hadn't said no. "It's legal advice, sort of," I said. "How much evidence do you need for the police to look into something? Will they do anything based on hearsay? Is that what you call it?"

"Oh, Lucy." He set down his drink, and his pale eyes filled with worry. "What's this about? Is it Cheri again?"

"Yes. I've actually heard some things, seen some things. I don't have any real evidence yet, but I think I can get some. I just wondered what would happen if I told the police now, told them what I know without being able to back it up."

Ray ran his finger around the rim of his glass. "What you've got to consider is who you're telling it to. The sheriff and his boys are related to hundreds of people here in the county, and if you're making accusations against their kin, they might not take it so well. Even if they're not related, who's to say they're not in bed with your suspect, so to speak. Taking bribes. Buying drugs. I'm not saying our law is corrupt, but you never know how it might be compromised. You've got to be sure you can trust whomever you're telling, that it won't come back on you."

"How can I be sure?" I asked.

He smirked. "You can't be, in Henbane. Therefore, I wouldn't try anything on word alone. When you have something solid—and in saying this, I do not by any means imply that you should go out investigating, because you shouldn't—but if you do have some real evidence, you can go over their heads and contact the state police. In fact, I'd be happy to do it for you."

I considered asking him if the necklace alone was enough, without the trailer or proof of who rented it, but I kept it to myself.

"It's noble of you, Lucy, trying to help your friend. I'd love nothing more than to see this case solved, to bring her killer to justice. But Cheri's gone. And in another year you'll be out of this town, making a life for yourself. Whatever mess Cheri was in, you don't want to get stuck in it. Nothing you do will put her back together."

So I was supposed to forget about Cheri now that she'd been laid to rest. Was I supposed to bury my mother, too, since I couldn't bring her back?

"Do you ever think about Lila?" I asked.

His expression stiffened. "I do," he said. "Every time I see your face."

"Did you believe she killed herself? Did you try to figure out what happened to her?"

He rubbed his forehead. "Losing her was hard on everyone who knew her. Myself included. I never wanted to believe she killed herself. But like I said before, people surprise you. I did have my own ideas about what happened. And I did talk to the sheriff about them. Nothing came of it."

"Because you were wrong or because they didn't listen?"

"I had no proof," he said. "Just things she'd implied. But the dead don't bear witness." *Dead.* He sounded so sure. And still pained by it.

"What did she tell you?"

"Why does it matter now?"

"Why *wouldn't* it matter?"

"You're still a child, Lucy," he said. "You're not old enough to understand that there are things you'd rather not know. Knowing won't make it easier. You think you can set wrong things right, but it's rarely so simple."

"I just want to know what happened to her," I said, slumping on Ray's desk. He watched me with a mixture of longing and sadness, and

I knew, looking at me, he was seeing her. Goose bumps pebbled my skin.

He sighed, fixing his gaze on the datebook spread out before him, each line adorned with his graceful, curled script. "I don't suppose anyone knows the whole truth, dear. We're all missing pieces of the puzzle. All I can tell you is to open your eyes. Look at whom you know and think about how well you know them. Open your mind to the possibilities; rethink things you've taken for granted. Like we tell the kids in Sunday school: Just because you don't see the devil doesn't mean he isn't there. He doesn't carry a pitchfork. He hides in plain sight."

Ray's words disturbed me. Question everyone, everything. I went home and opened my journal to "People Who Knew My Mother" and put asterisks next to all the names.

I wanted to call Daniel, but I didn't have a number where I could reach him. He'd been gone for a few weeks, and I missed him. More than I'd thought I would. I'd lie in bed replaying the night he kissed me, imagining that things had gone further, trying to conjure the shared heat of our bare skin pressed together, the tangling of his fingers in my hair. I didn't know why he wasn't interested in being more than friends. The one time I'd caught his eyes roaming over my body, he'd quickly looked away. Was he holding back because he felt protective of me? Did he think I was too young?

Work was lonely despite the flow of tourists on the river. Occasionally, one of the float-tripping college guys would invite me to join him and his friends after work, sit by the campfire, drink a few beers. They were all the same, their shirts and hats advertising their allegiance to fraternities and sports teams, their intentions clearly visible in their flirtatious smiles and flexing biceps. I can't say I wasn't sometimes tempted to take them up on their offers. It was enticing in a way, an anonymous encounter with someone who knew nothing about me, who would require little conversation and be gone the next day. But I knew that any of them would be poor substitutes for Daniel, even if I closed my eyes and imagined him there instead.

Bess and I had started spending more time together again, like we used to. After her last encounter with Sorrel, she'd taken a more personal interest in Cheri. We sat on the porch swing one night in late July, drinking lemonade and trying to figure out a way to get Sorrel to talk.

"I haven't seen him around town," Bess said, "but I think he's still here. If he took one of those other jobs and already moved, we'd have heard about it. So I could just call his house. I wouldn't even have to see him."

"What would you say to him?"

"I dunno. Too bad I couldn't act like I was pregnant. Go for the blackmail."

"That kind of thing wouldn't work. He'd want proof. He's not stupid. He wouldn't do what you say just because you call up and threaten him."

Bess's nostrils flared. "I'm trying to help," she said. "I don't have any other ideas."

"I'm sorry," I said. "I've been thinking about it for so long, and it's all a bunch of dead ends. Nothing we do will make him tell us anything." Bess started moving the swing sideways, like we did when we were kids. Birdie always warned us we'd go flying off the porch, but that just made us swing harder to see if she was right.

"Hey," she said. "What if we record my conversation with him, like people do on TV? Maybe even if he doesn't want to admit to anything, he might say something we can use. I can try to trip him up. He's not *that* smart."

I smiled at her, shifting my weight so I squished her as the swing went in her direction. She did the same when it swung back my way, and we giggled like little kids. "I like it," I said. I couldn't remember from all the crime shows I'd watched whether it was illegal to record a phone conversation or if you couldn't use it in court. But I wasn't worried about technicalities. We needed *something*. Enough to jump-start the investigation into Cheri's murder.

Two days later, Bess worked up the nerve to call Sorrel. I sat next to her and listened in while she recorded the conversation on the answering machine. He was quiet as she unspooled a story about her mom finding her journal and reading about everything she and Sorrel had done together, including his mention of Cheri. Her mom, she said, wanted to take it to the police. There was a long silence at the other end of the line. Bess and I stared at each other, her hand latched on to my arm, and we waited.

Sorrel let out a long sigh, like he was deflating. "You're obviously a troubled child," he said carefully. "We both know how easily you could fake something like that, but I'm not sure you realize what a bad idea it is. You wouldn't want to end up in juvie, would you? Or jail? That's what happens when you falsely accuse people, falsify evidence." Bess's face flushed with anger. "I'll give you time to think this over," he said. "If you want to meet with me, discuss this in person, call me back next week."

He hung up without revealing a single incriminating detail. And he'd twisted things around on Bess to make her feel like she was the one who should be worried. "He's bluffing," I said. "He wants to intimidate you into backing down."

Bess sank into the couch, shaking her head.

"We'll get him," I said, squeezing her hand. I knew I didn't sound convincing.

"We're running out of time. School's starting soon."

I pulled the remote out of the crack in the couch and turned on the TV. "I'm going to Crete's," I said.

Bess grabbed the remote from me and pressed mute. "What're you gonna do over there?"

"Snoop. He didn't have anything about the trailer in his office, which means he must have that information at home. He writes everything down. It has to be somewhere."

"Why don't you wait and see if I get something out of Sorrel first?"

"You just said yourself that we're running out of time. Summer's almost over. We can't let Sorrel go back to the junior high. And I can't stop thinking of the guy Jamie told me about. Emory. If he really is selling girls, more of them could end up like Cheri. It could be happening every minute we're not doing anything."

"I'll go with you," she said.

"No way. Then who'd come looking for me if something happens?"

Bess looked at me. "You're serious, aren't you."

I shrugged. I'd meant it as a joke, but part of me knew it was true. I wasn't sure what we were getting ourselves into.

CHAPTER 25

Birdie

Birdie was suspicious of Lila at first. Her own people had lived in Henbane since the 1800s, and after a while you forgot that your family was ever from anyplace else, that a hundred-odd years ago they were from Kentucky, and *they* were the new folks in town.

When Lila came, there weren't many new folks, nothing to bring them in—certainly not jobs. Every once in a while retirees would show up, looking to live out their golden years in the Ozarks, but most of them figured out pretty quick that it was nothing like the brochures. They all seemed confused not to be welcomed with open arms, but it took time to let people in. Sometimes it took generations. There were people in Henbane who'd never seen a Negro or an Oriental. Back when she was little, before Birdie had seen anyone much different from herself, her uncle came home from a street fair in Arkansas and talked about seeing a real live black man on the Ferris wheel. Birdie and the other kids likened it to seeing the bogeyman. When Lila showed up in town, supposedly from Iowa, folks saw right away that she wasn't any ordinary midwestern girl. Something about her looked exotic, that thick black hair and those unusual pale green eyes and what looked like more than a tan. It had folks guessing, was she one of those half-breeds? Part Indian? Arab? Some sort of Mexican? That was before they started in on the witch talk and worse. She was different; people gossiped. Birdie was one of them, and she wasn't shy to admit it.

She'd heard Carl had been flirting with the new girl over at the restaurant, had seen him driving her over to his house, and she didn't know what to think. Boys'll be boys, for one—they see something pretty, they go on point. She didn't guess it was more than that. She never thought a Dane would up and marry an outsider. And she sure as heck didn't want the girl living right down the road from her.

Rumors had started up, witchcraft and all that. You only had to look at the girl to imagine something supernatural at work, like a spell to make herself irresistible. Hogwash, mostly, but Birdie had no plans of getting anywhere near her until Carl called and said she was in a bad way and needed doctoring. Birdie had never turned down a Dane's request for help, and even though she wasn't a real doctor and hadn't taken any kind of oath to help people, she loaded her supplies in the truck and went on over. She wasn't trying to be saintly. Part of it was plain old curiosity, not unlike her uncle staring at the Negro on the Ferris wheel.

Carl told her that Lila had been attacked, but he didn't say who had done the attacking. Birdie shooed him out of the room while she examined the girl, who lay there limp as a flour sack. Though her bruises weren't fresh, it was hard to say how old they were. Once Birdie got under her clothes, she saw a bigger problem. The bite on Lila's breast—it had to be human, though that was a hard fact to swallow—hadn't been cleaned up right. It wasn't as bad as it could have been, but it could get worse without care. Birdie set to work mixing a poultice of tobacco and mullein leaves and called her cousin for antibiotics. For nearly a week she tended to Lila, applying fresh poultices and doling out pills. Whenever Carl came in to see Lila, Birdie made sure she was covered up. As the swelling and redness eased, she could see more clearly the marks on Lila's breast, the individual lines and points, and though she knew plenty of people with crooked teeth like the ones that had made those marks, she immediately thought of Crete. Some while later, when she heard that Joe Bill Sump had disappeared around the time she was called to treat Lila, she wondered if he'd been the attacker. Then she remembered he was missing teeth up front and couldn't have been the one who had left the mark.

Birdie was a bit perturbed, seeing Lila in Althea Dane's bed while Althea herself was stuck in a nursing home. Even when Althea's health started to decline, she was a good neighbor. She was cordial, kept her distance, and brought pies at all the right times. Birdie and her husband, Sy, used to make music with Althea and Earl back in the days when their kids were small. Sy played dulcimer and taught Birdie, though she never got to be as good as him.

A couple weeks after Lila recovered, she came knocking at Birdie's door just like an ill-mannered traveling salesman. Birdie opened the door but stood in the crack so Lila couldn't see inside.

"I brought something for you," Lila said. "Carl said you like squirrel."

Birdie looked at the foil-covered plate the girl carried, Althea's china pattern peeking out. Lila didn't look like somebody who could cook good squirrel, though Birdie had no choice but to let her in, since she'd brought something.

"They're dumplings," Lila said, carefully setting them down on the kitchen table. "My grandmother's recipe. Except for the squirrel." She smiled hesitantly.

"Much obliged," Birdie said, walking back toward the front door.

"I can't thank you enough," Lila said, "for helping me. I truly appreciate it." Her eyes were all watery, and Birdie hoped she wouldn't bring up the unspoken confidences between patient and healer. Birdie hadn't said anything to anyone about the bite and had no desire to talk about it with Lila, either. Just then the girl's eyes caught on something behind Birdie, and her face lit up.

"I've never seen an instrument quite like that," she said.

Birdie moved out of the way so Lila could get a better look. "It's a dulcimer," she said. "My husband's."

"I play piano," Lila said. "Played. Not in a long time. I was sort of terrible."

Birdie didn't offer to let her hold the dulcimer. "It's nothing like a piano," she said. "You set it in your lap and pluck it. He had a hammered one, too, you play with the little mallets, but I passed that one on to my oldest boy."

"Maybe you could show me how it works sometime. I'd love to hear it."

"I'm no good," Birdie said, showing her out the door. She felt a little guilty after the girl left. She'd brought an offering of thanks, after all, and Birdie had been less than neighborly. Alone in the kitchen, she peeled back the foil and examined the dumplings. She thought about scraping them into the dog dish outside the back door, but she lifted the plate and sniffed first, and they smelled decent. She licked one, tasted butter, and took a bite. It was better than any regular dumpling. Better than *her* dumplings. Over the next few days, she ate them all, wondering how that strange girl had performed such a miracle with squirrel.

CHAPTER 26

Carl

There was a moment, as Lila told him about the baby, when everything went haywire.

It felt like his heart had stopped pumping blood and let it all drain
down to his feet. He was warm and woozy, on the verge of passing out.
His eye twitched. His ears rang. Lila seemed to wilt as she waited for
him to speak, and he gathered her in his arms and held her. It was all
he could do. *I love you*, she said. He told her he loved her, too, which
the good Lord knew wasn't enough to describe his feelings, but he
couldn't say the other things he was thinking, the greedy, giddy, kid-

on-Christmas-morning thoughts that were flashing through his brain. *I got her. She's mine. She'll stay.*

There were practicalities to tend to: fix up a nursery; get Lila to a doctor for some of those horse-pill vitamins; visit Mama at Riverview and share the news. Before any of that, he was going to marry her. He left her there on the landing and sped over to Crete's house to ask him for Grandma Dane's wedding ring, which he knew good and well his brother had no use for. It took a bit of haggling, but Crete finally gave in.

Later that night, as Carl was checking his closet to see if he still owned a tie, Joe Bill, who mostly drifted in a dark current of his consciousness, floated to the surface. He didn't know what had happened between Joe Bill and Lila, what he had done to her, but the possibility was there. He didn't want to bring it all up again, drag her through painful memories, but he had to know.

He went to her room and curled up next to her on the bed. She was awake, and she took his hand and kissed the calloused knuckles, then gently pressed her warm mouth against his palm. They hadn't made love since the attack. It was hard to believe there'd been only the one time, at the homestead, and he wanted, needed, that feeling again, to be enveloped by her, her scent, her taste, her heat. First he had to know. *It doesn't matter,* he said. *It doesn't change anything, not my feelings for you or the baby.* She let go of his hand, waited. *Joe Bill, when he . . . did he . . . did he force himself on you . . . ?* She looked him in the eye. *No,* she whispered, her mouth moving toward his, kissing him in a way that drove all thoughts of Joe Bill below the surface. And then she was slipping out of her nightgown, helping Carl out of his clothes, and he pressed against her for the first time in so long and felt that everything was right, everything was as it should be. It was true what he'd said, that his feelings for her wouldn't change. But though he never would have admitted it to her, he'd lied about the baby. He wanted a child with her, but he wanted it to be his, theirs. When she told him Joe Bill hadn't raped her, it was like being yanked back from the edge of a crumbling cliff. Rescued. Because he didn't know how he could have lived every day looking at a child with another man's face, knowing what that man had done to his wife and what he himself had done in revenge.

They got to work on the house right away. Once he gave Lila free rein, she wasn't shy about freshening up the place. She was careful with family mementos, not moving a single thing in the china cabinet except to dust it, leaving Mama's room just the way it was. Everything else, she tackled with a vengeance. Gabby came over and helped her scrub the place down. They left no crevice untouched, wiping out every cabinet, drawer, and closet, oiling creaky hinges, polishing woodwork, dusting ceilings. Furniture was rearranged, slipcovers sewn, rugs aired out, curtains washed and mended. They spent one whole weekend taking all the pictures and knickknacks off the walls, rolling on fresh paint, and then hanging everything back up. When they finished, each room was a different color: yellow kitchen, green bedroom, pink bath. The halls were bright robin's-egg blue, the baby's room delicate lilac, because Lila felt certain she was having a girl. Carl wasn't a fan of the rosy bathroom, but he would have let his wife paint polka dots on the roof if it made her happy. All the windows stayed open while the paint dried, and the house felt fresh and new; it would always be his old family home, but now it was Lila's home, too.

Carl came home one evening after a day of baling hay—he was taking any job he could that would keep him close by—and found Gabby and Lila in the kitchen with the music blasting, dancing around like a couple of crazies. Lila both aroused and intimidated him with suggestive moves unlike anything he'd seen at local dances, but when he asked where she'd learned how to dance like that, she just laughed and grabbed his hand, and they tried out a line dance Gabby had taught her. It was something, to see her so at ease, laughing and having fun. He could have watched her like that all night. He was glad she had Gabby to keep her company. As flaky as Gabs could be, she was a good, loyal friend.

Carl visited Mama several times after the wedding, trying to smooth things over, but he imagined it was hard for any mother to accept that her son had gotten a girl pregnant and married her at the courthouse. It wasn't the proper way to do things, no question. The situation was made worse by Mama's condition, which had deteriorated to the point that the mother he remembered rarely made an appearance. Mama had become the angry, paranoid woman he'd seen in brief flashes throughout his childhood, though Dad and Crete had hidden her episodes as best they could.

From the very beginning, Lila had a hard time with the idea of his mother being separated from the family. He came to realize she hadn't left the bedroom untouched purely out of respect but because she expected Mama to move back in. She begged him to bring Althea home, promising to take care of her. He argued that it would be difficult to take care of a parent and a baby at the same time, but he knew it didn't make any difference to Lila. She'd lived with her grandma from the time she was little and couldn't imagine childhood without her. *Your mother is still alive*, she said, and he could see how much it hurt her that her own parents were dead, that they'd never know their grandkids. He didn't have high hopes that it would work out, but he couldn't argue with Lila. He couldn't *not* give her what she needed from him, if he had the power to give it.

Lila wanted Althea's room to be perfect for her homecoming. She scrubbed the wood floor and made the bed with fresh linens, fluffing the pillows against the headboard and folding the chenille duvet across the bed just so. She cut zinnias and asters from the garden and arranged them in Mama's milk-glass vase on the dresser. Carl kissed her goodbye, and she smiled in the way that made him want to keep kissing her instead of leaving her behind to make the drive to Riverview. She had plans to bake bread and fix vegetable soup from Althea's own recipe so dinner would be ready as soon as they returned. She'd even picked mint from the herb bed outside the kitchen, so she could try to make tea like Ransome's.

Mama sang to herself the whole way back to the house and seemed in good spirits. Maybe it was the right thing to do, Carl thought, bringing her home. Lila was four months pregnant, and there would be plenty of time to work things out before the baby came. Maybe they could somehow be the family his wife wanted. Lila opened the door for them as they stepped onto the porch, and he saw her smile waver as she laid eyes on Althea for the first time. His mother barely resembled the curvy, laughing blonde in the old family photos he'd shown Lila; her hair was thin and gray, cropped short like a man's, and her flesh kept close to her bones. Her mouth puckered into a frown.

"So there's the witch," Mama said, stopping to glare at Lila. "I ain't scared of you."

Lila pressed her lips together, shot Carl a determined look, and held the door open wider.

CHAPTER 27

Birdie

She'd heard Althea was back but didn't see her until the umpteenth time she walked down to the Danes' to return Althea's plate. Birdie couldn't ever think of those dishes as Lila's, though Lila was the one bringing them over, piled high with dumplings. The first time Birdie returned the plate, she felt almost ashamed. One, that she had been so unneighborly in the first place, and two, that she'd eaten the dumplings so fast. She told herself she was being ridiculous. There was no need for Lila to know she'd eaten them all. For all the girl knew, Birdie was just in a hurry to return the plate. It took Lila a while, that first time, to notice her hollering from the road. She had a queer look, running toward Birdie like something was wrong. It took a minute for Lila to figure out what was going on, that Birdie wasn't having a heart attack or losing her marbles, she was simply calling hello before setting foot on the property. It was polite, Birdie explained, to warn a person of your arrival, instead of showing up on the doorstep unannounced, like young folks now tended to do. She looked pointedly at Lila when she said that, but the girl didn't seem aware of her own bad manners; she just looked relieved that everything was okay. Birdie hadn't planned on saying how much she enjoyed the dumplings, but when Lila asked, she saw no reason to lie. After that, Lila brought dumplings around every week.

She didn't know how many times they'd been through the routine, Lila bringing the food, Birdie returning the plate. They always did it that way, never thinking to put the dumplings in one of Birdie's Tupperware bowls and send the plate back home with Lila. To be honest, she was starting to enjoy the girl's company. Usually, when Lila came by, she'd be full of questions, and Birdie felt good about having all the answers. Lila would ask her things like *What do you do with those berries?*, the ones growing yonder in the yard, and Birdie would say, *That's pokeweed, it's poison, but you can eat the young shoots in spring if you boil them three times and change the water in between.* Lila scribbled it down in a notebook and drew a little picture of the plant to remember. One day Lila led Birdie over to the tree line to show her some nightshade, and Birdie explained the medicinal uses and the deadly ones, then got to rambling about other names for nightshade—belladonna and devil's cherry and henbane and so on. She left out how belladonna was said to take the form of a beautiful, deadly woman, because certain folks in town had drawn that comparison to Lila.

This particular day she'd brought some morning glory seeds along with the plate, because Lila was always admiring hers, and now was a good time to scatter seeds for next year. She'd be sure and tell Lila those seeds were poisonous, too, and she started thinking how funny it was that so many beautiful things were poison, and then she wondered if maybe she ought to keep her mouth shut about all the poison plants. What was to stop Lila from cooking up a batch of tainted dumplings and doing away with her? She almost laughed at herself, at such a thought. She'd been listening too much to witch talk from folks who didn't know Lila.

She stood out at the road calling hello, but Lila didn't come out. Birdie figured she was home, because the girl hardly went anywhere unless Carl or Gabby took her into town. And Lila should have been expecting her. Birdie actually felt a little hurt that Lila didn't come to the door when she called. She knew she shouldn't do it, but she talked herself into walking through the yard to see if the girl might be digging in the dirt somewhere and hadn't heard her. When she got up close to the kitchen garden, she saw some lettuce and peas growing, which meant Lila had taken her advice on fall planting. The weeds were getting out of hand, though, and Birdie couldn't help herself, she set the plate and the bag of seeds in the grass and squatted down and started pulling. That was when she heard the shouting, and she recognized the voice and knew Althea was home.

Something smashed inside the house, and Birdie pressed her face up against the kitchen door. "Hullo!" she called. "It's Birdie. Returning your plate." More smashing and a scream. She banged on the door a few times and then thought to hell with manners, she was already at the door hollering and might as well go on in. Somebody might need help. And she had a tiny fleeting thought that maybe what people said about Lila was true and she was in there putting some sort of spell on Althea. Birdie hurried toward the racket and found Lila in the front room, shielding herself behind the wingback chair while Althea ripped picture frames from the wall and hurled them to the floor. There was blood on the rug where Althea had walked barefoot through the broken glass.

"Althea," she hollered. Althea turned around, and Birdie could tell that her old neighbor recognized her. A faint smile crossed Althea's lips. The wildness didn't leave her eyes, though, and it hurt to see her that way.

"Hello, Birdie. Was I expecting you?"

"Oh, yes," Birdie said. "I thought we'd do some singing today. I've been meaning to get out the dulcimer." Lila stared at the two of them, her eyes wide.

Althea clasped her hands. "Of course. That sounds lovely. I just need to get this witch out of my house—"

Birdie gently grabbed hold of her arms. "Let's go to my place," she said. "I made tea and cookies just for your visit."

"Hmm." She looked confused. "Well, yes, how good of you to fetch me. I lost track of time."

Birdie led her out to the front porch and sat her on the swing, telling her to wait. Back inside, she gathered bandages and antiseptic and a pair of slippers for Althea to wear. Lila was waiting at the bottom of the stairs when Birdie came down.

"She won't take her medicine," Lila said, wringing her hands. "This is just one of her bad days; it's not always like this. She'll calm down. She's fine when Carl's home."

"She can't stay here," Birdie said. "I'll take her to my place to wait for Carl."

"No! Please don't tell him. I'll try harder, I'll find a way to get through to her."

Birdie shook her head. "Oh, child. She ain't getting better. How do you expect to deal with this when there's a baby in the house?"

Lila grabbed her sleeve. "I want my little girl to have her grandma."

Birdie didn't know what Lila expected from a grandmother, but she wouldn't get it from Althea. "It'll be all right," she said, patting Lila's hand. She left the girl alone to clean up the blood and glass.

Althea was fine once Birdie got her away from Lila. The two neighbors sang hymns most of the afternoon, as they had often done on

Sundays when their husbands were alive. Birdie set the dulcimer on her lap and plucked the strings, and Althea had no trouble remembering the words to their favorite songs. Afterward, they drank tea, and Althea told her how the witch had roosted in her home and cursed it. Lila had trapped her son and she carried an evil seed, her belly bloated with sin. It all sounded crazy, but she said it with conviction.

Birdie had been among those folks who thought Lila was something dark, something *other*. But she had seen the lost look in the girl's eyes when she took Althea away. Lila was just a scared kid finding her way in a strange place, and Birdie felt ashamed for not helping her more. Carl came to get his mother that night after work, and once Birdie told him all she'd seen and heard, he decided to drive her straight back to Riverview.

Birdie went to see Lila the next day, to help pack Althea's things. Lila looked tired and didn't say much. As they carried boxes down the upstairs hall, Birdie noticed that one of the bedrooms had been cleared out and painted lavender. "Is this the baby's room?" she asked. Lila nodded, and they peered into the cozy space. "I can do grandma things," Birdie said. She'd been thinking about it all night, how this was one little way she could help. She had four grandsons of her own, two by her preacher son who lived over in the Bootheel, and two by her son in Oklahoma, but she didn't get to see them near enough. "For the baby. I can make cookies. Read books. Tell long boring stories."

Lila dropped the box of Althea's clothes and hugged her, her thin arms stronger than Birdie expected, her full belly pressed to Birdie's empty one.

CHAPTER 28

Lucy

Uncle Crete had an Elks club meeting the first Thursday night of every month, and I figured that would be a good time for me to sneak into his house. Crete didn't particularly like the Elks. He'd joined mostly to spite some local businessmen who would have preferred to exclude him, and he rarely missed a meeting if he was in town. I told Bess I'd call her when I got back home, and that if I hadn't called her by morning, to worry.

"Worry like call the police?" she asked.

I shook my head, thinking of Ray Walker's advice. "Worry like call my dad. I don't expect anything to happen, though. I'm just going out there to see if I can find anything useful. I'll be in and out before he gets home."

It was a long walk to Crete's, and the August heat was stifling even in the dark, but I didn't want to borrow Bess's car and risk being seen. In my backpack, I carried a flashlight, the Swiss army knife Dad had given me for Christmas, and a bottle of water. I thought it might be smart to have some sort of weapon, just in case, but I wasn't going to haul a shotgun along. The knife would have to do. I started thinking through scenarios in which I might need a weapon, and they were all ridiculous. I was overthinking things. It couldn't be that dangerous to sneak into my uncle's house. We were family, after all. He'd never treated me poorly a day in my life. I shook out my arms, tried to clear my head. I was going to Crete's house. No big deal.

But it was sort of a big deal, because even though we were family and he came to our house any time he wanted, I hadn't been to Crete's place in years. The house was a smaller version of ours, built for Grandpa Dane's spinster sister. It sat empty after she died, until Crete inherited it with his chunk of land and decided to move in. When I was in grade school, Crete built a more modern addition onto the back of the house, including a deck and aboveground pool, and even though woods surrounded the place on all sides, he'd installed a privacy fence around the backyard. One day when Dad and I went over to swim, we found a bare-naked woman sprawled facedown on the deck. Dad told me to cover my eyes, but of course I didn't. He rolled the woman over and felt for a pulse. Blood streaked from her nostrils down into her mouth, and I wondered if the blood was from snorting something or falling on her face. Dad leaned over her to listen for breath, and she came to, laughing and coughing and throwing her arms around him. As soon as Dad untangled himself, he dragged me straight back to the truck, and we left. Later that night, I heard him tell Crete on the phone that we wouldn't be coming over to swim anymore. He added that Crete was always welcome at our house, so long as he didn't bring a date.

When I came up on it through the woods, the house looked much as I remembered, except there was now a chain-link dog run bordering the privacy fence. Two pit bulls lunged at the walls of the pen, barking. The front door was locked, which was strange for anyone living so far out in the woods but not surprising for Crete. The windows along the porch wouldn't budge. I climbed on top of the dog run, further aggravating the dogs, to get high enough to boost myself over the fence and into the backyard. The sliding-glass door off the deck was locked, but it looked like one of the windows upstairs was open. I let myself out of the backyard through the gate, and there, on the side of the toolshed, hung the extension ladder that had been there for as long as I could remember. I carried it to the house and ratcheted it up until I could reach the window. Luckily, the screen was flimsier than the old-fashioned kind at our house, and I was able to push the frame in with a little effort.

I hoisted myself into a sparsely furnished bedroom and popped the screen back in place before stepping out into the hall. I was looking for an office or storage room but didn't find one on the second floor. I crept downstairs and poked around and didn't see anything useful. I opened the door to the basement and flicked on the light. There was another, heavier door at the bottom of the stairs that closed behind me when I passed through it. I was in the new part of the basement, which was completely unfamiliar to me, so I started opening doors until I found a storage room filled with neat stacks of boxes. I immediately started prying open the boxes; they were crammed with notebooks and files. I allowed myself to believe that I would find what I'd been looking for. Somewhere in these papers, I'd discover who had rented the trailer. I just had to hurry.

I skimmed through several boxes, scanning the tabs on the file folders and peeking inside the few that looked promising. The papers were old, and I hurried from box to box, worried that they were all out of date. I was down to the last stack of boxes when one of the tabs caught my eye. *Petrovich, L.* Petrovich was my mother's maiden name. In that moment, I didn't care about the rental contracts. I didn't care that the clock was ticking and Crete would be on his way home. I opened the folder and sat down to sort through the pages. Clipped inside the cover was a black-and-white picture of my mother, a photocopy. After a lifetime of studying the same few pictures of her, I was shocked to see a new one. She looked different. Still beautiful, of course, but missing the smile from all her other pictures. Her expression was mischievous, and her hair fell around her face in a messy, seductive way. She wore a bikini, and for the first time, I saw how she looked beneath her clothes. Seeing her that way felt almost unbearably intimate. Someone had been cropped out of the photo, leaving a phantom hand at my mother's waist.

I had to tear myself away from the picture. There were some magazine clippings, the little ads you find in the back. Agencies that placed nannies, housekeepers, models. I unfolded a sheet of paper, some sort of questionnaire. My mother's name was at the top, but the form was filled out in someone else's handwriting, and I quickly realized this wasn't an ordinary job application or medical form. *Hair color: Dark brown. Hair length: Long. Eyes: Green. Height: 5'6". Weight: 120. Chest: 34D.* It was noted that she was an English-speaking American with no STDs or tattoos. A section for additional information read *No family/Orphan/EXOTIC 10+.*

I knew Crete had hired my mother through an agency. He freely admitted that he couldn't find a local willing to do all the work he wanted for the wage he offered to pay. My uncle was always looking to save money. But he hadn't been seeking a typical hired hand. He'd chosen the most beautiful, the most exotic. An orphan. Was that part a coincidence, or had he wanted to make sure no one would come for her, that she had nowhere else to go? I spread out the rest of the papers and had started to read what looked to be her employment contract when I heard a muffled thud.

I tensed, trying to home in on the direction of the sound, and stepped into the hall. I heard the sound again; it was definitely coming from somewhere in the basement, not overhead. I checked my watch, estimating that I had at least an hour before Crete returned. "Hello?" I said. I had no idea what I would do if I came across someone in Crete's basement, but if there was anyone here, I hoped it was one of his drunk girlfriends—someone I could easily lie to and escape from. Maybe it was Becky Castle, if she and Crete were still seeing each other. I could make small talk about her daughter, Holly, and ask if she was still raising rabbits.

"Hello." I said it louder and waited through the silence until I heard another thump, then another. I followed the hall until it ended in a shadowy storage area, the shelves lined with cases of beer and soda, plastic barrels of pretzels, jugs of bleach, rolls of paper towels. Had it been better lit, it could have passed for an aisle at Walmart.

More pounding came from behind the shelves, and after deciding that was impossible, I realized the original basement lay on the other side of the wall. I started pulling down bulk packages of toilet paper and detergent, and as I did, the middle section of shelving began to roll. It was set on casters. I swung it out of the way to reveal a steel door with a keypad.

My skin prickled, just like it had when I discovered the safe hidden in the floor of Crete's office at Dane's. Unlike the safe, this locked room made no sense. What was he going to such great lengths to hide?

"Is somebody there?" I held my breath, listening, but there was no reply. I tried the door, which wouldn't budge. Then I heard more thuds. It could have been something mechanical, like an old pump acting up. I hadn't heard any voices. I was letting my imagination get the better of me.

I looked at the keypad, but it offered no hints. It didn't seem likely that Crete would choose an easy code, but it couldn't hurt to try. I punched in 1234. A tiny red light flashed on and off to let me know I was wrong. It would have been helpful to know how many numbers were in the code. I tried 12345, just in case. Again, the red light. My next guess was Crete's birthday. On the third mistake, the keypad made a beeping noise, and the light turned red and stayed red. Whatever was on the other side of that wall, Crete didn't want it found. That made me all the more determined to figure out what it was.

There had to be some way in. Then I remembered there was access to the old cellar from outside, two slanted doors set into the ground at the foundation. I ran upstairs and out the door, and the dogs started barking again. I made my way around to the side of the house. The cellar doors I remembered had been torn out, and in their place was a thick slab of concrete—an awkward porch adorned with empty flower-pots.

I was running out of time, and I had to accept that I wouldn't be getting into the locked room tonight. I needed to get out of the house, replace the ladder, and leave before Crete came back. My search hadn't accomplished anything except to make me more suspicious. It was creepy, the way he'd brought my mother here. I knew he was in some way, directly or not, involved with what had happened to Cheri. And now this sealed room. Whatever he was up to, it didn't look good.

I returned to the basement and hastily cleaned up the evidence of my visit. When I was done, I grabbed my backpack and opened the door to the stairs. There, on his way down, was Crete. I tried not to panic. He had caught me, and there was nothing I could do.

"*Lucy,*" he growled. His face burned with anger and disbelief. "I half-expected to find that Cole boy in here, after what he done at my office. I wouldn't have pegged you to be setting off my alarm."

An alarm? Maybe one had been triggered when I entered too many wrong codes in the keypad? Crete curled one hand into a fist, the muscles of his forearm tightening. He was my uncle, and he had never hurt me. I still wanted to believe that he wouldn't. I repeated it over and over in my head, *He won't hurt you*, but I was shaking.

"Why don't you tell me what it is you're looking for."

I searched for a believable lie. "My mom . . . I know she worked for you. I thought you might have . . . mementos or something."

He shook his head. "I don't have anything of hers. But if that's what you wanted, why didn't you ask? Have I ever denied you a single god-damn thing?"

"I'm sorry," I said. "It was a dumb thing to do. I just wasn't really thinking it through. I better get home."

"Why were you trying to get into my locked room?"

I tried to sound casual, but my hands were trembling. "I thought maybe you kept your papers in there, something that would tell me more about her. Or just something with her handwriting on it."

He looked me dead-on. He knew I was lying. "I keep valuables in there," he said finally. "Nothing of interest to you."

"Sorry," I said. "I wasn't going to steal anything."

He chuckled drily. "I know, you're not that kind of kid."

"I'm really sorry," I said. "It won't happen again."

"It won't," he said. I stared at him expectantly, waiting for him to move out of the way and let me by. Instead, he reached down and took my hand. "We got something to talk about." My heart stumbled and then resumed its frenetic pace.

Uncle Crete's grip was firm but not rough. He led me up to the kitchen and sat me down at the table. He got himself a beer out of the fridge and cracked open a soda for me. My throat was dry and I took a sip, holding the can with both hands to keep it from shaking.

"I know you been worried about that girl Cheri Stoddard," he said, sitting down in the chair opposite me. "I remember back when she first left, you couldn't believe she'd run away. And you were so upset when they found her. It hurts me to see you hurting, I hope you know that." My limbs felt detached, like they didn't belong to me. I wondered, if I got up to run, whether I'd be able to. "I never wanted you in that trailer. That was Judd's fault, and I should have talked to you right after, cleared some things up. But I didn't realize then what you were putting together. Not until you started asking around town about Cheri. From what I been hearing, you're out there playing Nancy Drew."

I wanted to get up from the table and run out the door. I wondered if he would stop me.

"I have to tell you some things I didn't ever wanna have to tell you. I been keeping 'em to myself so nobody'd get hurt, but it looks like I'm gonna have to let you in on it."

I stared numbly. I was thinking of the saying *I could tell you, but then I'd have to kill you*. I glanced at my watch. Nowhere near late enough for Bess to call my dad.

"Your friend Cheri, she had it rough. Left home of her own free will. Somebody came to me to help her out a bit, and she did stay in that trailer. But I had nothing to do with anything that went on over there. I collected my rent and kept out of their business. From what my renter told me, that girl was as happy as a pig in mud to be out of her mama's place. I didn't ask details."

I thought of what Jamie had told me, how Cheri had been running for her life down the river. Maybe she had decided to leave home on her own, but her decision-making skills were poor. She could have gotten talked into anything, even into a situation worse than the one she was trying to escape. I had a hard time distinguishing what part of Crete's story was true, if any. He could have been lying about everything.

"Now, it kills me to say this, but I don't see what choice I got." He leaned in close and took my hand. "Your daddy was the last person to see Cheri before she was found in that tree. He's the one who put her there."

I was hollow inside, a gulf opening up. "That's not true," I said.

"Ask him," he said. "See if he can lie to you." He sat back and finished his beer. "So if you were planning on talking to anybody else about Cheri, you should know you could get your daddy in a whole lot of trouble. I reckon they'd take him away. Now, if that happens, you're always welcome here. You're family, and I'll always take care of you, no matter what, just like I always done. But I sure would hate to see my baby brother locked up. Or worse."

I stared at the soda can, struggling to form coherent thoughts. He could be lying to protect himself. That made the most sense. Dad couldn't have been involved. But what would my dad say if I asked him? If he lied, would I know he was lying?

"This ain't the first time I've had to cover up for him," Crete continued. "He killed a man that fancied your mother. There were witnesses. Go ahead and ask him. There are all sorts of things that could send your daddy to prison if they came to light. I'm sorry I had to tell you, but you're old enough to hear it now, and it's better if you know. I've only ever tried to help."

I sat in the chair for a long time. Crete cleaned the kitchen up a bit, throwing beer cans in the trash and moving dirty dishes to the sink. After a while it seemed that he wasn't going to keep me from leaving. He'd already tethered me with his words. No noises came up from the basement to break the silence. At last I stood up and slung my backpack over my shoulder.

"You need a ride home?" he asked.

I stiffened.

"You ain't gotta be scared of me," he said. "Or your daddy, neither. He'd never do anything to hurt you. We're blood, and we stick together. Now, you remember everything we talked about. I know you'll do the right thing." He ruffled my hair and walked me to the door. "Careful out there. I'll be keeping my eye on you."

I stumbled out into the night, and when I hit the trees, I started running. I ran until my breath seared my lungs and my side hurt enough to double me over, and when the pain subsided, I ran some more, all the way up the back steps of the house and into the kitchen, where Dad sat at the table with a beer, horribly reminiscent of the scene I'd just left. Crete's accusations clamored in my head. *Your dad killed a man. He put Cheri in that tree.*

"Look who's grounded," he said. I stared at him, wheezing, trying to catch my breath. There were several crushed beer cans and a dwindling bottle of whiskey on the table. How long had he been sitting here, drinking, waiting for me? "I bet you're wondering why I'm home." I didn't say anything, but he continued anyway. "I got a call from Daniel Cole today up in Springfield, and we got together to talk a bit. He's worried about you. Said you're trying to track down Cheri's killer, and he's afraid you'll get yourself in trouble without one of us here to keep an eye on you."

Anger kindled inside me. Daniel hadn't bothered to call me since he'd moved. What right did he have to call my dad?

"Birdie had some things to say, too. Seems there's been traffic out here at odd hours. Past curfew. What's going on with you, Lucy? And where were you? Out with Bess? You better not have been drinking." I didn't answer. He circled me, sniffed my breath, my hair, laughable, considering the fumes coming off him. "At least I know you weren't out with some boy, since your boyfriend's outta town."

Boyfriend?

"Though now I think I'd probably rather you were out with him. He's older than I'd like, but he seems like a smart kid. Trustworthy. I really wish you would have had the courtesy to introduce us."

My breathing had almost returned to normal, though my heart was pumping overtime. I'd barely begun to process everything that had happened at Crete's, and now Dad was in my face, raving drunk, talking about Daniel and scaring me enough to make me wonder about all the things Crete had said.

"It's late," he said. "We're gonna have a nice long talk in the morning. I've got the next few days off work."

I nodded, finding my voice. "I just need to call Bess, let her know I made it home." I didn't want her worrying, or worse, calling my dad because she hadn't heard from me.

"No," he said, grabbing the phone as I reached for it. "I'll do it. I haven't decided yet if you're losing your phone privileges." He squinted at the list of phone numbers taped to the fridge and clumsily jabbed the buttons to dial. "Bess? Lucy's home. And you might not see her for a while, because she's gonna be grounded for breaking curfew and God knows what else."

He listened for a minute, exasperated by whatever Bess was saying. He tried to break in, but apparently, she just kept going and he relented with a frown. He shoved the phone at me. "She's gotta tell you something," he said. "You have one minute, and then your ass best be in bed."

"Lucy?" I couldn't tell if Bess was whispering or crying. I wished Dad would leave me alone so I could talk to her, tell her what had happened, but he stood at arm's length, glaring, tapping his watch like a prison warden.

"What is it?" I asked, turning my back to Dad.

"It's Sorrel," she said. "He hung himself. He's dead."

I lay in bed until I heard Dad snoring, then crept across the hall to the bathroom and took a long shower. When the hot water ran out, I sat down in the claw-foot tub and let the cold spray pelt me until my teeth chattered. Back in my room, I tried to make sense of things in my journal. I didn't yet know how to categorize everything that had happened, everything I was feeling, so I wrote it all down in one jumbled list. I wasn't convinced that my dad was a murderer. It didn't feel right. The man Crete accused Dad of killing—it could have been self-defense. And when I replayed the conversation, he hadn't exactly said that Dad had killed Cheri. Just that he had put her in the tree. But it was hard to believe anything Crete said at this point. I had no idea which parts were true.

I couldn't stop thinking about the sounds that had come from the hidden room. Though I had no reason to assume a person was trapped in there, the thought lingered in my head. Not so long ago, such a thing never would have occurred to me: that my uncle, whom I often felt closer to than my own father, might have someone locked in his basement. I knew it wasn't likely, but I realized with horror that I believed it was possible. If he had something to do with what had happened to Cheri or my mother, who knew what he was capable of.

CHAPTER 29

Gabby

Lila kept saying she didn't need a baby shower, but Gabby knew for a fact there wasn't a single damn thing in that baby's room, and Carl was working like a dog trying to save up money. It was already January, and Lila was nearly seven months along, so Gabby told her there'd be a shower whether she liked it or not, and she'd have to sit there and open gifts and let people rub her belly. The problem was, Gabby didn't know who to invite, because Lila didn't get out much, and since most folks didn't know her, they naturally saw her in a bad light. Half the town was caught up in witch gossip, whispering some nonsense about her and Joe Bill Sump. So it wasn't easy to come up with a guest list. There were

Birdie and Ransome, of course. Birdie said she'd talk to the ladies at First Baptist and come up with something. There was no way Gabby could back out on the shower after pushing Lila into it, so she vowed that even if only the two of them showed up, they'd have a good time.

She'd been to only one baby shower, for her friend Darla who got pregnant junior year, so Gabby was basing everything on what she remembered from that. They'd need sherbet punch, cake with frilly icing, and some dumb games—but not drinking games, like at Darla's shower. She knew Birdie and Ransome and Lila wouldn't want to drink, but the more she thought about the shower, the more *she* wanted a drink, so she had one, and another, and then Duane, the guy she was seeing, came by and they messed around for a while. He always kept his eyes closed, and Gabby couldn't tell if he was thinking of her or imagining someone else. When he came, he reminded her of a soldier, grunting, thrusting his bayonet in the enemy. In world history, one of the few classes she'd stayed awake for, men killed their enemies and raped their enemies' women. She wondered why men fucked what they hated and fucked what they loved and fucked what they didn't give a fuck about. Maybe they wanted to fuck everything, nothing to do with the way they felt, just an uncontrollable urge. Thrust, grunt, conquer.

When Duane finished, he pulled his pants back on and asked her to loan him some cash. For once she said no. She was saving to buy something nice for Lila, for the shower. She didn't know what, because Lila needed everything, but it would be something good. *Bitch*, Duane muttered before the camper door slammed. Gabby curled up on the wet sheets and pretended she didn't want him to come back. She would pretend hard enough to make it true.

The day of the shower, Gabby went over to Birdie's early to decorate. She had pink and blue crepe paper, even though Lila kept saying she was having a girl, because Gabby knew it was never a good idea to get your heart set on something that might not work out. Birdie had made the sheet cake and had it sitting out on the sideboard, still in the pan. She'd done it up in plain white without any sort of sprinkles or frosting flowers or anything. It looked like the sort of cake you'd get to celebrate joining a convent.

"You got any sprinkles?" Gabby asked. "Colored sugar, something?"

Birdie frowned. She was wearing a stiff black dress, to carry on the convent theme, Gabby guessed. "What for?"

"Nothing. Never mind." Birdie fussed with the punch bowl and cups while Gabby twisted the crepe paper and taped it across the front of the sideboard. Two gifts sat next to the cake, one from Birdie and one, in a green paper bag, from Ransome Crowley. "Ransome's not coming?" Gabby asked.

Birdie shook her head. "No, she dropped that by yesterday. That woman is plum wore out. Didn't feel up to the festivities."

Festivities? A few people eating cake in a deathly quiet house? Gabby wanted to drive over to the farm and drag Ransome's bony ass to the party. Not like she'd liven things up, but at least Lila knew her. They heard somebody pull up outside, and Birdie hurried to the door to see if it was her church friends. Gabby's pathetic attempt at decorating was all done, so she followed her.

Ray Walker's truck sat in the driveway, and he was in the back untying a bentwood rocking chair. "Hello, there," he said, stepping down from the tailgate. He wore a crisp button-down shirt like he did every single day of his life—probably slept in one, too. "I apologize for arriving unexpected," he said, his voice warm and smooth, like good bourbon. "But I heard about the shower, and I wanted to bring something." The first party crasher. Gabby could only hope there'd be more. "If I can just take this inside, I'll be on my way."

"That'd be fine," Birdie said.

"Let me help," Gabby said, hopping into the bed of the truck before he could stop her. They got the chair lowered to the ground and carried it up to the house. "This is some chair," she said as they set it down in Birdie's front room.

He rubbed his hand over the polished armrest. "I wanted her to have something nice. A keepsake." Red splotches spread across his face, and Gabby realized he was blushing. Even the civilized Mr. Walker had a hard-on for Lila. Gabby wasn't going to let that love go to waste.

Birdie was still out front, sweeping the walkway of dirt that only she could see. "Come here," Gabby said, dragging Ray by his shirt cuff. "We need some help." She gestured at the cake, the limp streamers. "It's depressing. We need sprinkles. Flowers. Balloons. Anything."

He cleared his throat. "I suppose I could run into town. Pick up a few things."

"Great," she said. "And you have to stay for the shower. We need bodies in here. Bring your wife, too, if she wants to come." Gabby knew that Mrs. Walker was infertile and either avoided baby showers or cried her way through them, but now that Ray was coming, it felt rude not to invite her.

The church ladies arrived while Ray was gone. There were five of them, all with identical old-lady haircuts. One brought a tray of sugar cookies that fit right in with the rest of the bland display. At least the gift table was filling up a bit, though one of the ladies had the nerve to wrap her gift in newspaper. The women all stood in the kitchen with Birdie, talking about some churchy thing or another, shooting Gabby bitchy looks through the doorway.

Ray came back alone, loaded down with goodies. He'd brought a package of sugar roses and tubes of colored icing for the cake, a fruit tray and a deli tray from Ralls', and a rainbow of helium balloons tied with ribbon.

"Nice work, Ray," Gabby said, making him blush again. There was something handsome about him, something sexy behind that button-down shirt, and she wondered briefly what he was like in bed.

When Lila and Carl showed up, Lila went on about how great everything looked, giving Gabby a huge tearful hug. Lila hugged Birdie, too, which horrified the church ladies. They clutched their punch cups in front of them with both hands, lest she try to hug them, too. Gabby didn't know how Birdie had talked them into coming but guessed one or two had shown up just to lay eyes on the witch of Toad Holler Road. Ray stared at Lila with a reserved smile, taking his eyes off her long enough to shake hands with Carl. The way he looked at Lila wasn't pure lust—Gabby recognized that well enough—there was something more to it, though she wasn't sure what. She fetched Lila some punch and a plate of food and got her situated in the bentwood rocker.

"Attention, everyone," Gabby said, clanging a fork on her cup. "It's time for a few games, and then we'll get to the presents and cake." Birdie herded the ladies into the front room, and everyone found a place to sit on the sofa, recliner, or folding chairs. The small room was pretty well filled up, and despite the crabby expressions on a couple of ladies' faces, the shower was starting to feel festive, just as Gabby had wanted it to be. She handed out pens and strips of paper. Crete slipped in the front door just as she was about to explain the rules. She hadn't invited him, but the more, the merrier. "Hey, look, it's the uncle-to-be," Gabby said. He rolled his eyes at her and took a spot standing in the corner, his arms crossed over his broad chest.

Gabby went on, "Okay, write down what you think the baby will be—boy or girl—and what day you think it'll be born. Whoever gets closest to being right'll win a prize." She was hoping everybody would forget about the prize by the time the baby came, because she didn't have any prizes. She collected all the scraps of paper in an envelope and handed it to Lila. "Why don't you read 'em out loud?" she said.

That would kill some time, if they were lucky, because she had only one other game.

Lila didn't look right. Her hand shook as she held up the little pieces of paper. Half the guesses had the baby coming way after the due date—the old ladies trying to scare her, most likely. When she got to the last one, she opened her mouth to read but then quickly folded the paper in her palm and slid her hand down into her pocket. Gabby waited a minute, but Lila just sat there staring at her lap, so she went on to the next game. She'd have to ask Lila about it later.

"For this one, we need a roll of toilet paper. You're gonna tear off as much as you think'll fit around Lila's belly. Then you have to wrap it around her, and we'll see who gets closest."

The old ladies looked embarrassed to be holding toilet paper in public and were unwinding the roll so slow that Gabby couldn't stand to watch. She glanced over at Lila, who'd all but turned to stone. Carl had gone to the kitchen for more punch. Gabby walked over and nudged Lila's foot, and she about jumped out of the chair. "You okay?" Lila nodded unconvincingly. "Sorry these games are kinda dumb," Gabby said. "We'll be done in a minute."

Lila stood in the center of the room while everybody took turns wrapping toilet paper around her. Ray went first, and from the warm smile that brightened his face when he touched her belly, Gabby could see what she'd missed before. He wanted Lila, all right, but in a different way than the rest of the jerks in Henbane. Ray and his wife were wrecked over not being able to have kids. He spoiled that niece of his, Janessa, like she was his own child, but she'd left town a few years back and never even came to visit. So poor Ray must have been thrilled when a pretty orphan like Lila showed up. In his head, he'd probably already adopted her.

Crete and Carl were too manly to take part in the game, and one of the church ladies won. She asked what her prize was, and her face turned all sour when Gabby said, "Bragging rights." Birdie served cake, and Gabby carried the presents in and set them next to Lila's chair. Lila opened Ransome's first. It was a baby quilt made of what looked like old shirts. Lila ran her hands over the squares of plaids and florals, staring hard like she recognized the fabric. The quilt was backed with a soft flannel teddy-bear print. Lila folded it so the bear side showed and stuffed it back in the bag.

It turned out the church ladies had sewn matching pieces for the nursery: a crib skirt and bumper, curtains, pillow shams, and a diaper-changing pad. Birdie had made a rag rug for the floor and a cloth doll with an embroidered face and yarn hair. Lila couldn't talk, she just sat there with tears running down her face, so Gabby went over and hugged every one of those old ladies hard enough to crack their brittle ribs, because it was such a nice thing they'd done, even if Birdie had made them do it.

Next Gabby announced that the chair Lila was sitting in was a gift from Ray, and he hugged Lila and brushed at her tears, but they just kept coming. Finally, with Ray's help, Gabby brought in her own gift, a crib from the secondhand store that she'd cleaned and painted white. Lila kept saying it was too much, too much, but Gabby knew it was just right. She looked around for Crete, but he was gone and hadn't left a gift. Carl and Ray loaded everything into Carl's truck while the rest of them sat around eating. Gabby didn't get a chance to talk to Lila in private about the unread scrap of paper, and after a while she forgot about it. She was feeling good, a little high, even, that she'd pulled off the party. She, a piece of slut trash from the holler, had hosted a successful shower. Even Birdie looked at her with newfound respect.

CHAPTER 30
Lila

It was like a punch in the stomach when Crete showed up at the baby shower. For a while I'd managed to pretend I wouldn't have to face him again, but I knew better. He wasn't through with me. *Bastard*, his scrap of paper had read. Not *boy*, like most of them, or *girl*, like Birdie and Gabby had written. From that moment, uneasiness festered, the sickness of waiting to see what he wanted and what he would do.

I was angry that the joy of Lucy's birth was marred by thoughts of Crete. As soon as she left my body, I felt a fierce animal urge to protect her. Whether or not she was Carl's—and I told myself she was—she was *mine*. All the doubts and the dark thoughts I'd had during my pregnancy dissolved when I held her. I'd been so worried that I wouldn't love my baby. Birdie had told me not to fret if the love didn't come right away, that it often took time but almost always showed up when the baby did. She winked at me as she wiped blood and goop from Lucy's tiny body. She could see my love had arrived.

Birdie showed me how to nurse Lucy, how to bathe her, how to care for the stump of umbilical cord that stuck out from my daughter's belly button, a potent reminder of her connection to me. I cried when the stump fell off.

Carl stayed home with me and Lucy for the first week, and then he had to go back to work. We needed the money. I was wiped out from lack of sleep and constant nursing, still wearing my nightgown when Crete showed up one afternoon. Carl wasn't home, and I wouldn't open the door.

"It ain't locked," he said. "That lock don't even work." I stood there, terrified, ready to run for a butcher knife if he came in. "I'm not here to do anything to you. I'm just here to talk. We both know that baby . . . that baby right there"—he pointed to Lucy, who, as always, was wrapped securely against my chest—"she could be mine. And you can't keep her away from me. One way or another, we're family. I'm gonna be in her life, whether or not you like it. That's how it is. You can tell Carl anything you want, he knows what family's all about. He's tied to me. I drown, he drowns. You drown. All of us." We stared at each other through the screen. "Or just you. We could get rid of you, and everything'd be fine between me and him. Up to you, really, how you want it to play out."

I felt sick, being so close to him. Could it be true that he wanted to spend time with the baby? Be in her life? How could I allow that after what he'd done to me? How could I trust him around Lucy? I loved her more than I ever could have imagined. Maybe it was true, what

Carl said, that being an uncle would soften Crete. Maybe it would change him. I doubted it. To me, he'd always be a monster.

I rode into town with Gabby one afternoon so I could drop off a thank-you note for Ray. The rocker sat by the window in the baby's room, and I loved to look out over the hills as I cuddled Lucy in the chair, singing lullabies. Ray's gift had been incredibly thoughtful, and I'd been too emotional at the shower to thank him properly.

"What a grand surprise," Ray said as he ushered me into his office. He took Lucy's carrier from me and eased it to the floor. "What brings you by?"

"I just wanted to tell you how much Lucy and I love the rocker. She quiets down every time we sit in it."

"Warms my heart to hear it," he said, gazing admiringly at Lucy. "That child is a living doll."

I adjusted the baby quilt Ransome had made, tucking it under Lucy's feet.

"How are you feeling these days?" Ray asked gently. "Are you getting enough sleep? You're . . . You look awfully thin, my dear."

"I'm fine," I said. "The baby keeps me busy. I barely have time to sit down and eat."

"Have you been to a doctor since the baby came?"

"Birdie's been checking on me," I said.

"I know she delivered Lucy, but the woman's not a real doctor. Heck, she was never even a real veterinarian. She gets prescriptions illegally from the vet she used to work for, some relative of hers. Now, I have a friend in Springfield, Dr. Coates, I can get you an appointment for tomorrow—"

"I don't need to go see a doctor," I said, my voice rising. Lucy squeaked in her carrier, and I burst into tears.

"Oh, sweetheart." Ray slid out of his chair and knelt beside me, taking my hand. I leaned over and sobbed on his freshly ironed shirt. He smelled comfortingly of dryer sheets and old-fashioned aftershave. "It's all right. Everything's all right. It's completely normal to feel overwhelmed with a new baby. But you should really see someone, just in case."

"It's not that," I said, my voice muffled by his sleeve.

"Then what is it? You can tell me. Maybe there's something I can do to help." There was genuine kindness and concern in his voice, and that made me cry harder.

"I can't tell you. I haven't told anybody. If I tell, it'll just make everything worse."

Ray pulled a crisp handkerchief from his pocket and handed it to me. His initials were embroidered on it with gold thread. "It's Crete, isn't it," he said softly. "Did he threaten you somehow?"

I didn't answer. I'd been warned not to tell, and I knew Crete wouldn't hesitate to follow through on his threats.

"I was worried there might be some retaliation for breaking the contract." Ray sighed.

I was confused. My work contract? I hadn't thought about that in a while. Carl had told me not to worry about it, and I assumed Crete had let it drop. Though I should have known better than to assume Crete would let anything go.

"Most likely, he's just bullying you for fun," Ray said. "He has no reason to be peeved—Carl did everything he asked. Signed over the deed to the house and his share of the land to Crete, to buy you out. I tried to talk Carl out of it, told him the contract couldn't possibly be enforced, but he insisted. He wanted to do it Crete's way, make sure his brother was happy."

I felt like I might throw up. Carl hadn't told me that he'd sold everything to set me free. Or that Crete now had control over us, could kick us out of the house, off the land, on a whim.

"We could try to get a restraining order," Ray continued. "You'd need to talk this all over with Carl. I understand you might not want to tell me what's going on, but you've got to discuss it with your husband."

"Not yet," I said, still reeling at the news of Carl's sacrifice. "I don't know what to say."

Ray sighed. "Well, honestly—unfortunately—restraining orders don't work best on those who need them most; they rely on rational thinking and fear of the law. But you do need to protect yourself. You have to be prepared in case something happens and Carl isn't there to stand between the two of you. I hate to say it . . ." He paused and looked down at Lucy, who drifted between sleep and wakefulness. "You need a gun. Do you know how to use one?"

I shook my head. I'd never even held one.

"You're no match against him physically, and he knows that. If you had a gun, the game could almost be fair."

Though I couldn't see myself toting both a baby and a gun, what choice did I have? If a lawyer was sitting here telling me I couldn't rely on the law?

"Ask Carl to teach you with one of his little handguns. If he won't do it, I'll teach you myself, but I bet you can talk him into it. Tell him you're worried about snakes while you're out with the baby; you want to learn how to shoot to protect yourself and Lucy. It's not completely untrue."

It was a lawyerish thing to say, a slippery way of viewing truth and lies. But I was already lying to Carl in my own way, by hiding the truth. This was no different. I wiped my eyes and nose on Ray's handkerchief, careful to avoid the embroidery.

"One more thing," Ray said. "Promise, if it's anything more than big talk, you'll let me know. If Crete ever lays a hand on you, you'll tell me right away."

"Promise," I lied.

CHAPTER 31

Gabby

From the start, Lila seemed to know what to do with that baby of hers. Any time Lucy cried, Lila would swaddle her up so tight, Gabby worried she couldn't breathe. Then she'd pop a nipple in the baby's mouth, and after a minute of nursing, the kid would be asleep. Gabby asked what the deal was. Did Lila put a spell on Lucy? Did she have magic milk? Lila said all mothers' milk was magic.

A few months after Lucy was born, Lila had lost all her baby weight, though her boobs were bigger than ever, thanks to the milking operation she had going. Meanwhile, Gabby's pants grew tighter. Under her apron at work, she wore her cutoffs unbuttoned, then unzipped. Nobody special had come around to replace Duane, and she was moping, going to bed alone every night with a box of Velveeta and a fork.

She felt better when she was around Lila. Somehow her friend's newness hadn't worn off, and now she had that new little baby, too. Gabby soaked up as much of them as she could. Over the summer, Lila decided to take up shooting, and Gabby went along with her. Carl and Ray gave them lessons until they trusted the girls not to shoot themselves or each other. A couple times a week, Gabby and Lila would drop Lucy at Birdie's house and head out for some target practice. Both of them could knock cans off a log, though Lila could do it from a much greater distance. Gabby got bored with the shooting after a while, so she'd set up the cans and watch Lila shoot. Lila never got tired of practicing. She wanted to try skeet so she could work on moving targets.

One day Gabby was standing off to the side, watching the cans jump off the log, when she felt a gassy flutter in her stomach. She didn't think much of it as she set out the next round of targets, but when Lila pulled the trigger, the sensation in her gut grew stronger, a tapping, then a knocking. She pressed her hands against her bloated stomach where it ballooned under her dress, and she knew. She'd been dumber than Lila, not paying attention to what was happening in her own body. She should have been over the moon at the thought of someone new coming into her life—she did love new things, after all. And Lila was managing just fine with a baby. But unlike Lila, Gabby didn't have a house or a husband, and she didn't want anything to do with Duane, who was likely the father. She lived alone in a camper and had no instinct for kids. And a baby was only new for a little while. It was bound to you forever.

Gabby went home that day and drank. She drank every last drop she had in the camper—beer and tequila and Mad Dog and peppermint schnapps—so much that she was sure the baby would be washed out, poisoned, or, by some weird trick of anatomy, thrown up. The next day, still dry-heaving, she forced herself out into the woods and started running. Nature was a poor housekeeper, just like her, and the ground was littered with dead leaves, mushrooms, fallen branches, bugs. Layers of life and death piling on top of each other, growing and rotting, tangling under her feet. She let it all trip her up, fell down hard, and gagged. She pushed through the undergrowth, dehydrated, woozy, up into the hills and back down till she was covered with scratches and ticks and burrs. She lay in her narrow bed in the camper and waited for blood, but none came.

Sarah Cole confirmed what Gabby feared: The baby was glued tight as a nit. It refused to be flushed from its hidey-hole, not before it was ready. *You're worried you'll be a bad mother,* Sarah said. *But that's a good thing. The bad ones don't give it a thought.*

Lila was happy for Gabby. There were no gifts at the shower she threw; instead, she and Carl collected and scraped together enough money for a down payment on a trailer. It was close enough, Lila said, that they could walk to each other's houses through the woods. By that time, the soft tapping in Gabby's gut had become a whale rolling over in the confines of her innards, carelessly shoving organs out of its way.

Bess was born prematurely, in the thick heat of Labor Day, screaming on the way out and every day after. She screamed whenever Gabby tried to nurse her, so Gabby gave up and switched to the bottle. Lila tried to swaddle her, but she screamed through that, too. Whenever Bess screamed, Lucy would get worked up and start bawling. Finally, Gabby and Lila discovered that if the babies were swaddled together, they'd both fall asleep, peaceful so long as they were touching.

They didn't see each other as much over the winter, so Gabby couldn't say for sure if Lila was depressed. It seemed more like she was preoccupied. Gabby was preoccupied, too. That first year with Bess was a long, bitter haul, and it took all she had to keep going. Mothering didn't come naturally to her, like it did for Lila; plus, Gabby was doing it on her own. She was lucky if she had time to shave her legs. She had tunnel vision. She didn't see what was coming. And she'd never, ever forgive herself for that.

CHAPTER 32

Birdie

Birdie had four grandsons, two by each of her boys, but she didn't get to see them like she wanted. Her oldest son followed the Lord, preaching at a church way over in the Bootheel, and the other followed the weather, chasing hail across the country for a paycheck fixing dents. She always figured her kids would stay in Henbane, like so many did, but there weren't enough churches or hailstorms to keep them.

Lucy was the only little girl Birdie ever took care of. She wasn't sure at first what to do with her but realized right quick that Lucy was no different from her baby boys. She liked to be rocked and sung to, liked to gnaw Birdie's overall buttons. Lila never left her for too long of a stretch, because she hated to be away from her. That, and Lucy didn't cotton to the bottle. She liked Birdie just fine till she got hungry, and then she'd cry for her mama.

A couple of things changed after Lucy was born. One, Carl went back to working construction. He'd kept close while Lila was pregnant, doing odd jobs around town. Now he was spending more time away, trying to make more money. They wanted to save for Lucy's college, Lila said. The other thing that changed was Crete started coming around more often. Birdie hadn't seen his truck rumble past her house much since he'd moved out of the house on Toad Holler Road a few years ago. Now it was back, here and there, no predictable time or day. Not many vehicles traveled their fork, so she noticed when they did. She wondered about Crete coming by when Carl was gone, but Lila never mentioned it. Birdie went so far as to ask one time, knowing it wasn't her business, and Lila said that now and then he brought them groceries from Dane's. Without really knowing why she was doing it, Birdie started keeping track of his visits, making tally marks on the back of the bookmark she kept in her Bible. Months went by, and she thought about mentioning it to Carl or bringing it up to Lila again, but she didn't. Still, the neat rows of lines on the bookmark made her uneasy.

One fall afternoon she took Lucy so Lila could get caught up on housework. Most days were still warm enough to run around in shirtsleeves, but nights came early and brought a whiff of wood smoke. Persimmons had started dropping, the air woozy with ripeness and rot, and Birdie aimed to gather up a bucket or two for her cousin's horses, who ate them like candy. She set Lucy's busy chair in the sun and buckled her in so she could bounce around and make noise while Birdie worked. *Buh!* Lucy said, smiling and drooling all over the place. *Buh.* That was her word for Birdie.

Birdie filled a bucket, working till sweat dripped down all her crannies, and then sat next to Lucy to rest. The baby's little hands grabbed at Birdie's shirt, and Birdie held up a plump persimmon, showing Lucy the waxy skin, all rose and orange. Lucy reached for the fruit, and Birdie let her hold it. She took another from the bucket, split the sticky flesh with her fingernail, and dug for seeds. She cleaned one seed on her apron and sliced it along the seam with her pocketknife, splitting it in two, hoping the white spot at the center would be in the shape of a fork, predicting a mild winter. She would have settled for a spoon, which meant snow. But this seed and all the others she cut revealed a knife, straight and sharp. *You best bundle up, child*, she said to Lucy. The winter would be long and bitter.

She was sorry to be right. Lila disappeared early in April, not quite twenty years old. Birdie could barely remember such an impossibly young age, a time before all her various parts began to rust and fail. As the years piled up, the betrayals of her body grew more humbling. First, a dulling of the senses: sight, hearing, smell, taste. Then the innards started to go. Her bowels wouldn't cooperate. Her joints wanted to pull apart or grind together, depending on their mood. She couldn't sleep at night but nodded off all day when she was trying to get things done. One afternoon she took the clippers and hunched over to make sense of her toenails, which had brittled and yellowed like old piano keys. Afterward, her back refused to uncurl. She sat there for a bit, helpless in the cage of her own bones, feeling like the Tin Man in *The Wizard of Oz* before Dorothy showed up with the oil.

It occurred to her then that there was a reason age drained the pleasure out of life, slowly stripping away all the things you enjoyed or took for granted. It was so you wouldn't need convincing when the time came. You'd be ready, because everything good in life was gone.

By the same turn, Lila's end would never sit right with Birdie. She had been nowhere near that downhill slide. She was a child, practically. No matter how hard Birdie prayed, it just didn't sum, how you could snuff out a light like Lila's and leave Birdie's, a guttering flame.

CHAPTER 33

Lucy

The morning after Uncle Crete had caught me breaking in to his house, I woke up exhausted, like I'd been hauling rocks in my sleep. I wanted to stay in bed, but I had to get up and face my new reality. I was grounded, and Dad wouldn't let me out of his sight. I wasn't supposed to use the phone. Dad was hungover and threatening to send me to a Christian boarding school in Arkansas. It seemed a bit extreme for breaking curfew, if that was really all he thought I'd done. He dragged me into town with him to get some groceries, and I begged him to let me go to the little library in the courthouse.

"I thought you said they never have anything worth reading," he grumbled. "Isn't that why I'm always stopping at the Trade-A-Book?"

"Please. I finished all the books you brought me. Can't I at least have something to read if I'm gonna be stuck at home?"

"Fine," he said. "But I don't know how much time you'll have for reading, with all the chores you'll be doing."

I climbed the steps to the courthouse, and instead of heading down to the basement library, I went straight to Ray's office. He wasn't in, so I borrowed a piece of paper and an envelope and scribbled a note to him. *Need to talk to you ASAP.* I sealed the envelope and left it with the receptionist, then hurried down to the library and grabbed a book at random before heading back to the truck.

Dad was sitting in the cab with the newspaper spread across his lap. "Junior high vice principal hanged himself," he said.

I tried to sound surprised. "What does the article say? Did he leave a note or anything?"

"Don't say much at all," he said. "Happened sometime yesterday." He glanced over at me. "What'd you get?"

I inspected the book cover along with him. It was an old Harlequin romance novel with a picture of a bare-chested man and a corseted woman groping each other. Dad looked at me like he had no idea who I was, and I gritted my teeth to keep from defending myself.

On the drive home, he lectured me about staying on the right path. He laid out the next few days, which would consist of woodchopping and brush clearing, soul-saving tasks for a wayward youth. We had plenty of firewood for the winter, but we needed to get next year's supply cut so it could cure. He repeated his favorite and most annoying adage, that wood warms you three times—when you cut it, when you haul it, and when you burn it—and I didn't bother pointing out that it was August and I didn't want to be any warmer. I had mostly tuned him out until he brought up his return to work, which would be the following Monday. He didn't want me home alone anymore. I would be staying with Birdie.

Dad didn't waste time. He sent me to my room to get ready as soon as we got home. I dressed in jeans and a thin flannel shirt, laced up my work boots, and pulled back my hair. We doused ourselves in bug spray, and I packed a small cooler with sandwiches and apples while Dad loaded up the truck with his saws, ax, and shotgun. I grabbed two frozen water jugs from the deep freeze, and we headed into the woods on the narrow road we'd cleared through the timber.

Dad felled three oaks and set to work slicing off the limbs and cutting the branches into manageable pieces. I dragged all the useless parts to the brush pile while he sectioned up the tree. When I was done with the brush, I would start loading wood into the truck to haul it home, following this pattern over and over until we were too worn out to continue.

The humidity was in full bloom, my entire body sticky with sweat. I sat down on a log and took off my thick leather gloves, hating the musty smell they left on my hands. I wiped sawdust off my face and drank meltwater from the jug. The buzz of the chain saw lulled me into a drowsy state, and I wanted to curl up in the cab of the truck and fall asleep, forgetting everything that was going on. The chain saw stopped abruptly, and the sudden silence was unsettling. Dad set the saw down on the tailgate and got out his sharpening kit. "I could use a hand," he said. When he worked on the chain saw at home, he clamped the bar to his workbench with a vise, but out in the woods, he needed me to hold it steady. He drew a file through the chain's teeth until the edges shone sharp. "I've been meaning to talk to you about something," he said. "I thought about it last year when you . . . you know, with the pastor's boy. But when I saw that boyfriend of yours the other day—"

"He's not my boyfriend."

"Well, Daniel, whatever he is, he cares about you, and he's older, and . . . You know I've taught you to keep your pants on, and I haven't changed my mind about that. I hope you realize he's over eighteen and you're not, and if I found out anything happened, I could have him prosecuted."

"Dad! We're not even— He's . . ." I didn't know how to explain my relationship with Daniel, and it wouldn't do any good anyway.

He kept filing. The grating of metal on metal vibrated through my bones. "What I'm saying is I tried to raise you right. But I don't know how good a job I did. People make mistakes. I don't want you fooling around with that boy, but more than that, I don't want you getting pregnant and ruining your life. You need to go to college, get yourself some fancy degree, and make a decent living. I'll do whatever it takes to make that happen."

I thought carefully about what I wanted to say to him. "Did it ruin Mom's life when she had me?"

Heat reddened his ears, stained his throat. "She was coming from a completely different place. She wanted you more than anything."

I'd heard that before. "Didn't she want to go to school?"

Dad slid the file back into its plastic sheath. "If her life had gone differently, if it hadn't got thrown off the tracks, she'd have been in school somewhere. She never would've met me or had you. But things happened. And she told me she wouldn't have changed any of it; she wouldn't have given you up for anything. All the good parts missing from her life, she wanted those for you. She said there was plenty of time for her to go back to school when you were older."

Except there hadn't been time. "So she had plans. She wanted to raise me and go back to school. . . . What happened? What changed all that?"

"I wish I knew," he said. "She was depressed about something, but she wouldn't talk about it. And then she was gone." He gassed up the saw and pulled his gloves on. "Back to work," he said.

"Speaking of work," I said, "I'm scheduled to go in tomorrow. Will I still be under house arrest?"

"I seem to remember, when you took that job, you promised to follow some basic rules. Which you broke. From here on out, you work for me."

"You've got to be kidding. I was late one time! You can't take away everything just for breaking curfew."

He yanked the cord, and the saw grumbled fitfully. Dad's expression dared me to keep arguing, and when I didn't, he turned his back and resumed deconstructing the tree.

After three days of hauling wood and splitting last year's logs, I was worn out and getting cabin fever. I hadn't been able to talk to Bess, and I hadn't heard anything from Ray. I'd practically given up hope of Daniel calling. I didn't know if Dad had given him the sex talk, too, but whatever he'd said surely hadn't helped. I was still angry about my overblown punishment, though secretly, I was relieved not to have to go to work. Just thinking about Crete made my stomach hurt.

It was Dad's last night before heading back to work in Springfield, and he was drinking, like he usually did after talking about Mom. It wasn't the best time to ask him a question, but I couldn't wait any longer for the answer.

"Hey," I said, poking my head into the living room, where he was listening to an old bluegrass album. "I need to ask you something." He looked up, his expression blank. "You know how I've been trying to figure out what happened to Cheri. Would you tell me something if you knew? I can keep quiet just like you. You know I can. It's important to me to know the truth. You might not realize how important."

He got up and crossed the room to the stereo, where he flipped clumsily through a stack of records. "Sure, I know something. She was killed and chopped to bits. End of story."

"Dad." I waited until he turned to look at me. "Somebody thinks you had something to do with it. I don't believe it. . . . I know you didn't kill anybody . . . but she was my friend, and I—"

He dropped the record he was holding and moved toward me, unsteady on his feet. I had pricked a nerve. "*Somebody?* I can guess who that might be. What else did *somebody* tell you about me? Huh?"

I took a step back. He'd scared me a few times when he was drinking, and I'd seen him plenty angry, but rarely had he ever directed such anger at me.

"He tell you I killed somebody?" His whiskey breath soured the air.

"I didn't believe him," I said quietly.

"You're wrong," he said, gritting his teeth. "I killed a man once." He clamped his hands on my shoulders and pushed me back against the doorframe. "It was an accident that haunts me every day of my life. *Somebody* convinced me to keep it quiet, took care of things for me. So I owed him a favor. When he needed my help, I came running." I squirmed, but he didn't seem to realize how tight he was gripping me. "He's my brother, and he needed my help, so I helped him. I'm the gravedigger in the family, and it was just another job. Except when I got there and saw . . . it was her."

"Cheri? Crete killed her?" I felt a rush of anticipation. I was so close to the answer.

Dad shook his head. "He didn't kill her, and he didn't tell me who did. He just called me to clean up the mess. He said the whole thing started out as an accident, but it happened on his property, and he didn't want to get messed up in it. She was already dead, no point calling the law."

He let go, and my shoulders ached where he'd clutched me. "But you didn't bury her."

"No. I tried, but I couldn't. She didn't deserve to disappear like that."

"You . . . you put her in the tree?"

"Right across from Dane's," he said. "Crete is family, and I'd never turn him in, but I wanted him to know it wasn't okay. I won't go around burying murdered little girls, no matter what he has on me."

"How do you know he didn't kill her?"

"He's never been afraid to tell me the truth. He don't hide who he is, not from me."

That didn't mean Crete wouldn't mislead him. He had known the truth about Cheri all along, yet he'd tried to make me think Dad was the guilty one. He'd twisted the truth about my mother, about how she came to be here. He wouldn't have shown Dad the papers I'd seen in her folder. Wouldn't have admitted that he'd handpicked Lila as his own. And I didn't believe that Crete would tell my dad if he'd had something to do with her disappearance.

"What are we going to do?"

"Nothing," he said. "We're gonna keep quiet. There's no bringing Cheri back. Crete got my message loud and clear, I'm not doing him any more favors. School's about to start. Your job is to stay out of trouble and graduate, and you don't need to worry about anything else. You can let Crete think you believe him . . . hell, he didn't really even lie to you. No doubt I'd get thrown in jail right along with him if any of this came out."

"Do you think he did something to Mom?"

"In all the years she's been gone, I've thought through every imaginable possibility. So I thought about it, yeah. I even asked him once, straight up, did he have anything to do with her leaving. I asked everybody the same thing. I don't believe he did. I know him better than anybody. His idea of right and wrong might not be the same as yours or mine, but he stands by his family. I took a risk when I laid Cheri out like that. He was pissed. He could've taken away everything we have in a heartbeat, but he didn't. He won't. He was disappointed when I told him you wouldn't be working for him anymore, but he didn't argue." Dad sank into his recliner. "Everything's gonna be fine now. You can focus on school, and you'll be safe and sound at Birdie's while I'm gone."

"I thought I was safe and sound here," I said. He unscrewed the lid on the Southern Comfort and took a swig straight from the bottle. "How long's this punishment going to last?"

He looked tired, dazed. The lamplight sallowed his skin, aged him with unflattering shadows. "Everything's gonna be fine," he repeated. *Fine* got swallowed up in the bottle as he took another drink.

He was worried. My missed curfew might have scared him, but it wasn't the only reason I was headed to Birdie's. He wanted to protect me, to lock me back in a box I no longer fit inside, though he knew as well as anyone that it wasn't possible to move in reverse; no matter how hard we fought against it, time flowed in only one direction.

CHAPTER 34

Crete

Crete had been on his way to St. Louis when Sorrel called. Sorrel called only when he needed to make an appointment, and since he was supposed to be *at* an appointment at that very moment, Crete knew the call was no good.

Sorrel was a kinky bastard. Crete had seen that right away when he showed up with props. Most guys did their business and got out. One, he knew, didn't even touch the girl; he just liked to look at her while he jerked off. But Sorrel would spend hours in the trailer, doing things Crete didn't care to hear about.

Sorrel was blubbering on the phone. His story came in gurgling spurts, taking longer than Crete had patience for. From what he could make out, Sorrel had hooked the girl up to some electrical device and given her a few little shocks, and he may have also held her head underwater—none of this intended to truly hurt her, all this shit just turned him on, and he needed it to get hard enough to fuck her. Well, the girl started jerking around and collapsed like she was in cardiac arrest, and Sorrel didn't think she was breathing. He panicked and grabbed the biggest kitchen knife he could find, thinking he'd cut her up and carry her out in a suitcase and everything would be fine. He started with her leg, hacking away at the hip joint, but somewhere short of bone, the girl came to, puked, and started dragging herself across the room. She was bleeding real bad by this point, and before Sorrel could figure out what to do, she ran out of blood and breath and collapsed in a swamp of her own fluids. He went back to work cutting off pieces, but the knife was poorly suited to the job, and the realization of what he was doing caught up to him.

Fear made his voice shrill. He was scared not just of what he'd done but of what Crete might do to him. *You owe me*, Crete told him. He hung up and called Carl.

He gave his brother an abbreviated, partly true rundown of the situation: A whore had been operating out of a trailer on his property, and the whore was now dead. Possibly very messily dead. The whole thing was an accident, he said. *Like with you and Sump*. Which rankled Carl, who didn't agree that killing a hooker was anything like what had happened between him and Joe Bill Sump. Carl was getting worked up on the phone, and Crete knew he was pushing his brother dangerously close to the line where he could no longer keep his mouth shut and look the other way. It would be worse when Carl got to the trailer. But Crete trusted him, and there was nothing to be done for the girl at that point, no reason to tangle with the law. *I'd clean it up myself if I was there*, he said. *But it can't wait. If you take care of it, we'll call things even on Joe Bill. I'll throw out that wallet and license plate of his and be done with it.*

Crete kept Sump's belongings locked up in a shed along with some other things he needed to hold on to but didn't want people to see. Though he'd never planned to use his collateral against Carl, he liked having it there all the same. In truth, Crete would have disposed of a dozen bodies for his brother and not expected anything in return. Not that Carl was likely to need such a favor.

It was unfortunate that Crete couldn't call on Emory to clean up the mess, since he was the one to blame for it. Emory had gotten a bit too involved with methamphetamine and was starting to get sloppy. He'd had a little blond boy with him a few times, and Crete hadn't asked whether it was Emory's kid or if something entirely different was going on. He didn't want to know. Crete had been furious when Emory showed up with Cheri, a girl who lived down the road from Lucy and hung out with her when they were kids. Taking a local girl was risky in the first place, but keeping her nearby was even worse. Emory promised she'd be on Crete's property only temporarily, that he would get her set up at his own place as soon as he was able, but it hadn't happened soon enough.

Crete wasn't happy with how things had played out, but his cut of the girl's profits was a small consolation, and now he no longer had to worry about keeping Cheri hidden. There were plenty of other things to hide, so many secrets burrowing down into the dark like roots knotted deep in the earth.

CHAPTER 35

Lila

Sometimes Crete didn't even stop the truck. He just drove by slowly, eyeing the house. Making me nervous. Other times he brought things for Lucy, little toys and gifts. If Carl was home, I had to let Crete in. I made excuses to feed Lucy, put her down for a nap. Watching him hold her cramped my stomach. I told myself the novelty would wear off. That he had no real interest in my baby. That he was doing this to scare me, and if I didn't act scared, he'd stop.

No matter how I acted or what I said, he kept coming around. And he wasn't looking at me. He was looking at Lucy. He was gentle with her, soft-spoken, and she smiled at him the same sweet way she smiled at me. That was the most painful part. She wasn't old enough for me to explain the danger he represented. I was failing her. I stood there, helpless, as he impressed himself in her life.

I'd been practicing my shooting, as Ray had suggested, and had grown comfortable with Carl's guns. I felt prepared to protect myself and my baby if anything should happen, but Crete had yet to break into the house or threaten me in a way that justified self-defense. In fact, he hadn't made any threats since the day he came to warn me that I couldn't keep him away from Lucy. The worst thing he'd done was get close to her. As much as I wanted to be rid of him, I couldn't just shoot him as he walked into the house for a visit.

An unseasonable cold snap hit right before Lucy's first birthday, and freezing rain fell through the night, knocking out the power. The world glittered the next morning, every surface smoothed and rounded, encased in a half-inch of ice. I'd never seen anything like it. Carl and I dressed Lucy in her snowsuit and slid around the glassy yard with her, her eyes wide with wonder. At the moment she turned one year old, the three of us were snuggled on the couch, basking in the heat of the stove by candlelight. Carl and I sang "Happy Birthday" to Lucy as she dozed in my lap.

When Lucy was born, I thought maybe I'd finally found the direction I'd been missing. Here was something I was good at, something I could devote my life to: being her mother. The first year of her life had been the best year I could remember. The love I felt for her dwarfed everything else, even Crete. Life was not perfect, but it was better than I'd dared to hope. I had friends, a devoted husband, and a healthy child. I wavered between utter joy and the fear that it could all be taken away.

Spring weather returned the day of Lucy's party, and sheaths of ice fell from the trees, the hills echoing with the sound of breaking glass. Birdie came, and Gabby and Bess, and Ray brought his wife. Crete was there, too, with a rocking horse for Lucy that wasn't safe for a child her age. Everyone was eating cake when I remembered the ice cream and went to fetch it from the freezer. Crete followed under the pretense of helping and cornered me on the back porch.

"There's a way," he said, "to see who her father is. A test you take. I wanna know."

"What does it matter?" I sputtered. "She's mine. She's Carl's. You get to see her, what more do you want?"

"It matters," he growled. "I got rights."

"You don't want Carl to know what you did to me. Why would you want to do something like this?"

He chuckled. "You haven't had any trouble keeping that secret. I think *you* don't want Carl to know. Maybe he'll think you cheated on him. Or be mad at you for lying. Maybe he'll be mad enough to kick you out, send you back where you came from, and keep Lucy here with us. I already know he'll forgive me—are you sure he'll forgive you?"

"What if I won't do the test?" I hissed.

"Oh, I don't really need you," he said. "I just need Lucy."

My skeleton tingled inside my skin. If he was her father, I never wanted her to know. I didn't want anyone to know. "Please," I said. "Don't do this. Don't."

"You can't stop me," he said.

The ice cream was numbing my fingers. I wanted to get back to Lucy. "I can't even talk about this right now. This is her *birthday party*."

"It's gonna happen," he said, "unless you got something to convince me otherwise. Maybe we can find a way to work this out. Huh?"

"Never."

"Suit yourself," he said. "But if you change your mind, you can meet me out at the cave Monday noon. Nice and private out there, no chance anybody'll see us. I'll give you one last chance to talk me out of it. I told Carl I got a nice little birthday trip planned for Lucy later this week. Figured she'd like to go to Springfield with her uncle and see the zoo. Then we can swing by a doctor's office and see about that paternity test."

I turned and walked away from him. "Monday noon," he repeated. I rejoined the party in the kitchen, scooping ice cream with trembling hands. I plucked Lucy out of her high chair and hugged her tight, her frosting-covered fingers knotting in my hair, her sticky mouth smearing my cheek with kisses.

That night I rocked Lucy in the bentwood chair, singing softer and softer as her body relaxed into sleep. I was reeling from my encounter with Crete and didn't know what to do. If I told Carl the truth, that Crete had raped me, would he believe me over his brother? I wanted to think that he would. But he'd been loyal to his brother his whole life, and I knew how Crete could lie. It would be easiest, I thought, to go along with the test. Maybe if Crete found out he wasn't the father, he'd back off and quietly accept the role of uncle. Yet I couldn't risk it turning out in his favor, granting him legal rights to my child.

I wondered if Crete was serious about meeting in private to "work things out," or if he'd suggested it because he enjoyed watching me squirm. Did he really think I'd be willing to trade sex for his silence? That was what he'd implied. More likely, he thought I'd show up for one last desperate attempt to talk him out of the paternity test, and once he had me there, he'd take the opportunity to intimidate me, hurt me, remove me from his family the way I'd wanted to remove him. Why else would he choose such a secluded location? Whatever he was planning, he didn't want anyone to see him near my house that day, didn't want anyone to spot us together. But that could work to my advantage, the two of us alone in the cave. No one knowing we were there. Crete possibly unaware that I was smart enough to bring a gun or strong enough to use it.

I thought of the long-ago night when I'd slashed my cousin's face with a kitchen knife as he reached under the covers to touch me. I was capable of hurting someone else to protect myself. I could live with blood on my hands. Crete had the advantage when he attacked me in the garage, but this time I was ready for him. And I had something more to fight for now, something bigger than my own life. My daughter. Lucy. I could go to the cave and put an end to the one thing that threatened to destroy my family.

I dropped Lucy off at Birdie's Monday morning, kissing her little pink mouth and giving her an extra-long squeeze. I told myself that when I came back for her, everything would be different. She'd be safe, and we could live our lives without Crete's shadow hanging over us. I didn't allow myself to think I might not come back. That wasn't an option.

The ice had all melted, and the sun shone in a pale sky. I'd been to the cave a couple of times with Gabby when we were out in the woods, but we'd never gone much farther than the cavernous room near the entry. She'd shown me the passageways that funneled into the darkness, warning me that any of them could be dangerous but that one in particular plunged down to an underground river. A conservation agent had fallen through a false floor in that tunnel, and his body was swept away in the current.

I reached into my jacket pockets, seeking reassurance in the flashlight and the gun. The confidence I'd felt with Lucy in my arms had waned, and I was nervous. I believed that I could shoot Crete if he gave me the chance, if I had time to aim and pull the trigger, but that wouldn't be enough. I couldn't just shoot him at the entrance and leave him there in plain sight. It was possible that no one would suspect me; Crete surely had other, more capable enemies. But I figured I'd have a better chance of getting away with it if his body wasn't found right away or ever. As much as I wanted to protect Lucy from Crete, I was selfish; I wanted to be with her. I didn't want her to grow up visiting me in prison. Crete's body would be too heavy for me to move very far, and the only way I could think of to get him deeper into the cave and out of sight was to lead him there. I knew that he wasn't stupid, that he might not follow.

As I approached Old Scratch on wobbly legs, not knowing whether Crete was already inside, I wondered if it would be better to turn around and run. I could go straight back to Birdie's and wait there with Lucy, then tell Carl everything when he got home from work and hope for the best. Then I thought of Crete with his hands on my throat, the look in his eyes, and I knew I had to go through with it.

I stepped into the darkness. It took a moment for my eyes to adjust. Enough light seeped into the wide entry that I could see the old beer cans and cigarette butts that littered the floor of the cave. I walked farther in, eyeing the passages that gaped open like throats on the far wall. They looked more similar than I remembered, and I searched my memory for the one Gabby had singled out. I slid my hand into my pocket and gripped the pistol.

"Didn't think you'd really come."

The voice, so deep and familiar, so entangled with fear in my brain, came from behind me. I spun around, pulling out the gun, my hands shaking. My plans scattered, like papers dropped in the wind.

"Don't be dumb," he said, grabbing for my wrist. I stepped back just in time, out of reach, and he lunged at me. I wheeled around and ran for the nearest opening, knowing, and fearing, that he would follow.

CHAPTER 36

Lucy

When Dad headed back to Springfield on Monday morning, Birdie came to pick me up in her truck, which was hardly necessary. She rarely drove anywhere, let alone the short distance to our house, and I had only one bag to carry. I could have walked. Then I wondered if she didn't trust me to go down the road alone without taking a side trip into trouble. Would she have her eye on me every moment of the day and night? I didn't know what Dad had told her, but she clearly took the task of watching over me seriously.

I set my bag down in the bedroom once shared by Birdie's sons, the room I'd slept in so many times. Birdie had put away all the little knick-knacks I once kept on the dresser—the jar of buttons, the yarn-haired doll, the children's Bible that I'd defaced with crayons—though my favorite pink afghan still lay across the bed. The room was sweltering, and it would only get worse as we sank deeper into the heart of August. I opened the window and looked out on the empty pasture and the hills that rose beyond it. I had nowhere to go and nothing to do. If I got desperate, I could crack open one of Birdie's musty *Reader's Digest* condensed books, but for once I didn't feel like reading.

The phone rang, and Birdie came to tap at my door. "He's on your approved phone list," she said. Great, there was a list. I was surprised there was anyone on it but Dad.

"Is it Ray?" I asked, following Birdie to the living room, where her old-fashioned phone sat tethered to a tiny table in the corner.

Birdie shook her head, positioning herself in the armchair across from me. "It's that boy."

I picked up the receiver and sat down on the arm of the sofa. "Hi," I said.

"Hey." It was good to hear Daniel's voice, even if I was mad at him. "Your dad told me where you were."

"Nice of you to call." I hoped I sounded aloof.

"I finally got a phone. Sorry."

"So what do you want?"

"To know how you are, for one. I can't believe how much I miss you and how much time I spend worrying."

"That's your own fault," I said. "You're the one who left. And I never asked you to worry about me."

"I guess you're mad at me for talking to Carl. I don't blame you. But I wasn't trying to get you in trouble, I was trying to help."

"Hold on," I said. I looked up at Birdie, who was feigning interest in her yarn basket. "Could you please, please let me talk to him in private for just a minute?" I asked her. "It's kind of embarrassing fighting in front of you."

Birdie took her sweet time getting up and walking across the room to the kitchen. She clicked on her little radio, which was set to the gospel station, and shot me a stern glance through the doorway. She'd probably report this to Dad later and see if I was allowed to talk unsupervised. I spoke low enough that I hoped she couldn't hear me. "Look, I'll be honest with you. I miss you, too. I wish you were here, but even if you were, there wouldn't be anything you could do to help. Everything's a mess."

"What's happening?"

I filled him in the best I could, explaining that I didn't know who killed Cheri, but Crete knew and had lied to me about it. And my dad was involved, which complicated things. I couldn't tell him what I knew about Sorrel, because Bess had sworn me to secrecy.

Daniel groaned. I envisioned him raking his hand through his hair in that aggravated way of his. "Wait. Back up a minute. I didn't follow half of that, with you whispering. How did you end up talking to Crete about Cheri? Did you ask him point-blank and expect him to tell you the truth? And how do you know he's lying if you don't know what happened?"

"I sneaked into his house to see if I could find anything out about the trailer, and he came home and caught me in his basement. He knew I'd been asking around about Cheri, and he said he wanted to clear some things up with me."

"You broke into his house? Are you kidding me? What the hell made you think that was a good idea?"

"I don't need you to lecture me right now," I said. "There's something else." I peeked at Birdie, who was wiping down the already clean kitchen table. She adjusted the knob on the radio, switching it from gospel to weather. "When I was digging through his papers, I came across something of my mom's. It looked like a job application, but it had all these weird comments on it about her looks and the fact that she had no family. It felt wrong. I'm wondering if Crete brought her here for the same reason Cheri was in that trailer."

"Oh . . . wow." He was silent for a moment. "Lucy, I'm sorry. I know you're already mad at me, and I don't want to make things worse, but don't you think it's time to turn this all over to somebody else?"

"I will. I mean, I'm going to talk to Ray. I'm waiting for him to get back to me. He knows somebody with the state police."

"Why are you waiting? Just make a call and be done with it."

"It's my dad," I said, coiling the phone cord around my finger. "He didn't really have anything to do with it, and even with the body, he was just trying to send Crete a message. But I'm worried he'll get locked up, too. I'm trying to figure out how to keep that from happening."

"I know you don't feel like he should go to jail, Luce, but Crete and whoever else was responsible, they have to pay for what they did. You can't spare them to keep your dad safe. You can't just let them go."

"Dad doesn't want me to call the cops."

"Your dad's a good guy," Daniel said. "I know you, though, Luce, and you always want to do the right thing."

"I want to do my version of the right thing," I said.

"I'll be back this weekend. If you want to talk to the cops, then I'll go with you. I was in the trailer, too. I can back up your claims. Then you can let this go. It's not up to you to figure it all out. Let someone else handle it."

It sounded easier when Daniel laid it out. Simple, almost. He couldn't get here soon enough.

"I'm glad you're coming," I said.

"Me, too. We have a lot to talk about."

After I hung up the phone, reality seeped back in. I knew nothing would be simple after I talked to the police. My dad and uncle could be taken away, the family business destroyed, the Danes forever tarnished. Staying here would be unbearable, and I had nowhere else to go.

I hadn't told Daniel everything; I hadn't mentioned the noises in the basement or the locked room. No need to make him worry more than he already was.

I joined Birdie in the kitchen as she got out the flour and lard to make biscuits. "Radio says we're in for some bad weather the next few days," she said, wiping sweat off her forehead. "We're already under a thunderstorm watch. Merle's getting all antsy, like he does when hail's coming."

I was glad she didn't ask what Daniel and I had talked about. "I was thinking I'd go out looking for gooseberries," I said. "See if I can get enough for a pie."

Birdie measured baking powder. "Awful late in the summer for gooseberries." We both knew I wouldn't find any, that I just needed a reason to get out of the house. I handed her the salt, pulled milk and eggs from the fridge. "Don't go far, I guess." Birdie sighed. "Bucket's on the porch."

Merle sat at the back door and watched me cross the pasture. Birdie was probably watching, too, from the kitchen window. I didn't know her woods as well as I knew my own, so I wandered along the tree line until I found a stone ledge big enough to stretch out on. I stared at the hazy sky, watched two vultures with their white-tipped wings circle slowly, deliberately, waiting for something somewhere to die.

Although I was closer than ever to finding out what had happened to Cheri, I still didn't know what had become of my mother. I had so many unanswered questions about Crete's connection to the two of them.

I closed my eyes and inhaled deeply, the air so thick that I imagined it could drown me. Being outdoors hadn't calmed my nerves, like I'd thought it would, so I decided to head back to the house. As I sat up, I got the feeling that I was being watched. Ordinarily, I would assume it was an animal, most likely a deer, but I was feeling more jittery than usual. I looked all around and saw nothing. Then Merle's insistent barks rang out across the field, and I was on my feet, fighting the urge to look behind me. I jogged back to Birdie's and found Bess sprawled in the grass, searching Merle's ears for ticks.

"Are you on my list of approved visitors?" I asked, flopping down next to her.

Bess rolled her eyes. "Hard to believe. I don't guess anybody else is gonna come see you here in lockdown."

"Tell me you brought news of the outside world."

"Well," she said, ducking her head to pat Merle's belly, "you already know about Sorrel."

"Are you doing okay?" I asked.

"You know, I don't miss him or anything like that. It's a relief, in a way. But I can't help wondering if he'd have killed himself if I hadn't called him."

"We can't be sure he did it himself," I said. "Somebody could have done him in. The paper said he didn't leave a note." The article had referred to his wife as "estranged" and said she couldn't be reached for comment.

"Let's hope, if he talked to anybody, that he didn't mention me. I'm having enough trouble sleeping as it is. I heard down at Bell's that there'd been a fire in his burn barrel. Probably him or somebody else burning anything that connected him to Cheri. Or to me."

Any evidence from Sorrel, any confessions pent up inside him, were now gone. I didn't want to think about it. "Any other good gossip at Bell's?"

Bess perked up a bit. "Yeah, your friend Becky Castle's back." Crete's girlfriend, or ex-girlfriend, though I thought of her more as Holly's mother.

"I don't know why you call Becky my friend. I don't even know her."

Bess laughed. "I thought you guys would get to be pals while you were working for Crete, but she hasn't been around much this summer."

"I never saw her once," I said. "Where'd she go?"

"I don't know. Visiting relatives, I guess. Pam was bartending, and I asked her how Holly was getting along, and she said Holly was staying with her grandparents and wouldn't be back at school this year. Pam also said Becky was high as could be. Twitching and scratching like her skin was on fire."

"Maybe it's better for Holly, then, not to be here. Remember that 4-H show when we were nine or ten? Her mom just dropped her off there by herself with that enormous rabbit cage."

"Yeah, I remember. Birdie kept poking us and saying we should be more like Holly, because she was always so quiet and serious." When Becky didn't show up to take Holly home, the little girl had set out walking, balancing the cage in her scrawny arms. Birdie had stopped and given her a ride.

"We sucked at 4-H," I said, and Bess cracked up laughing. I was glad to see her in a good mood again and grateful that she'd come to visit me. I'd missed her.

I blew Bess a kiss as she backed out of the driveway, and she smacked it like it was a mosquito. I blew a dozen more, and she swatted those away, too, before giving in and blowing one back.

"Thanks," I said to Birdie when I came inside.

She nodded. "A girl needs time with her friends. And you've only got the one."

I started to tell her indignantly that I had more than one friend. But I didn't, not really, unless you counted Daniel. And then it was only two.

"No gooseberries, I take it," she said.

"No."

"A season for everything. Walnuts will fall before you know it." She poured two glasses of tea and gestured to the kitchen table. "The biscuits are almost ready. I got some apple butter up from the cellar just for you."

I sat and she stood, waiting for the timer to buzz. She hustled two steaming biscuits onto plates, and we sat there together until they cooled enough that we wouldn't burn our mouths.

"Tell me again about the day she left," I said, dipping a spoon in the apple butter.

Birdie pulled her biscuit apart and stared at the pieces. "You haven't asked for that story in a while."

We ate in silence, and when our plates were empty, she started talking. "She left you with me when she went. She said, 'Watch her for me, Birdie, please?' The way she said it was just like she was going to the store, except she almost always took you along anywhere she went. She hated to take her eyes off you. I went over it in my head so many times after, the way she said it, the sound of her voice, the look on her face. I blamed myself, because I was the last one to see her, and maybe I could have stopped her. But there was nothing for me to notice except the fact that she wasn't taking you along. She didn't say 'watch her,' like she wasn't coming back, like she was laying a lifetime of responsibility in my hands. She just said it like she had something to go do, something none too interesting but it had to be done, and it wouldn't take long because she hadn't left any of her milk for you. You squawked and kicked when I tried to get you to drink cow's milk out of a cup, like it was the worst sort of torture and you just wouldn't bear it."

I'd heard this part before, how I'd given Birdie no choice but to wean me with sweet tea.

"It took me a long time to accept that she wasn't coming back; I just didn't believe it. She wouldn't leave you. I knew her near as well as

Carl or Gabby did, and I knew she wouldn't leave on her own. Truth be told, plenty of folks were glad to see her gone, had no interest in looking for her, but I walked those woods every day for weeks, hoping she was somewhere lost or hurt and I could bring her back home. Your dad, they got him all talked into postpartum depression and post-traumatic stress from her living in foster care, all these ridiculous things that sounded like they could've been true but weren't. They told him he shouldn't blame himself for teaching her how to use the gun, for believing her story that she wanted to protect herself from snakes in the woods when she was really planning to shoot herself. He'd seen his mother go through so much, with her fragile state of mind, I guess he was more readily convinced that such things were possible, that it could have been going on without him seeing it. And that filled him up with guilt, near smothered him. He didn't know why he hadn't seen it coming, but I did. There was nothing to see. She was happy. She loved you, both of you. She was troubled sometimes, but she wouldn't say why. I figured it had to do with what happened to her right before she and your dad got married." Her eyes sank. "I don't suppose your dad ever said anything about that."

I shook my head. Was it possible she was going to tell me something new after all these years?

"She was attacked, I guess you'd say. Beat up. She got bit, and it got infected. I nursed her, that's how I knew. Nobody said anything. I don't even know if your dad knew about the bite, though I'd guess he would have eventually seen the scar."

Someone had *bitten* her? "Who was it?"

"I don't know, not for sure. She wouldn't say. Neither would your dad, if he knew. There was talk around town that Joe Bill Sump had been to see her. That was right before he took off, and I considered maybe that was why he left. But the bite . . . the mark it left . . . well, this is just a guess on my part, but I always wondered if it was Crete who did that to her."

I picked at my fingernails, not wanting to look at Birdie. Sarah Cole had claimed my mother wasn't sure who my father was. What if Crete *had* attacked her? What if he was the other man, the one whose child she didn't want?

"I did like she said," Birdie continued softly. "Kept an eye on you. I always have. I always will. You're like a granddaughter to me, Lucy." It was strange to hear her say that, yet it made perfect sense. "You grow up feeling the weight of blood, of family. There's no forsaking kin. But you can't help when kin forsakes you or when strangers come to be family. Lila found her home here. She belonged with us. She didn't kill herself, I just can't believe it. I don't have proof of anything, but I've always had my suspicions. Crete loved her or hated her—don't really matter which. Either one'll drive you crazy if you let it. Now, it ain't my place to tell you what to think of your own family, but you've got to look past what you've always been taught and listen to what you know in your bones to be true."

CHAPTER 37

Jamie

Thirteen-year-old Jamie Petree could work the dogs just as good as his older brothers, and they knew it. They let him go hunting on his own whenever he wanted, so long as he shot something they could eat. Jamie didn't give a lick about playing with other kids, he just wanted to be out in the woods treeing coons, shooting birds, and splashing in the creek. His mama homeschooled him, mostly math and religion, so he had plenty of time outdoors. He had four hunting dogs in his pack: Josh and Calvin's two blue ticks, his little brother Gage's black-and-tan coonhound, and his own yellow cur, Custard, raised from a pup.

He was wandering the hills around Old Scratch Cavern, even

though his mama had told him not to. She said the witch lady haunted that cave. She'd been saying that a good long year—ever since Lila went missing—and that was exactly what drew him here. He *wanted* to see the witch lady again. He remembered vividly the first time he'd seen her over a year ago, in Ralls' grocery, when she'd rescued him from Junior and bought him a candy bar. No one ever looked at him the way Lila had. Her gaze took in everything about him, inside and out, good and bad; she had seen all that and smiled.

To his mama's dismay, Lila had also sparked in him an uncontrollable urge to touch himself. He was hexed, Mama said, bedeviled, and she did her best to whip the evil out of him. But the witch lady had powerful spells. She wouldn't let him be. In his waking dreams, Lila was a seductress. She crept into his sleep as well, though in those dreams, she did nothing more than hold his hand and smile.

It was his favorite time in the woods, near dusk, when everything was still and shadowed and cool, not yet dark enough for the bugs to start singing. It seemed to him the best time for spirits to show themselves. He watched for Lila. Loose rocks and dead leaves covered the ground, and the soles of his boots, worn slick, threatened to slide out from under him if he didn't mind his footing. Some of the ravines here were so steep, they never saw sunlight.

The dogs had moved on ahead, sure-footed and eager. Jamie ran his hand along the bark of a fallen tree and knelt to see if there might be any early morels on the lee side. Then he heard a yelp and its answering chorus of bays and shot up in time to see the ruckus at the top of the rise. He didn't get a look at the quarry, but the blue ticks were on to something, and the other two lit out after them. Was it her? Had she finally come back to him?

By the time he got to the ridge, Custard was hauling ass for Old Scratch, and the others had already disappeared inside its black maw, their howls echoing out into the holler. Jamie wasn't sure what to do, so he waited and watched for Lila. He knew he couldn't catch up. The dogs were smart, too smart, probably, to get themselves lost in the cave, so they might turn around and come back. But they were also determined, single-minded. They might well chase their quarry down the Devil's Throat and never come out again. What were they after, if not a ghost? Something that didn't naturally tree, he guessed. A mountain lion? A bear? He'd never seen one in these parts, though plenty of other folks had. He no longer heard barking.

Tears stung Jamie's eyes, and he rubbed them away with grimy hands. The dogs would be all right. But if they weren't? He'd only turned his attention away for a minute, to look for the mushrooms. He hadn't expected them to go for the cave, and by the time it occurred to him to whistle and call them back, it was too late. He was trying to figure out how to tell his brothers—who'd skin him for sure, and who could blame them?—when the dogs' muted yawps rolled through the holler. The sound wasn't coming from the mouth of the cave, where Jamie stood. It was coming from the other side of the hill.

Jamie hightailed it through the trees, slipping and skidding and catching himself and pushing on, the barks becoming clearer but less frenzied as he approached the far side of the hill. He still couldn't see the dogs, but he followed their sound down into a gap he hadn't explored, its entrance narrow and cloaked with underbrush. The path was steep, and he clutched roots and vines to slow his descent. When he reached the bottom, he found himself standing in a shallow creek bed. The dogs ran toward him, muzzles frothing, coats filthy, ropes of slobber draped over their snouts. Custard came up to lick his hand as the other dogs lapped the thin stream of water at their feet.

Jamie sank down and clung to Custard, bawling with relief. He wiped his face on the dog's fur and sat back to take in his surroundings. He couldn't see the opening where the dogs had left the cave, though he knew it had to be there, that perhaps this very stream trickled out of it. There was no sign of their quarry, either. "Lila," he said. She'd protected them, but she wouldn't show herself.

Flowers filled the little glen despite the lack of sunlight, purple and blue and yellow, frilly things Jamie had no names for. He pressed his hands into the stream to rinse them off, rubbing them over the stony bottom to scrape away the dirt. He noticed one rock with a strange shape, like some sort of fossil, and held it up to the fading light. It wasn't a fossil, he decided. A bone. A small one. He lined it up with his own finger and came close to a match. Something panged within him. He didn't know what animal it came from, but it looked different, special. He ran one gentle fingertip over the length of it, examined its delicate contours, considered taking it home to sit on the bedroom windowsill with his other treasures: a four-leaf clover pressed in waxed paper, a shell lined with mother-of-pearl, a Matchbox car he'd stolen from a kid at church.

The dogs whined, anxious to get home and eat. Instead of putting the bone in his pocket, Jamie set it back down in the stream. On his walk home through the darkening woods, he imagined a big rain coming, a good old gully washer. He pictured the underground river in the cave flooding, gushing out into the ravine, and lifting the bone along with it. Who knew how far the bone could go, from the stream to the North Fork, from there to the Mississippi, way down through the port of New Orleans, the Gulf, out to sea. Not that it mattered where the bone went, because he could tell when he held it that the spirit had been washed free.

CHAPTER 38

Lucy

The next day was humid and still. We ate tomato sandwiches for lunch, and Birdie studied her Bible. I sat on the porch for what felt like hours, trying to read the condensed version of *Old Yeller* and wondering how *Reader's Digest* decided which parts to cut. I had trouble rooting myself in the make-believe world on the page. I was thinking about Crete. I couldn't reconcile the two different images in my head: the uncle who loved me and the man Birdie suspected of attacking my mother. I tried to remember what the noises in his basement had sounded like, but I wasn't sure I could trust my memory not to be overwhelmed by my imagination. Another thought surfaced, over and over, but I did my best to push it back down. I didn't want to think about the possibility that Crete could be my father.

Birdie came out on the porch late in the afternoon and took down her bird feeder. "It's gonna blow later," she said. "Storm's coming in." I helped her move the hanging petunia onto the porch floor. We sat down on the steps to watch the clouds bloom in the sky to our west.

"Bess and I were talking about Holly Castle yesterday," I said. "Remember her?"

"That poor girl." Birdie shook her head. "Such an earnest little thing. Didn't she win a blue ribbon for one of her rabbits at the fair way back when?"

"Yeah," I said. "Bess and I didn't even place."

"I know you didn't," Birdie said. "You and Bess should've taken lessons from Holly. I always did feel sorry for her, though, having Becky for a mother."

"Bess said Holly's gone to live with her grandparents. So maybe things'll work out better for her there."

Birdie fixed her gaze on me. "That girl don't have any grandparents. Becky never knew who the dad was, and her own folks passed a long while back. Your dad buried 'em."

I shrugged. "Maybe it's some other relatives, then."

"I thought her other family lived in town."

"No clue," I said.

Birdie clicked her tongue, ruminating. "Well, I guess she couldn't do worse than Becky."

I wondered if it was a relief to Becky, doing whatever she wanted now that Holly was gone . . . somewhere. It was easy for girls like Cheri or Holly to slip away, to vanish, without anyone asking questions. No one was looking out for them. No one would guess that they might be locked away in a trailer. Or a basement. The noise I heard at Crete's—

could it have been Holly pounding on the door with those spindly arms that I still pictured clutching a rabbit cage?

It sounded crazy, and I was probably wrong, but I knew in my heart that it was *possible*. I couldn't keep on doing nothing if there was even the slightest chance that Crete had someone in his basement. If Holly or some other girl were in there, I had to help her. It couldn't wait. She could end up like Cheri if I waited. I needed to call Ray and have him contact the state police. They were more likely to listen to such a bizarre claim coming from him.

"If a big storm's coming," I said, "I should get over to the house and make sure all the windows are closed." I didn't want to explain everything to Ray on the phone with Birdie listening in. It had been hard enough the first time, with Daniel.

"Good idea," Birdie said. "I'll drive you."

"The sun's still shining, worrywart. I'll run home and check on things, and as long as the weather stays clear, I'd like to get some work done in the garden. I bet it's already full of weeds. If you want, I'll bring back some zucchini and tomatoes, and we can do some canning later."

Birdie glanced at the horizon. "Keep your eye on the weather. I expect you back before a drop hits the ground."

I set off at a jog, taking nothing with me. The humidity sapped my strength, mimicked dreams where I ran in slow motion, the landscape barely moving no matter how hard I pushed myself. What I was about to do could tear my family apart. I wasn't prepared for that. But I knew it had to be done.

Finally, I reached the house. It looked more abandoned than usual, as though the moment we left, paint had sloughed off, dry rot spread, shingles peeled and dropped. Queen Anne's lace had reclaimed the yard, the frilly heads bobbing in the breeze. I walked into the kitchen and picked up the phone to dial Ray. His secretary answered, and I discovered why he hadn't called me back. He'd blown out his knee playing golf in Branson and was staying at his lake house there while he recovered from surgery. "I'll give you the number," she said after I swore it was an emergency. "But I guarantee he's out on the boat." She was right, apparently, because no one answered.

I hunched over the phone, trying to decide whether to call Bess or my dad or Deputy Swicegood, who played poker with Crete once a month. *Lucy.* A voice wavered in the stillness of the empty house. I didn't know whether I'd heard it or if it was only in my head. I turned around, and a shape materialized in the shadows. It was Jamie Petree. Fear tingled across my chest and down my spine as my body prepared to fight or flee. I hadn't seen Jamie since the day at the river when he'd kissed me, but I recalled the crush of his body against mine, the vise of his arms, with clarity.

"I don't mean to scare you," he said. "I been waiting to get you alone."

Not the best choice of words if he didn't want to scare me.

"I almost had you yesterday, at Birdie's. In the woods."

"You've been *watching* me?" I judged the distance between us, weighed it against the number of steps to the gun rack in the hall. Jamie eased closer, and I saw a flash of brushed metal peeking out from the waistband of his jeans. A handgun, the kind I'd seen only on TV.

"We need to go now," he said.

"I'm not going anywhere with you." My voice sounded wispy, unconvincing.

Jamie held up his arms like he was surrendering. "I'm not here to hurt you," he said.

I couldn't take my eyes off the gun, and he realized that I had noticed it. Slowly, he lowered one hand and slid the weapon from his waistband, repositioning it at his back, out of sight, as if that would ease my fears.

"Just listen, okay?" I couldn't do much else; my feet were not convinced that I should run. "I have a business meeting I thought you'd be interested in. You remember the guy I told you about? Well, he decided he wants some of my inventory. And he don't want to pay for it. So he offered up a trade, a pretty little girl with long white hair, all mine for one evening only. Because she's such a prized pussy, she'll soon be moving to larger markets. His words." He watched for my reaction. Holly had to be that white-haired girl: at fourteen, barely more than a child. "The meeting," Jamie continued, "is at your uncle's house."

"Why are you doing this?" I asked him. "What do you care about helping that girl?"

He swallowed hard, his Adam's apple dipping and rising in slow motion. "It's not her," he mumbled. "It's *you*."

"You want to help *me*?"

He looked away uncomfortably. "You ever have the same dream over and over? Like it won't leave you be? Like it's trying to tell you something?"

I watched him expectantly, waiting for more.

"Forget it," he said. "Just returning a favor, I guess."

Jamie didn't owe me anything. Our exchange on the riverbank, when we kissed, had been an even one. There was a possibility that he was lying to me, luring me into any number of undesirable situations, but when he met my gaze, I saw something there and knew he was telling the truth.

"Let's go," he said, and I followed him out the door.

Jamie had left his souped-up Charger just out of sight, around a bend in the road. Save the vinyl upholstery on the seats, the interior of the car was stripped to a bare metal skeleton. The engine roared so lustily that my internal organs buzzed with its vibration, and together Jamie and I sped toward Crete's house beneath rapidly darkening clouds.

I hollered to be heard over the engine. "What do we do when we get there?"

"You don't do anything but stay out of sight. If he leaves me alone with the girl, we throw her in the car and haul ass."

"And if he doesn't?"

He glanced at me, his hair swirling in his face. "You're smart," he said. "I figured you'd think of something."

Honeysuckle bushes crowded the narrow road as we neared the turnoff to Crete's. He would be heading home from Dane's soon, if he were on his normal schedule. My nerves jangled, but Jamie maintained the drowsy expression he always wore, like he wasn't the least bit scared by what we were about to do.

"You should get down," he said. "Stay hid unless I need you."

I crouched on the floorboards, wondering how I'd know if he needed me and what I would do if he did. I had nothing prepared, no magic spells, no plans. Jamie parked the car and unloaded something from the trunk. Emory greeted him—I recognized the voice from the time he'd yelled at me and Daniel by Mrs. Stoddard's trailer—and Jamie, not much for social graces, moved right into negotiations.

"It's a lot of product," he said. "You know it's worth more than a fuck."

"You'll change your mind when you see her," Emory said. "Besides, it's in your interest for us to develop a working relationship. There's give and take, but you gotta consider the long term. What's in it for you."

Silence while Jamie pretended to think about it. "So how does this work?"

Emory laughed, a harsh scraping sound. "Don't tell me you never had a whore, boy. I can see that's a lie."

Jamie, unruffled: "I just meant, do we trade up front? You take the stuff, and I take the girl to my place for a few hours?"

"Well, no." Emory's laugh dried up. "You're not taking her anywhere. You come in and do your business, and I'll be here, making sure you mind your manners."

"How do I know I can trust you once I hand over my part and walk into that house? No offense, you understand. But I could be walking into a bullet."

"Trust takes time, son, I get that. Trust'll come from working together for our mutual benefit. But right now we both need what the other's got. So what can I do to put you at ease and get this deal done?"

"I wanna see her," Jamie said. "The girl. Bring her out so I know she's really in there. That she's everything you said."

Emory groaned. Plainly, he wasn't used to accommodating demands. "All right," he said. "I'll give you an eyeful. And you can give me a sample of your wares there. Insurance for both of us."

I heard the door to the house open and close. Jamie stepped back and leaned against the car. "Get ready," he murmured. The gun was nestled in his waistband at the small of his back, hidden by his shirt. I hadn't gotten a look at Emory, but he surely had a weapon, too.

The door slammed again. Emory's voice, off to the side: "I'll help myself to that sample now. Go on and have your look."

"Jesus," Jamie muttered. "She even old enough for titties?"

I raised my head high enough to peer out the window, and there she was, behind the screen door, real and not real, Holly and not Holly. She swayed like a puppet on a string. I threw open the car door and sprinted toward the house.

"What the fuck is she doing here?" Emory howled, registering who I was.

If Holly was confused or scared or grateful when I yanked open the screen door, I couldn't tell. Her eyes rolled, and she slumped against me as I reached for her, her body light and malleable. I locked my arms around her rib cage and pulled her out of the house. When I turned around, Emory stood in my way. Behind him, Jamie had drawn his gun, but he held it at his side, waiting to see what I would do.

"What the hell, little girl?" Emory said. "Crete know you're out here?"

Wind gathered in the surrounding trees, shuffling the leaves and building into a low mournful keening. It swept over us with an unexpected chill. "I called the state troopers," I lied. "You want to clear out, go now."

His eyes narrowed, nearly hidden by tufted gray brows. "You wouldn't turn in your own uncle."

"Not without warning," I said. "He's already left town." I didn't know the strength of their bond, didn't know if he'd believe his partner would turn on him to survive. With each passing moment, Crete drove closer. If his truck pulled into the driveway, everything would fall apart.

Emory's arm sliced through the air and dealt a backhand smack to my face, his knuckles smashing into my cheekbone. My grip faltered, and Holly sagged to the ground, a pale puddle at my feet. Jamie lunged toward us, but Emory was already on the run, slowing down just enough to grab the box Jamie had brought and toss it into the van. He peeled out, heading for the compound at Caney Mountain, I guessed, or maybe straight out of town. I wondered how much time we had before he called my uncle.

We had to go. Jamie and I hustled Holly to the car and laid her in the backseat. Her lips moved as though speaking, but not in a voice we could hear. Likewise, her eyes flitted to things we couldn't see. She was drugged, adrift, her hair sliding across her face like a veil.

"Shit," Jamie hissed as we piled into the front seat. "She's a fucking *kid*, for Christ's sake!"

Lightning stripped the world of color in one vivid pop. If thunder followed, it was lost in the rev of the engine as Jamie launched us down the road. Rain pecked the windshield, slow at first, then relentless, a barrage of firecrackers. We rolled up the windows.

"She should see a doctor," I said.

"We'll take her to Birdie's."

"No." There was a good chance Crete would find out what had happened from Emory, or that he'd piece things together on his own, and I didn't want anyone else to get hurt when he came for me. "The hospital in Mountain Home."

"We can't take her there." Panic edged into Jamie's voice. "I can't drive some drugged-up kid across state lines. What do you think'll happen? What the fuck are you gonna say when we sign her in?"

He was right. "Take her to Sarah Cole's, then. You know where she lives?"

He nodded, biting his lip. We bumped off the gravel onto the main road. The blacktop steamed in the rain. Headlights ghosted by, but I couldn't make out the vehicle through the downpour. We watched the mirror nervously but saw no lights behind us.

"Drop me at my house," I said. He shot me a confused glance but didn't object. "I'll meet you at Sarah's as soon as I can. Just keep Holly safe." I placed my hand on his arm. His biceps twitched, and he made a loose turn onto Toad Holler Road, the car skidding and correcting as he braked and regained speed.

CHAPTER 39

Crete

Crete left a message for Carl, asking him to reconsider letting Lucy come back to work. He was sure he could wear his brother down, though it might require a bit of patience. He waited a few minutes past quitting time to see if Carl would call back, but he didn't, so Crete locked up his office and let Judd know he was leaving. Rain clouds hung low as he left Dane's, and thunder grumbled in the distance. He remembered how Mama used to say she could feel a storm coming. Her leg would ache along the seam where the bone had broken and knitted itself back together. She was right more often than not, but

Crete suspected it was all an act. His nose had been broken twice, and after it healed, it never ached in any kind of weather.

He rubbed a finger over the twisted bridge of his nose, feeling hard knots of bone where it had fused back together. It had been that way for so long, he hardly recognized old pictures of himself where it was straight. He was twelve the first time it got broken, and it was all Mama's fault. She had sat in the rocker in her bedroom for days, eating nothing but oyster crackers she lined up on the arm of the chair, using the toilet only when Daddy carried her across the hall. A bouquet of peonies browned on the dresser, petals dropping onto a doily and curling into themselves, and she did nothing except stare at those petals dropping, at the soft pile they made. Carl had taken sick, fever slicking his little body with sweat, and Daddy had driven him up the road for Birdie to take a look at, leaving Crete to keep an eye on Mama. She couldn't be left home alone when she was having one of her spells. The year before, she had thrown herself out of an upstairs window and landed in a viburnum bush, breaking her leg. After that, Daddy had installed new screens and planted viburnums under every window to catch her if she jumped again.

Crete checked on his mother, who had fallen asleep in the rocking chair, and then he went to sit outside on the porch. The night was warm and breezy, perfect weather to roll his sleeping bag out in the yard. He liked sleeping outdoors, listening to the night sounds all around him. He wasn't scared. Nothing outside bothered him, not even bugs, which rarely bit him. They didn't like his flavor, Mama said. Crete worried she was right, that something in his blood was bad. The bugs smelled it and stayed away.

He heard a loud crash and ran back into the house. On his way up the stairs, he heard another crash, then a moment of silence before Mama started screaming. He flung open the bedroom door and saw her straddling the windowsill, half-in, half-out, waving her arms as a bat flapped around the room. He guessed that the crash he'd heard was Mama kicking out the screen, and the bat must have flown in as Mama tried to get out. If she jumped, it would be Crete's fault, because he was supposed to be watching her.

Please, Mama, he said. *Come back in.* He grabbed her nightgown and pulled till she fell to the floor, cussing him. The bat flew back out into the darkness, and Crete closed the window. He tried to help Mama up, but she swatted at him.

I ought to throw you out that window, she sneered. *You're just like me, something wrong in that head of yours. I'd be doing you a favor.*

Her words burned into him. He wondered what would have happened if he hadn't come to stop her, if she had gone ahead and jumped.

Get out, she hissed, pulling herself to a squatting position and lurching toward him. *Get out!*

He backed to the doorway, and without warning, she slammed the door in his face. Blood spurted out of his nose. He went back outside and sat on the porch swing with toilet paper stuffed in his nostrils, listening, but nothing fell from the upstairs window into the bushes.

When Daddy got home, he handed a sobbing Carl over to Crete and thumped up the stairs to check on Mama. Daddy didn't want Carl to see her, not until he took her back to the doctor in Springfield and got her fixed up with some pills. Heaven forbid Carl learned the truth about anything that might upset him. They had to tell him pretty lies about Mama and Santa and the Easter Bunny. Carl loved their mother because he didn't really know her. It was different for Crete. He wasn't sure that he could ever look at Mama again without seeing the meanness he knew was inside her.

Carl settled down when Crete took him, snuggling his sweaty head against his big brother's neck. Crete took Carl's stuffed bear out of his hands and, with little ceremony, drop-kicked it off the porch. Carl's face quivered on the verge of a sob, so Crete set him down roughly on the swing and retrieved the bear before the crybaby could bawl loud enough to bring Daddy back down and get him in trouble. He would be in enough trouble when Daddy saw the busted screen. But Carl didn't cry. Crete handed him the bear, and his little brother gave it an awkward punch, knocking it to the ground. Carl sniffled and looked up at Crete with a wan smile. Crete held out his arms and let Carl climb back onto his lap and rocked him in the swing long after the boy fell asleep, swatting away any mosquitoes that dared land on his brother.

Decades had passed since the night Mama broke his nose. He'd looked out for Carl all these years, and his little brother had stuck by him, even when the only thing tethering them was blood. Crete trusted Carl more than anyone else, which was not to say that he trusted him completely; Carl's weakness—not of character but of constitution— could be a liability. Carl didn't know everything, for example, about the girls. He knew Crete was invested in some sort of escort business, but the true nature and extent of the operation would have turned his delicate stomach. Crete hadn't set out to hide it. He figured his brother would find out sooner or later, and then, as with most questionable things Crete did, Carl would manage to ignore it. Carl was good at blinding himself to what he didn't want to see, especially where his brother was concerned.

But then Carl had gone and gotten involved with Lila. And Lucy had come along. Crete didn't want Carl to know what he had done, because it might be the one thing his little brother couldn't overlook. He didn't dare work any of the girls in Henbane after that (Emory was to blame for the whole Cheri mess, proving again that it was a bad idea to traffic in your own backyard), though he brought new recruits to the farm as needed and kept them hidden for a few days or weeks until he could transition them to Springfield or Branson or other locations. He'd had girls in trailers and basements and back rooms, in the sticks, the city, the suburbs. It didn't matter where they were, because men would find them, and the money would follow.

He'd learned the basics from Emory, a mentor of sorts who looked more like a senile moonshiner than a businessman. They had met at an Amway meeting, though neither of them was there to join up and start selling vitamins and detergent door-to-door. Crete was there to confront a guy who owed him money, and Emory was there to scout for like-minded individuals who could expand his territory. At the time, business was slumping at Dane's, and Crete needed to make up for a few bad investments. Once Emory trusted him enough to talk details, Crete couldn't believe how easy it sounded.

Even with Emory's guidance, Crete made mistakes at the start. He picked the wrong kinds of girls. Girls who weren't desperate enough, hadn't resigned themselves to their situations, wouldn't cede. And he failed when it came to forcing them. He figured out quick enough that force wasn't necessary when he picked the right ones. There were plenty of ordinary girls who were poor or dumb or lonely, abused, addicted, confused. No need to import exotic beauties. Emory had told him that looks didn't matter—a guy would screw a goat if he got desperate enough—but that was another mistake Crete had made in the beginning, picking pretty girls, girls he'd want for himself. It had backfired with Lila in the worst way. He could admit later how stupid he'd been to think something would spark between them once she arrived. He had lost perspective, let himself feel spurned and jealous and vengeful. And instead of cutting his losses on a sour deal, he'd brought strife to his family, ultimately hurting his brother—the one person who had earned his love and loyalty. He wouldn't let himself be tempted to make that mistake again.

He thought about quitting early on, but it was easy money—which he sorely needed to keep Dane's afloat—and he couldn't argue with the business model. You could only sell a cow once, but you could milk it every day. And no matter how much people drank, they would always be thirsty again. Demand was unceasing, and the supply was bountiful. There were so many girls, like milk cows, giving and giving until they gave out. He took them in, spoiled them with compliments and attention and clothes, and sometimes recouped his investment in under twenty-four hours. Someone told him that way back in slave times, a girl might cost you a thousand bucks. For reasons he didn't question, women's worth had plummeted, and Crete could buy one for a few hundred dollars. And he didn't always have to buy them; sometimes he got lucky and found one on his own.

After a while, the thrill dulled and he didn't touch the girls anymore, even when they tried to touch him. He'd slept with some of them after Lila, hard little creatures with broken parts inside that caused them to malfunction, to seek comfort in his lies, to kiss his stubbled neck, remove their clothes, and kneel before him, an empty offering to a false god. But that was how all gods were, he figured: blind, deaf, and dumb, unconcerned or unaware of what people begged of them. It wasn't guilt that made him stop sleeping with the girls, it was the pointlessness of it. Sex with a broken girl was hardly better than jerking off. He wanted something he couldn't find in girls as empty as he was. Nothing plus nothing equals nothing, he thought, an equation that served no purpose.

The only girl he truly cared about was Lucy. He barely trusted Carl to watch over her, doubting his brother could be ruthless enough or smart enough to protect her. And so he was there, always, for Lucy when she needed him. He was there rocking her to sleep while his brother drowned in grief. He was there, with his eye on her, while Carl wandered for work. Carl wanted to send Lucy off to college, but Crete wanted her to stay in Henbane and take over the family business— Dane's, not the other, the buying and selling of girls. He would rather she saw none of that but the assets, the money he had set aside to provide for her and keep Dane's running as long as she liked without worrying about its actual profits. That was a reason he gave himself for continuing in the business when he no longer needed the money; it was a better reason than the simple fact that he liked having control over the girls. The flip side was that Lucy wouldn't want the money if she knew where it came from. She had the same moral compass as Carl but lacked his ability to ignore unsavory things.

When Lila was alive, Crete had been determined to find out if Lucy was his daughter. He was driven by selfish anger and a blind urge to claim what belonged to him. But with Lila gone and Carl floundering, things changed. No one stood between him and Lucy; she was closer to him than ever. He knew that after the loss of his wife, Carl couldn't take a second blow, the one he would suffer if Crete took away his child. He wouldn't do that to his brother. And this way, he didn't have to face the possibility that Lucy *wasn't* his. He would rather not know for sure. Though what would a test result matter? It was just a bunch of letters and numbers. It wouldn't change his love for her. It was real love, true and effortless: stronger, simpler, and more important than what he had felt for Lila or his mother or any other woman. And she loved him back. He gave Lucy everything, and she was enough, a solace for all the other things he knew he couldn't have.

Crete's nose had been broken a second time when he lied and told Carl he'd slept with Janessa Walker. He stood there and let Carl hit him, because he knew he deserved it. Janessa was the first girl to turn down his advances in favor of his little brother, and while he felt bad about hurting Carl, he couldn't stand to let Janessa go unpunished.

Crete was almost home when the sky let loose. Rain blurred his windshield as the wipers struggled to keep up, and he flicked on the headlights. A few minutes later, he pulled into his driveway, parked the truck, and made a run for the house. He fumbled with his keys as he reached the front porch but quickly realized that he wouldn't need them.

Crete stood there in the wind and rain, fully soaked, staring into his house. Beyond the screen, the front door gaped open on the dark and empty hall, and he knew right then, before he ran inside and down the stairs to check the basement, that the girl was gone.

CHAPTER 40

Lucy

Though the rain let up as soon as I got in the house, the sky stayed dark. Birdie would be worrying. I fetched the rifle from the front hall and checked the chamber, knowing the gun was little more than a rattle on a snake, a warning—a plea—to stay away. I wasn't so worried about Emory, who'd already shown that he valued survival above retribution when he sped away from Crete's. But Crete might not believe I'd call the law, that I'd forsake my family to save a girl I barely knew. He wouldn't run on speculation; I'd never known him to run from anything. He was a man of confrontation. If Emory told him what I'd done, he'd want answers from me.

I dialed Birdie, and she picked up at half a ring. "I got caught in the rain out in the garden," I said. "I'm gonna get cleaned up, and then I'll head back."

"I'll come get you," she said. "Radio says it's gonna get worse."

"No!" It came out harsher than I intended. "I'm fine. I don't need your help. I'll wait it out here if it gets that bad."

Lightning flared, and her voice buzzed with static. "Well, at least turn on the radio." She wasn't happy with me, but that couldn't be helped. I had to wait at the house until it seemed likely that nobody would come. Then I could start cleaning up my mess. I'd have to call my dad.

I stepped out onto the porch and inhaled the damp electric scent of the storm. Bruised clouds bulged overhead, leaving a gap of clear greenish sky along the horizon. All through the hills, the treetops swayed like the coat of a giant beast being stroked by unseen hands. I heard no approaching engines, no man-made sounds, just the swell and creak of the house, the shuddering wind, the rustle of ten thousand leaves. *He's not coming*, I thought. *He is letting me go.*

A tender ache flowered along my cheek where Emory had struck me. I hadn't bothered to check my face in a mirror, but now that I had time to think straight, ice seemed like a good idea. I went back inside and cracked ice cubes into a kitchen rag to make a compress. Remembering Birdie's advice, I clicked on the radio and changed stations in time to hear the weatherman speak of a hook echo. His instruments and calculations had detected a pocket of rotation. I waited as he read the names of towns in its path: Theodosia, Isabella, Sundown, Howard's Ridge, Henbane. The list kept going. I wondered if the tornado siren was blaring in the town square; we were too far out to hear it.

A tornado had torn through town when I was in grade school, and for a long while after that, every time a tornado watch was issued for

Ozark County, I'd drag Dad out to the root cellar with me. We would huddle on the dirt floor and use the flashlight to count the preserves on the sagging shelves. *If Birdie don't quit with the pickled beets*, he'd say, *there won't be any room left in here for us.* I outgrew my fear, letting myself believe Dad's assertion that twisters skipped right over the holler due to geography.

Now I imagined the tornado warning's angry magenta blotch on the radar screen, and all my fears rose up inside me like floodwater. I didn't want to be here alone, waiting for something terrible to happen. I picked up the phone, and it crackled at me. I jabbed the buttons until I got a dial tone and called Birdie. When she didn't answer on the first ring, I knew she wouldn't answer at all. I'd told her I was fine. She was probably already in her cellar with Merle. I didn't want to consider the alternative—that Crete had shown up there looking for me.

I paced the kitchen floor in tears, marveling at my stupidity, my stubbornness. I was stuck here until the storm passed. I hoped that Jamie and Holly had already made it to Crenshaw Ridge, to some sort of safety. Outside the window, the trees were thrashing, eerie tendrils of cloud trailing down as the sky closed in. Hail pelted the yard, a scattering of pearls, and I knew that I should take shelter, just in case. I grabbed the rifle and opened the back door.

From the corner of my eye, I glimpsed the truck. And Crete stepping out of it. Staying in the house wasn't an option, so I dashed for the concrete mound of the root cellar, rain lashing me as I ran.

"Lucy!" He sprinted across the yard, catching up to me before I could push the cellar door closed. He wedged himself in the entryway so that I could neither escape nor shut him out. I backed into the darkness, holding the rifle in front of me, the safety still on.

"Lucy, honey, I just wanna talk to you," he said. "Put that down." He pulled the gun easily from my hands.

"Just leave me alone," I sobbed. "Please."

"I wanna tell you I'm sorry," he said. "There's been . . . misunder-standings. But I love you, and I'd never do anything to hurt you." He edged into the small space with me. The wind howled at his back, tugging at his hair and clothing. It was absurd, him trying to carry on a conversation as the storm bore down. I scooted into the corner, brushing cobwebs from my face.

"You wanna know the truth about her," he said. "Your mother. That's what all this is about, all your poking around and causing trouble." I covered my ears. *Truth.* It didn't mean much coming from him. He would say whatever was necessary to distort the things he'd done, to lay blame on everyone but himself.

"Listen!" he shouted. "What happened to her in the cave . . . she didn't kill herself. I know that for a fact. It was an accident, that's all. It was black as pitch, and she fell. She was gone, and there was no getting her back. There was nothing I could do."

I slowly grasped what he was saying. He'd been there when she died. He'd known all along that she was never coming back. He had known it my entire life and never said a word. If it truly was an accident, if there was some good reason he'd been alone in that cave with my mother when she died, he could have told me years ago.

I lifted my head and looked him in the eye. "*What did you do to her?*"

I felt the *boom* before I heard it, a reverberation in my chest, and then Uncle Crete fell to the floor, his face in the dirt. I thought at first he'd been struck by flying debris, but then Birdie dropped down into the cellar, her hair plastered to her head so I could see the pink scalp beneath. She set down her gun and wrestled Crete's legs out of the way so she could bar the timber door. I didn't move. My eyes struggled to adjust to sudden blindness. In the faintly lit circle beneath the ventilation pipe, Crete's blood crept across the floor. There was a shift in pressure, a horrible sucking at the pipe, and my ears popped. The door groaned but held. And then Birdie's arms were around me, cradling me so I couldn't tell whether her body was shaking or mine, and we stayed there while the roar outside died away and for some time after that.

We stepped gingerly around Crete's body and out into the gray evening light. "Are you all right?" Birdie asked finally. "I heard the warning on the radio, and I know you said you were fine, but I promised to look after you . . . and then I saw him there with the rifle . . ."

"He wasn't going to shoot me," I said. "It was my gun. He just took it away to keep me from doing something stupid."

"We don't know what he would've done," Birdie said sharply.

When the phones came back up, Birdie called Dad. He was already on his way, having heard about the tornado. Birdie took him out on the porch when he arrived, and I couldn't hear what she said to him. She had her hand on his arm and kept him facing away from the window so I couldn't see his face. He pulled away from her at one point, and his shoulders slumped, but she kept talking, and a minute later, she was following him to the root cellar. Birdie came in through the back door and took me by the hand. She was trembling. "I tried to explain . . ." she said, trailing off. "He needs time. Let's go to my place for a bit." We rode in silence, observing the storm debris—shredded leaves, snapped branches, a lawn chair in the ditch—without comment.

Birdie plied me with tea and sugar cookies that I didn't want but ate anyway, for the sake of doing something normal, familiar. Bite, chew, swallow. I could do that much. She didn't eat anything, just sat in her chair watching me from the corner of her eye, knitting needles working an endless skein of yarn.

When night fell, I knew Dad was taking care of Crete. Wrapping his body in a tarp and dragging it from the cellar. Cleaning up the evidence. Mourning the loss of his brother, who, despite everything he was suspected of, everything he'd done, was still Dad's blood, the last of his family. Except for me. I was and would always be a Dane, with all the good and bad that entailed, and like my forebears, I would keep the secrets entrusted to me until they slipped from my naked bones. But Birdie had taught me that I needn't be bound by the unspoken laws of kin; that I could have a family based not on bloodline but on love. She had kept her promise to my mother to look after me. I didn't know why I hadn't seen it sooner, that Birdie loved me as she loved her own children—enough to take a life to save mine.

Frogs started up their courting songs. After a while Birdie took out her worn Bible and read aloud in a quiet, soothing voice until at last sleep beckoned. *Yea, though I walk through the valley of the shadow of death, I will fear no evil.*

We took a somber tour of the storm damage the next day. The tornado had skipped through Henbane in typical fickle fashion, demolishing some buildings and leaving others untouched. A mangled pickup balanced precariously on the roof of the Great Southern Bank. One of the ancient gum trees on the courthouse lawn had toppled, smashing into the Donut Hole across the street. Sections of the blacktop road leading to the river had been scoured down to bare earth, and a handful of homes had been reduced to a confetti of insulation, splinters, and glass. The storm took pieces of Henbane with it, snatching up photographs and receipts and pages of books with greedy fingers and dropping them out of the sky as far away as Howell County.

Dane's general store was intact minus a few shingles and the patio awning, but the landscape around the building had been swept clean—the hand-lettered signs advertising firewood and night crawlers, the planters overflowing with petunias, the trash can and ashtray and wooden benches, the old wagon where Crete had stacked melons and pumpkins for sale. Even the morning glories that climbed the walls and gutters had been stripped away. Devoid of all its familiar adornments, Dane's appeared alien and unwelcoming. Cheri's tree, along with countless others, had been uprooted and tossed in the river.

Several people had been wounded by flying debris. Arleigh Snell had been rescued from her crushed trailer after hours spent pinned under the rubble, and one person remained unaccounted for. Whispers spread through town that Crete Dane was missing. A storage shed behind his house had been ripped apart, the contents lost to the wind, and it was thought that he might have been borne away in the funnel cloud. The sheriff expressed hope that Crete's remains would be recovered, but with thousands of acres of forest on all sides, it wasn't feasible to launch a search.

An anonymous tip led to a raid on Caney Mountain, but no trace of Emory was found. While it was possible, authorities acknowledged, that a significant trafficking ring had operated in Ozark County, they were unable to locate the victims. They couldn't even prove the existence of the suspect; his identity had never been captured on paper. I wanted Holly to come forward, but I couldn't force her. Much of the experience was blurry for her, and she wasn't ready to bring it into focus. I filled my journal with alternate endings, things I could have done to save her without letting Emory go. I felt the weight of the other girls I'd endangered with his escape. I hadn't seen Jamie since he'd driven off into the storm, but Sarah told me he'd stayed by Holly's side that whole night, watching over her, keeping her safe. He had stayed until I finally reached Ray and asked him what to do with her.

Ray had no trouble getting appointed as Holly's temporary guardian, something her mother did not emerge to protest. He and his wife had been looking for a child to dote on for a very long time, and if they had their way, they'd adopt her. I still thought of Holly with her 4-H rabbits, waiting on the curb for someone to take her home, and I was glad she now had a family she could rely on. I didn't know what it would take to heal her after all she had been through, but I believed the Walkers would do everything possible to mend her wounds.

CHAPTER 41

Ransome

In the weeks after Lucy Dane's visit to Riverview, Ransome fretted over the question she hadn't asked: She had wondered all these years if Lucy still had her baby quilt and whether the girl knew Ransome had sewn it. But she'd been so taken aback when she laid eyes on Lila's daughter that the question had dried up in her mouth. She knew it was Lucy who stood before her, but for a second she wondered if it was Lila's ghost, come to take her to the other side.

When Lila left the garage—when Carl carried her away—she didn't take anything with her. Ransome thought for sure Carl would come by to fetch her belongings, but he never did, and she wasn't about to drive

Lila's suitcase over to the house. It was best if she didn't see Lila or talk to her. After a while Crete told Ransome to clean out the garage. She was bagging everything up for the burn barrel when she pulled a ratty pink T-shirt out of the chest of drawers. It had belonged to the first girl. She pressed her face to it, trying to recall the girl's smell, but it was long gone, nothing left except the musty stink of old wood. She stuffed the shirt in the trash bag along with Lila's clothes and hauled it all up the hill to her house.

She looked forward to spending the winter in the front room by the woodstove, gazing out over the dead fields and working on her quilts. As soon as the first hard frost hit, she dumped the bag of clothes on the floor and started cutting. She'd heard by then about the baby. Birdie Snow had told her. Ransome stitched a crib-sized quilt, piecing together bits of Lila's abandoned jeans and shirts and nightgowns, and held back a square from one of the prettier blouses to use on another project.

She didn't go to Lila's baby shower, but she sent the quilt and let the gift speak for itself. She stayed home that day and sewed together the first two pieces of a new quilt: the silky square she had saved from Lila's blouse, and one she had cut from the first girl's pink T-shirt. *Maria*, she printed on the back of the pink square, and *Lila* on the other.

Over the years it fell to Ransome to clean up what the girls left behind, and they almost always left clothes. They shed their outfits like old skins, leaving them in piles on the floor. She tried to pick something she remembered the girl wearing, something to link a face and name, and she'd cut a square and sew it to the rest. Her quilt of lost girls. It felt right to keep a record, guilt stitched into the seams. She touched the squares and said their names, like a Catholic worrying rosary beads, so that when the time came to sew on the backing, she could still recite them by heart.

CHAPTER 42

Lucy

A few weeks after the tornado struck, Daniel and I sat on a blanket at the mouth of Old Scratch. It was an unlikely spot for a picnic, but the cool air from the cave was soothing in the late-August heat. I had brought a bouquet of wildflowers for my mother and placed them in a patch of sunlight nearby. One good thing had come out of the storm: Daniel had found work clearing debris, allowing us some time together before he had to go back to Springfield and start classes at the tech college.

"You ready for school to start?" Daniel asked, eyeing the remains of my lunch.

"Yes and no," I said. I gave him my half-eaten sandwich, and he stuffed it in his mouth. "I'll miss you around here. But it's good that you're going, I guess. At least my dad thinks so."

He smiled. "Good that I'm going to school or good that I'll be gone?"

I punched his arm. "You'll visit, right?"

"Until you're sick of me."

We sat in silence for a while, staring into the cave. I didn't know which, if any, of Crete's last words were true, but I chose to believe that my mother hadn't meant to leave me. I didn't need to know everything about her to know how much she had loved me.

Daniel brushed my hair back over my shoulder. By now I'd stopped cataloging all the times he touched me; not that the thrill had worn off, just that I had lost track. He'd shown up at my house the day after the storm, walked up to the door, and pulled me into his arms without saying a word. He had kissed me right there, in front of my dad, who hadn't even protested.

"You getting used to working for Carl?" he asked.

"He's annoying," I said. "But it's kind of nice having him around." However hard it was for Dad to sit at Crete's desk every day, surrounded by reminders of his brother, he was unapologetically delighted to have a job that kept us tripping over each other every day. *We'll be spending a lot of time together before you leave for college*, he'd said with a bittersweet smile.

I was worried about my dad. He couldn't bring himself to say much to Birdie, though he knew she had shot Crete only out of fear for my life. I'd told him what I had found in Crete's basement—the folder with Mom's picture and her unsettling job application. Everything left his face: color, emotion, awareness. He retreated to his room to drink, and I went to stay with Bess and Gabby for a few days. They had stuck to me like a couple of seed ticks, constantly asking if I was okay.

While I was there, Gabby took me out to the woodpile to see the one remaining possum from the litter of babies I'd brought her back in May. Its siblings had all disappeared into the woods, but the last possum appeared to have formed a bond with its adoptive mother, the mama cat, and it had chosen to stay. Gabby got all teary when we found the cat and the possum curled up together to sleep, and Bess rolled her eyes and told her to go light a joint.

When Dad came to pick me up and take me home, he reeked of smoke, and his eyebrows were singed. He'd spent a whole day at Crete's house, burning things. He'd carried all the boxes of paperwork out of the basement and set them on fire. He looked rough, but he was sober, so I got in the truck with him. Neither of us said anything on the ride home, but I figured when he was ready—if he ever was—he would talk.

Many things were in limbo. Ray said that, without a body, it could take years for Crete to be declared legally dead, yet he insisted that I see the will right away. Both houses, the store, the land, the insurance, an astonishing assortment of bank accounts: all in my name. *For Lucy, who is like a daughter to me.* However I tried to interpret them, those words hit me hard. I didn't know for sure whether Crete had attacked my mother—and whether it was possible that he was my father—but I knew I was nothing like him and that Carl would always be my dad. Still, as much as I wanted to, I couldn't escape the fact that Crete and I were family. We had loved each other. I had loved a monster, and a monster had loved me.

It was a relief for my dad to have our home and property restored to us, and while he'd never imagined himself a shopkeeper, it was clear he felt a sense of pride in taking over his father's business. The cash was another matter altogether. In addition to the bank balances, there was the safe under Crete's desk. Dad had drilled it open and found it packed with stacks of bills. I had no way of knowing how much of it was made off girls like Cheri and Holly. Girls like my mother. I wouldn't keep it. I wanted to use it to help other girls escape, or to keep them from being trafficked in the first place. Ray promised to help me find the best organization to give the money to, and I would make the donation in Cheri's name.

I hadn't expected to feel guilt snaking through me as I read Crete's will. The things he had left for me meant nothing compared to all that I'd lost, all that he'd taken away, and I hated him for it. He deserved to pay for what he'd done. But I'd never wanted him dead. I remembered how he had sung to me, though sometimes I wished I could forget.

It was well past lunchtime. Daniel and I needed to be heading back, but neither of us was in a hurry to leave.

"So, do you think you'll come back here after college and take over the family empire someday?" Daniel asked.

I didn't know the answer. The Ozarks did have a way of calling folks home, though I'd never thought I would be one of them. All my life I had told myself I didn't belong here. Henbane was a map of the devil, his backbone, eye, and throat, its caves and rivers a geography of my loss. But I hadn't taken into account how a place becomes part of you, claims you for its own. Like it or not, my roots tangled deep in the rocky soil. I would leave Henbane, but home sings in your bones, and I wondered how far I could go before the hills would call me back.

"Maybe," I said, leaning in to him. "And if you're lucky, maybe I'll hire you."

I ran my fingers along the chain around my neck; they came to rest on the blue butterfly. I'd taken Cheri's necklace out of hiding, though I didn't feel right wearing it. It would always belong to her. I unhooked the clasp and rose to place the necklace with the flowers. *I'm sorry*, I whispered. *For everything*. I hoped that somehow she could hear me.

I turned away from the cave. I couldn't stare at it any longer, expecting answers that wouldn't come. I was done waiting for ghosts. I pulled Daniel down onto the blanket and kissed him, hard.

"I haven't been replaced by Jamie Petree?" he teased, trailing his fingers along my cheek.

"Hardly," I said. "He's a terrible kisser."

Daniel wrapped his arms around me and drew me close to him, almost as close as I wanted to be. On the blanket, in the filtered light, doves lamenting in the trees, I felt at home—with my world, myself, with him. I let myself get lost in the moment, looking neither forward nor back, seeking nothing absent but embracing what was right in front of me.

A NOTE FROM THE AUTHOR

When I was seven, my family moved to a remote Ozark community where newcomers were rare and not necessarily welcomed. Everyone in town was interconnected, it seemed, by blood or marriage or life-long acquaintance, and naturally they wondered why we had shown up in their midst with no ties to the land or people. I didn't tell them that my father had chosen our new home by looking at a roadmap and circling a tiny dot in the middle of nowhere. He wasn't the only out-sider drawn to the region by a desire for isolation. We lived near the East Wind commune (rarely seeing any members save the topless woman who jogged past as we waited for the school bus) and the hid-den compound of an extremist group called The Covenant, The Sword, and the Arm of the Lord (which was later raided by the FBI).

The land itself was both beautiful and threatening. We were surrounded by wildflowers, thick forests, and rivers clear as glass. But buzzards circled low overhead and snakes sunned themselves on our porch. Scorpions crept into our beds at night, and darkness was absolute. From our craggy, wooded property, we couldn't see any lights or houses or people; we heard no traffic or other manmade sounds—nothing but insects and coyotes and wind. Never had I felt so removed from the outside world. The locals were content to live that way, rooted by their heritage and traditions and kin, but even as I made friends, it was clear that I would never be one of them. I was still a "foreigner." To belong in such a place, you had to be born there.

We moved several times throughout my childhood, but no other place haunted me like the Ozarks, and I attempted to bring it to life in *The Weight of Blood*. I wanted to expand on my experience of being a stranger in the place I called home, so I created mother and daughter narrators—Lila, who is an outsider in Ozark County, and her daughter, Lucy, who is native born but feels that she doesn't belong.

I was well into the first draft of the novel when I heard about an horrific human trafficking case that took place in the small town of Lebanon, Missouri. The case struck a chord with me because I had lived in Lebanon during my teens, and the victim was a teenaged girl. Multiple people had been involved in the girl's exploitation over several years, yet no one in the close-knit town seemed to have known about it. Small town folks are known to gossip and get into one another's business, yet this terrible secret had stayed hidden. *The Weight of Blood* begins with the discovery of Cheri Stoddard's body. The trafficking case made me rethink Cheri's character, and ultimately helped shape the story. Unfortunately, Cheri would not be as lucky as the real-life victim, who thankfully escaped and survived.

Laura McHugh
August 2013

ACKNOWLEDGMENTS

Thank you to the Runge and McHugh families, especially my mom, Veronica Runge, for everything, and my sisters, Lisa Gilpin, Diane Berner, and Ellen Runge, for their unfailing belief and love. Thank you to my in-laws, Barb and Bill McHugh, for their kindness and support.

My husband, Brent, deserves a huge thank-you for suggesting that I stop trying to squeeze my pregnant belly into an interview suit and instead use my newfound unemployment as an opportunity to write a book, like I'd always wanted. His love and support kept me going. Thank you to our daughters, Harper and Piper, for making me want to work harder.

I am forever grateful to my agent, Sally Wofford-Girand, for all she has done. She made my dreams come true.

Heartfelt thanks to my wonderful editor, Cindy Spiegel, who believed in the story and made it better, and to everyone at Spiegel & Grau and Random House who helped. Thank you to Selina Walker of Century Arrow in the UK for her invaluable insight and to E. Beth Thomas for copyediting.

Much love and gratitude to my writing group: Ann Breidenbach, Nina Furstenau, Jennifer Gravley, Jill Orr, and Allison Smythe. I'm lucky to be surrounded by such talented and generous friends. Special thanks to Jill for the endless encouragement and for sharing this journey with me.

I would like to thank everyone who read early drafts, answered questions, offered advice, or cheered me on: Paula Parker, Hilary Sorio, Elizabeth Anderson, Angie Sloop, Sally Mackey, Emily Williams, Jennifer Anderson, Liz Lea, Amy Messner, Julie Hague, Nicole Coates, Jessica Longaker, Scott Greathouse, Dan Sophie, Ryan Gerling, Thomas Jacobs, Keija Parssinen, and Paula Chaffin of New Horizons for Children. Thanks also to Taisia Gordon, my favorite photographer.

Thank you to the friends and neighbors who offered to babysit my children when I needed help, and last but not least, thank you to Daniel Boone Regional Library, where I spent countless hours drinking coffee and working on this book.

ABOUT THE AUTHOR

LAURA MCHUGH grew up in small towns in Iowa and southern Missouri, the youngest in a family of eight children. She holds a master's degree in library science and has worked as a librarian and a software developer. Her short fiction has appeared in *Confrontation* and *Big Muddy: A Journal of the Mississippi River Valley*. As a full-time mom, she spends most of her time doing laundry and playing My Little Pony, but she also likes to garden, sew, and watch zombie movies. McHugh lives in Columbia, Missouri, with her husband, two daughters, and dog.

www.facebook.com/lauramchughauthor
@LauraSMcHugh

ABOUT THE TYPE

This book was set in Electra, a typeface designed for Linotype by re-
nowned type designer W. A. Dwiggins (1880–1956). Electra is a fluid
typeface, avoiding the contrasts of thick and thin strokes that are preva-
lent in most modern typefaces.